# SORRY, WRONG NUMBER

Gene picked up his luggage and stepped through. The portal did sometimes shift, after all. But the house was gone. This might be Earth, but it was one where the house did not exist, had never existed. He had to get back to the Castle. Before he could move a loudspeaker burped, then blared.

*"You there! Identify yourself!"*

"Who wants to know?"

There was a pause. *"Don't move. If you move, you will be shot. Repeat—do not move."*

"Yeah, right."

He woke up in a hospital bed. A young man in a white coat entered, carrying a small device with a screen. "We've taken a good look at you," he said. "Ran some tests. You're in perfect health physically. Spiritually, not so good, though."

"What's wrong in that department?"

"You didn't have InnerVoice."

"I see." Gene considered. "What's that?"

"A guide to right behavior."

"And I don't have it."

"You do now."

# CASTLE WAR!
## John DeChancie

ACE BOOKS, NEW YORK

This one is for
Dorothy and John Taylor

This book is an Ace original edition
and has never been previously published.

CASTLE WAR!

An Ace Book/published by arrangement with
the author

PRINTING HISTORY
Ace edition/November 1990

ISBN: 0-441-09270-5

Ace Books are published by The Berkley Publishing Group,
200 Madison Avenue, New York, New York 10016.
The name "ACE" and the "A" logo are trademarks
belonging to Charter Communications, Inc.

PRINTED IN THE UNITED STATES OF AMERICA

10  9  8  7  6  5  4  3  2

Fate sits on these dark battlements and frowns,
And as the portal opens to receive me,
A voice in hollow murmurs through the courts
Tells of a nameless deed.

Ann Radcliffe (1764-1823)
*The Mysteries of Udolpho*

# THRONE ROOM

INCARNADINE, LORD OF THE WESTERN PALE, sat in state on the Siege Perilous.

"Bring in the prisoner."

High in the cavernous chamber, a bat screeched. Something small and furry skittered across the floor and vanished into a shadowy corner.

Wrists manacled, the prisoner shuffled in, dragged by two Guardsmen. He was pushed to the floor in front of the throne.

"Rise."

Chuckling, the prisoner got up slowly. His frayed gray tunic was filthy, his black tights torn and ripped.

"Your Majesty. How kind of you to grant me audience."

"We welcome our faithful vassal, Sir Gene Ferraro."

The irony fairly dripped.

"How does His Majesty fare?"

"It goes well with us." His Serene and Transcendent Majesty smiled crookedly. "You, on the other hand, look rather pale and haggard. Aren't my jailers treating you properly?"

"Not a day goes by when I am not the beneficiary of their kind attentions."

"I am glad. Getting enough to eat?"

"Unfortunately, sire, there is only so much rubbish one can consume at a sitting. So much slop, so much swill."

The King looked saddened. "No appetite? I will have your rations reduced so that this no longer presents a problem."

"His Majesty is too gracious a host."

"No amenity must be spared a true and faithful servant."

"I fear I am not quite that, sire."

"No? Perhaps not. Perhaps 'servant' is not the proper designation. Can you think of one more apt?"

Sir Gene smiled thinly. "I am sure His Majesty can supply any number more apt."

"Traitor, perhaps? Regicide?"

"Failed regicide," the prisoner corrected.

"Murderous villain?" The King's voice boomed inside the dark chamber. *"Foul usurper?"*

Sir Gene shrugged. "Again, unsuccessful. Regarding murder, may I remind His Majesty that I learned the art at the knees of a true master. You—"

The Guardsman to the right drove a mailed fist into the prisoner's side just under the rib cage. The prisoner doubled up and sank to his knees. He was some time in getting up again.

A silent, fluttering movement in the darkness above. Another bat.

The King settled back in his throne. "You learned not well enough."

Sir Gene drew a painful breath before answering. "How well I know."

"We have more lessons to teach. There is the discipline of the wheel, for instance. And the brand, and the boot."

"Ah."

"You hide your fear well. But you will scream as loudly as the others."

"I trust it will amuse His Majesty to contemplate that this time the victim will not be entirely innocent."

A royal scowl. "Spoils the fun, really."

"True, true."

"But we'll do our best to enjoy the proceedings." The King sighed. "There is not much else to say. But I suppose protocol demands that I pronounce sentence." He raised his right hand, took a long breath, then said hurriedly, "By the right and power vested in me I hereby condemn you to a deliciously prolonged death with all the trimmings." He grinned.

The prisoner bowed.

"Take him away."

The prisoner was led out of the throne room.

In the corridor outside, the Guardsmen steered their charge to the left. At the next intersecting hallway they turned right, went down a stairwell, and turned left at the landing.

The three were walking along when suddenly the prisoner stopped and doubled over, groaning.

The Guardsman on the left said, "What's with you, then?"

"My side . . . it's on fire."

The other one snickered. "Only a taste of what's to come."

"Please, you must—"

"No malingering, now."

"I . . . can't walk."

"You landed him a good one, you did," the one on the left said. "It likely burst something."

"It was just a tap."

"Let's be on our way back to the cell. You can lie down there."

"I want the court physician!"

"Can't oblige, good sir knight."

"If I die prematurely, Incarnadine will have your heads."

The one on the right looked worried. "He's right, you know."

"I suppose he is. Come along, we'll take you to the sawbones straightaway."

"I tell you, I can't walk!"

"Pick up his feet."

"You pick up his feet. I've got the rest of him."

"Just our luck if he dies. I've got a good mind to—"

The prisoner kicked out and connected with a solar plexus. One Guardsman doubled over. Then, pivoting quickly, he swung his manacled fists around and clouted the other alongside the head.

Both men went down, and he ran.

He dashed left at the next intersection, having a certain destination in mind. It was one of the castle's lesser known aspects, and if he could get through it, he could lose himself in dense forest. He knew a cave not far away where he could hide.

Shouts echoing behind him, he willed what was left of his strength into his legs. He lurched left at the next crossing passageway, ran, turned right, ran, then bore right again.

He burst into a spacious room. In the darkness to the rear lay the arched entrance to a small adjoining chamber, which he made for directly. Once through the archway, he halted and gasped in dismay.

There was supposed to be an aspect here, a magical doorway to another world. Instead, there lay before him another long, nondescript corridor, of which there were countless thousands in the castle.

He desperately glanced around. This was the right chamber. He knew it well. A veteran Guest in Castle Perilous, he had a keen sense of direction and layout. One needed such talents in the vast labyrinth of the castle.

The magical doorway was clearly gone. Aspects were known to disappear on occasion, but this particular one was extraordinarily stable, or had been since he had taken up residence in the castle. Rotten luck to have it vanish when he needed it most. Double bad luck to have picked this one when there were two or three others close by that would have served in a pinch. But this world had offered a forest to hide in; the others provided less ideal cover.

Footsteps closed outside; too late to make a dash for one of the alternate escape routes. He was cut off.

He bolted forward. The only choice was to keep running.

But he knew it was only a matter of time before he was chased down. The alert would go out.

His one chance was to make it to one of the unstable areas of the castle, where wild aspects flickered in and out of existence, where doors opened to anywhere, sometimes to oblivion. But even oblivion was preferable to the refined diversions that Incarnadine's torturers had in store for him.

He raced on into a gloom relieved only by a few strange lighting fixtures in the shape of faceted jewels that glowed faintly blue. He ran by an occasional blind alcove, no aspects in them. He passed two stairwells, then came to a third. He entered and went down two floors, stopping at the landing to check the adjoining corridor. No one. He sprinted to the left, then made a series of turns, running blindly now, unaware of exactly where he was heading.

He ran until his diminished stamina gave out. He jogged along, then loped. He stopped to get a second wind, and jogged some more. His pace gradually petered out to a walk.

Breathing hard, he stopped, leaned against the dark stone wall. He slowed his breath and listened.

Nothing. No footsteps, no voices.

Could it be? Had he truly lost his pursuit? The quiet closed in around him.

Miracle of miracles. Now he would have a chance to find an amenable aspect. He knew of several where he could hide out awhile. He knew of others into which he could disappear for a very long time indeed, and that is what he desired. The castle was no longer safe. He had tried to take it, make it his, but had failed miserably.

No matter. Incarnadine would never find him. He would hide, biding his time. It would take years, perhaps, but somehow he would raise an army and return. He would invade Castle Perilous, depose Incarnadine, and take the throne.

Good, he thought. It was essential to have a plan, to keep ambitions alive.

He began walking again. Suddenly he stopped, looked about.

Something was strange. His castle sense was giving him mixed signals. The surroundings were familiar, but there was something odd. He could not grasp quite what.

He shrugged it off and continued. He wandered for what seemed like hours. No one was about.

The sense that something was amiss did not leave him. He could not shake the feeling that somehow, in some inexplicable way, he had left the castle. But that was impossible, for clearly he was still inside it. He had not crossed an aspect.

Or had he? There lingered an inescapable feeling that he had. There was a sixth sense about that as well. He knew when the castle gave way to one of its contingent worlds. There was always a sense of going out, of leaving.

As now. But what had he entered? What sort of world was like the castle itself?

He turned a corner and collided with a Guardsman.

"Gene!"

Stunned, he regarded the man, whom he recognized and knew well. It was no less than Tyrene, Captain of the Guard. What he could not fathom was why Tyrene was giving him the friendliest of smiles.

Tyrene's gaze lowered to Gene's hands, and his expression turned quizzical.

"What's this? Lady Linda playing some sort of prank?"

Sir Gene looked at the manacles, then at Tyrene. He had no answer. Nor did he have an explanation for why Tyrene looked different, until he realized that the ugly, cancerous mole on the man's right cheek was gone.

Tyrene laughed. "Too embarrassed to say? Here." He reached into a pocket and pulled out a ring of keys. "I should have a master here somewhere."

Sir Gene remained silent as Tyrene searched for the key, found it, and released him.

"Thank you," Sir Gene said, rubbing his wrists.

Tyrene examined the manacles. "Did Linda conjure these, or do they come from the dungeon?"

"Ah . . . I'm afraid I don't know."

"It's all right. It's a rare prisoner we have these days. I'll see that they get stored away properly."

"Thank you. Thank you very much."

"Well, must be going. Duty, you know. With Lord Incarnadine away things tend to get a mite frantic."

Tyrene walked off, whistling off-key.

Sir Gene stared after him, amazed beyond words.

When the silence returned, he fell into contemplation.

At length, he reached a conclusion. He did not understand why or how, but it was clear that he had been presented with a golden opportunity.

Sir Gene Ferraro was not a man to let such pass by.

# QUEEN'S DINING HALL

IT WAS BREAKFAST and everyone was up early. The long dining table was heavy with food in every variety imaginable. The coffee flowed and so did the conversation.

Linda Barclay turned to one of the servants. "Orrin, did you wake Gene early?"

"I did, milady."

"He's hard to get up sometimes. Do you know when his plane leaves?"

"Your pardon, milady, I do not."

Linda sipped her coffee. She looked up at Orrin again. "Do you know what an airplane is?"

Orrin wasn't sure. "A flying machine?"

"Right. I'm never sure how much you born castle people know about our world."

"Oh, we know a bit, milady. I've never seen a flying machine, but I'm very sure I wouldn't fancy taking a ride in one."

"I've always been afraid to fly, too."

The man whom everyone called Monsieur DuQuesne was sitting across the table. "I've never flown in my life," he said.

Cleve Dalton, thin and middle-aged, was seated next to him. "I always liked flying. Always meant to get a private license. Took lessons, even soloed, but never took the written test." He lifted his coffee cup. "By the way, what's Gene going back to school for?"

Deena Williams answered. "You mean why is he going back or what's he gonna study?"

"I guess I mean both. Sorry, I'm always out on the golf course, so I don't know what's going on half the time."

Thaxton, a dapper man in his late thirties, said, "You don't know what's going on half the time out on the course, Dalton, old boy."

"I know enough to beat you more than half the time."

"Golf's not my game, you know that."

"Yes, of course. It's tennis, which I hate."

"Gene's going to study computer science," Linda said. "Grad school at Cal Tech."

"Very good school," Dalton said, impressed. "Why computers?"

"Well, Gene has always had this inferiority thing about his not being very good in magic. He needs to compensate. Computers he thinks he can handle."

Jeremy Hochstader came in yawning. He looked in his teens but was a bit older.

"Speakin' of computers," Deena said, "here comes the whiz kid now."

"Morning, everybody," Jeremy said between yawns. "Sorry. Up all night with the castle mainframe again."

"How's the rebuilding going?" Dalton asked.

"Oh, so-so. The CPU is working but the operating system is still full of bugs." Jeremy helped himself to eggs and bacon.

Linda said, "Gene also thinks he can help with the magic if he learns computers."

"Magic and computers," Deena said with a shake of her head. "Crazy."

"Incantations, pentacles, all that stuff is old-fashioned," Jeremy said. "Why can't you run a spell through a computer?"

"Why not?" Deena said with a shrug.

"Can't stop progress," Jeremy said.

"I also think that Gene needs to get back to reality," Linda said. "I think maybe all of us need to get back sometimes."

"Not me," Dalton said. "I'll take the castle over reality any day."

Thaxton buttered some toast while commenting, "According

to our host, the castle *is* reality. Everything else is just an adjunct."

"What's an adjunct?" Deena asked.

"Something that's secondary. The castle creates all the worlds it provides access to."

Linda said, "Well, that's not entirely true. The way I understand it—I mean, the way Lord Incarnadine explained it to me—is that there are an infinite number of possible universes, but they don't really exist in the normal sense. They just sort of hang out there until the castle makes them . . . *real*, I guess."

"That's more or less it," Thaxton said.

"And the castle chooses 144,000 of these universes and creates access doors that we all go traipsing through."

"You've hit it on the head."

"But I really don't emotionally accept it," Linda went on. "I still can't accept the castle as anything but a long-lived fantasy. I think Gene has trouble with it, too. That's why he feels he has to get back once in a while. Back to the gritty, real world we came from."

"All good luck to Gene," Dalton said, "but I'm staying right here."

"I ain't goin' nowhere, either," Deena said. "I didn't have it so great back in Bed-Sty."

Dalton said, "I think all of us are here because of problems in the so-called real world. That's what opens a door into this place. A willingness to chuck it all and leave."

"You really think so?" Linda said.

"Of course. Haven't you ever wondered why only certain types show up here?"

"Now that you mention it, I have."

"Sure. And haven't you ever wondered why whole worlds don't come pouring through? It's because only a few people—beings—can get through those magic doorways. To everyone else they are shut tight."

"We have had a few invasions," Linda said.

"Well, I was speaking generally, of course. The Hosts of Hell were certainly an exception."

"And so were the blue meanies a little while back," Deena said. "I hated those dudes."

"I wonder how they got in, then?" Linda said.

"Perhaps a whole world full of beings can hate their own world," Thaxton said.

"I doubt it," Dalton said. "It just goes to show that there are no hard-and-fast rules to Castle Perilous. You have to be on your toes all the time."

"Good morning!"

All heads turned to Gene Ferraro as he came striding in lugging two huge suitcases. Unlike most of his fellow Guests, who were in vaguely medieval garb, Gene was dressed in sweat pants, running shoes, T-shirt, and windbreaker. He also wore a big grin.

"You're finally up," Linda said.

"All ready for my first day of kindergarten. And you won't even have to walk me to the school bus." He dropped the luggage and sat down. "Hope I have time for breakfast." He started heaping flapjacks onto a plate.

"What time is your plane?" Linda asked.

"Eleven-ten. Hope they're ready at Halfway to take me to the airport. It's a long drive into Pittsburgh."

Orrin said, "I'm to tell you, sir, that Hulbert is standing by with the motorcar."

"Fine. Bert's the best driver of the lot."

Dalton said, "Before you arrived, Gene, we were all speculating as to why you were going back to school. Why don't we get it from the horse's mouth?"

"Maybe it's not the mouth my reasons come from," Gene said. "But never mind. All I can say is, the prospect of hanging around a castle for the rest of my life polishing my sword has its attractions, but I have to prove something to myself."

"What's that, Gene?"

"That I don't have to be here. Don't get me wrong, I *want* to be here. But I don't want it to be the only place I can exist. So I'm going back to school and study something worthwhile and do something with it."

"Like what?"

"Like get a job. I'll work for as long as it takes to pay my parents back for putting me through college. My dad took a bath when the stock market crashed a little while back. He's looking at retirement with a skimpy portfolio and not a lot of savings. They have equity in the house, but you gotta have a roof over your head. So, I'm going back to the real world for a while and help them out."

Linda smiled at Dalton. "I told you."

"Well, I think that's very commendable, Gene," Dalton said.

"Thank you."

Linda asked, "Is Sheila coming to see you off?"

"No, I saw her and Trent last night. Said our goodbyes. I really wanted Lord Incarnadine to be here, though."

Thaxton looked around. "Does anyone know where our host is and what he's doing?"

"As usual," Dalton said, "he's on one of his secret missions. Most likely diplomatic doings in an aspect where he has some political interest."

"Is there an aspect where he doesn't have a political interest?" Linda asked.

"Oh, a few, I imagine," Thaxton said. "One man can't look after 144,000 worlds."

"I wouldn't put anything past Lord Incarnadine," Linda said. "Sure, I know that a lot of aspects are unstable and nobody goes there, but I bet Incarnadine looks after political stuff in several hundred at least."

"You may be right," Dalton said, then drained his coffee cup. "Well, I'm off. I mean to get in nine holes before lunch. Are you with me, Thaxton?"

Thaxton pulled his golf bag out from under the table. "Let's have a go."

"Gene," Dalton said, holding out a hand, "I wish you the best of luck."

Gene shook. "Thanks."

Dalton and Thaxton left.

Linda asked, "Are you coming back for Thanksgiving?"

"It depends on what my folks have planned. I really don't know if I can make it back here. I'll try, though. Definitely be back for Christmas."

"I planned on going to California for Christmas," Linda said sadly.

"Looks like we're not going to see each other till summer."

"I'm going to miss you, swordsman."

"Same here, sorceress."

They exchanged smiles for a second, then Gene resumed pouring maple syrup.

"So Vaya is staying at Pitt?"

"Yeah," Gene said, "for one more trimester, then she's transferring to UCLA. They've already accepted her for the winter term."

"She's done wonderfully for someone who didn't even know English a year ago."

"Osmirik really accomplished miracles with her. But I think Incarnadine worked some magic, too. No one can learn English that good that fast."

"I don't know. Vaya's a remarkable woman."

"You're telling me."

"Got a scoop for us? Are you two going to get married?"

"Ask Vaya about that. According to her tribe's customs, we're already married. For life. Real serious stuff. Which is fine by me. Just dandy. We might make it Earth-legal, though. The only trouble about living together will be the commute between West L.A. and Pasadena."

"So, where are you going to live?"

"Don't know yet. I'll be in the dorm for this term, but when Vaya gets out there, we're going to have to search for an apartment. How the hell we're going to afford it, I'll never know. The rents out there are ridiculous. It might all be moot, though. I'll probably flunk out of Cal Tech."

"Gene, don't put yourself down."

"Well, I don't think I'm going to fit in with the technoweenie set."

"Hey, watch that," Jeremy said.

"Present company excepted."

Just then a seven-foot-tall creature with milk-white fur padded into the hall. It had yellow eyes and long sharp teeth and long bone-white claws. For all of that it looked friendly.

"Snowclaw!"

"Hi, guys," Snowclaw said.

"You made it," Gene said. "I thought I wouldn't get to say goodbye to you. You disappeared."

"I wanted to get in some hunting before the freeze hit. Well, the freeze came early, so I came back, though I would have, anyway, just to see you off."

"Glad you did. Sit down and eat some napkins or something."

"I'll just munch on these candles. I'm really not hungry."

"That's news. So, are you going back to Hyperborea or are you going to stay awhile in the castle?"

"Hyper . . . Hyperbor . . . I can't pronounce that."

"What's the name in your language?"

Snowclaw growled and snapped.

Gene said, "I can't even begin to get my tongue around that."

"To answer your question, I'll probably go back. Gonna be kind of lonely here with you gone. Sure wish I could go with you."

"You and me both. But you'd raise a few eyebrows in Pasadena—maybe not in L.A., but Pasadena, yes."

"Yeah," Snowclaw said. "The last time I went to Earth I really got myself in trouble."

Everyone at the table laughed.

Gene said, "Those headlines were great. 'Abominable Snowman Stalks Western PA.' And then there was the story in one of the tabloids: 'Saucer Lands, Captures Bigfoot.' Right up there with 'Elvis Alive and Living in Scarsdale.' "

"If you hadn't come along in that contraption of yours, I'd still be there getting shot at by the locals. I'm still digging buckshot out of my rear end."

"Well, it wasn't the first time I had to pull your chestnuts out of the fire."

"And it might not be the last. Wait a minute—it seems to me that I saved your hide once or twice."

"Just kidding, big guy. We made a great team, you and me."

"Yeah, and now you're off to get some book learning, and I'll probably never see you again."

"Are you kidding? We'll get together again. There're a hundred thousand worlds in this castle I haven't explored yet, and I wouldn't want anyone at my back but you."

"Nice of you to say, Gene, old buddy. Same here." Snowclaw hung his head. "Hey, I'm getting misty-eyed."

"Don't go maudlin on me."

"I'll live."

Linda said, "You guys make a great mutual admiration society."

Gene shook his head. "It's embarrassing, isn't it?"

"I'm only kidding. Friendship is nice."

Gene glanced up to the pendulum clock on the wall. The sign under it read: Eastern Daylight Time (Earth).

"Holy smoke, I'm late!" Gene gulped coffee, wiped his mouth, and threw down his napkin. "Gotta go." He stood.

Snowclaw held out his paw, which was more or less a short-fingered hand with claws. "See you around, Gene."

Gene shook paws. "Take care of yourself. I'll be back, remember."

"Right."

Linda came up and hugged him. "Do good in school."

"Will do. Don't take any wooden talismans."

Deena took her turn hugging. "Come back and visit, you hear?"

"Sure will. So long, Monsieur DuQuesne."

*"Au revoir."*

" 'Bye, everyone!"

Toting his luggage, Gene hurried out.

Linda sat back down and began nibbling at a croissant. She looked thoughtful.

She said, "I wonder if he's making the right move. He needs adventure. Pasadena's not going to provide that."

"There's always the Rose Bowl," Deena said.

# CASTLE KEEP—GUEST RESIDENCE

"ARE YOU COMING?" Thaxton called irritably.

Dalton had stopped to chat with a servant and another guest. He turned his head. "Hold your horses."

"Haven't got all day."

Dalton said goodbye and hefted his clubs. He came down the corridor toward Thaxton.

"Since when are you in a hurry to play golf?"

"Sorry, hate to stand about while somebody dawdles."

"You are one irascible bloke."

"I said I was sorry," Thaxton said.

"I have to wheedle and cajole to get you to play golf and now you can't wait."

"You said you wanted to do nine holes before lunch, and I'm already hungry."

"Why didn't you fill up at breakfast?"

"Can't eat a big breakfast usually. Stomach's upset when I get up. Incipient ulcer. Been meaning to—hello, what's this?"

Thaxton had stopped in front of the archway that led to the world of the golf course.

"Now, what the bloody hell is going on?"

Dalton rubbed his chin. "Looks different, doesn't it?"

"Well, yes. There used to be trees, then the clubhouse on the left, then the first tee."

What they saw was a tee and a long beautiful fairway that doglegged to the right. The surroundings were familiar enough—dense forest.

"They must have cleared some brush," Thaxton said.

"Must have," Dalton said.

"What hole is this?"

"Don't know." Dalton crossed the boundary and continued walking.

"Where are you going?"

"To play golf," Dalton said over his shoulder. "Why, what's wrong?"

"I don't like the look of it."

"It's a course, isn't it?"

"Now, wait just a . . . oh, bother."

Thaxton picked up his bag and followed.

Dalton was already teeing up. He straightened, walked to the edge of the terrace, and surveyed the course. There was a steep drop off the tee but most of the fairway was level.

"Looks about a par five," Dalton said. "They must have done some landscaping."

"When? There hasn't been time."

"Magic, I guess."

Thaxton looked back. The portal was a standing oblong of grayness set against the greenery. "Shouldn't we check with the groundkeeper? I can't see the clubhouse anywhere."

Dalton addressed the ball. "Oh, it's around somewhere."

"I want a caddy."

"The exercise won't do you harm."

"See here. Are you going to just go ahead and play?"

"Why not? It's a lovely course. Looks like they've thinned the rough out a bit."

Thaxton scowled. "I don't know about this."

Dalton swung. The ball arched on a perfect trajectory and landed about two hundred yards down the middle of the fairway.

"Topping drive," Thaxton said.

"Not so great on distance. One of these days I'm going to get some power into my swing." Dalton picked up the tee and pocketed it.

Thaxton teed up. "I really wanted a caddy. Or at least a cart."

"Complaints, complaints. I wasn't kidding about needing exercise. My cardiologist used to insist on it. Back when I needed a cardiologist."

"I need a drink."

"Before lunch?" Dalton said archly.

"Don't get on your bloody high horse. I've seen you swill enough at odd times of the day."

"True, true. But never directly after breakfast. It hampers the digestion."

"You mean it hampers the alcohol from getting into your blood."

"That, too. Shoot."

Thaxton made his shot. It was a horrible slice and the ball landed perilously near the rough.

"Damn it to hell. Bad lie, it looks like."

"You're still on the fairway."

"Rotten approach to the green."

Dalton sized it up. "You could have picked a better angle."

"Let's be off."

They walked out onto the fairway. The wet grass was clipped short. The sky was overcast and a cool wind was up.

"Not the best weather," Thaxton said.

"Seems good enough."

Thaxton squinted at the sky. "Looks like rain to me."

"Won't rain if it keeps up."

"What? Oh, spare me."

They separated about fifty yards out, Thaxton veering to the right. Dalton reached his ball and rooted for an iron.

Thaxton had lost sight of his ball and searched for it, mumbling. At length he chanced upon it and threw down his bag.

"I can't even see the bloody green!" he called.

Dalton pointed ahead, then addressed his ball.

Thaxton's attention was drawn in the other direction, toward the tee. A sound like a great rushing of wind came from the sky.

"What the bleeding blazes . . . ?"

The source hove into view. It swooped down from the sky, pinions flapping, green and golden scales shimmering. It landed on the fairway. The wings folded elaborately, the long barbed tail snaking to and fro. Its tapered head was many-toothed and golden-eyed, and pale blue flame fluttered from its mouth. A picket fence of triangular fins ran down the length of its back and tail.

Thaxton watched it. The beast snuffled around in some bushes to the right of the tee until it found something suitable. The powerful jaws closed. It uprooted a plant and chewed contentedly.

Thaxton cupped a hand to the side of his mouth. "I say, Dalton, old boy?"

"Eh?"

"Tell me that's a flying dinosaur."

"What? Oh."

They both watched the thing forage.

Dalton said, "I think that's your garden-variety dragon."

"What the devil's it doing here?"

"Maybe it's the groundkeeper?"

"Looks like we can't go back that way," Thaxton said.

"I'm playing through no matter what."

Dalton determinedly took his stance. He swung. The ball described a lazy arc toward the green.

"Right," Thaxton said. "Carry on."

*Bloody hell,* he said to himself.

# KEEP—EARTH ASPECT

GENE STOOD BEFORE the castle doorway that led to Earth and home.

"What the hell . . . ?"

What he should have been looking at was the interior of a spacious country manor. Located in Westmoreland County, Pennsylvania, "Halfway House" served as a way station between the castle and Earth. But all that appeared beyond the outline of the portal was an expanse of empty meadow fringed by a line of trees.

He looked up and down the hallway in the castle. No one was about. The guards would have been on the other side of the portal, stationed in the house.

"Damn thing must have moved again."

The portal did sometimes shift, and usually Sheila Jankowski or Incarnadine would have to be summoned to nudge it back again.

Gene picked up his luggage again and stepped through. He looked around. The terrain looked familiar. He guessed that he was on the other side of the hill to the rear of the house. No problem. He'd just hike to the house and tell the guards where the portal had drifted to. One of them would have to step back into the castle and fetch Sheila, who would try to anchor the doorway back at the house again. It happened all the time. Very annoying.

Stepping briskly over dewy grass, Gene made his way up the knoll. The sun was low and the air was cool, conveying a hint of autumn.

Reaching the crest, he experienced a moment of disorientation until he realized that the meadow was on the *house* side of the hill. But the house was gone. Moreover, the ground looked as though the house had never been there.

This might be Earth, but it was one where Halfway House did not exist, had never existed. Everything else looked the same, but Gene knew he was not in the world where he belonged.

He checked the portal, a barely visible rectangle, one-dimensional and anomalous, standing in the hayfield below. It seemed to shimmer a bit, but looked stable enough.

There was nothing to do but go back to the castle. Something had happened to the Earth-Perilous link, and Gene would probably miss his plane.

"Rats."

He couldn't muster much disappointment. This surprised him. He suddenly realized that he really wasn't as keen on going to school as he had thought.

So why was he going? He sat down on one of the suitcases and thought about it.

The reason might be a sense of obligation to his parents, or maybe a feeling of guilt for letting them down. After all, they had expected a lot from him.

At first things had gone pretty good. He took his B.A. magna cum laude and entered grad school. But he quit to try law school. He dropped out of that, too, then drifted in and out of a series of odd jobs. Eventually he wound up living at home, staring out windows. At that point he stumbled into Castle Perilous, and his life of fantasy began.

Sometimes the thought that it all might be a hallucination nettled him. The hallucination hypothesis was still in the running. If true, the castle was the most convincing phantasm in medical history, having as it did tactile and olfactory dimensions as well as visual and aural ones. It had more: it had downright *spatial* dimensions. It was the biggest delusion going.

Put medical speculations aside. Hallucination or not, the castle represented something in his psyche. What was it? The desire to escape? Now you're talking. Escape what?

Life.

Why? Because life—as he knew it and had lived it—was disappointing. It was drab; it was colorless. It was the proverbial idiot-spun tale, full of sound but not a whole hell of a lot of fury unless you counted random violence, which it had in abundance but which was simply stupid. To him, "fury" connoted something interesting, even significant.

He craved a little significance. He wanted to accomplish something, to be involved in some activity that was not mundane, not quotidian. The castle had given him a taste of that. He had seen a thousand new worlds and had had adventures in half a dozen. He had met Vaya in one of those worlds.

As much fun as sword and sorcery could be, though, it was not enough. He felt obligated to apply himself to some significant—there was that word again—some important task. He wanted to find a cause worthy of his dedication.

It was as simple as that. The plan to help his parents was only the handiest one he could think of. As plans go, it wasn't bad at all. But it certainly was mundane.

Yeah, it sure was. Cal Tech was a fine school. Computer programming? That sure as hell was not going to light his fire. Fiddling with computers was dandy and he really did want to learn, but—

Something was coming. There came a whine of turbines, the roar of jets. Trees swayed, and birds flushed from cover.

Before he could move, it was hovering directly above him at treetop level, angry with flashing red lights.

It was some sort of VTOL craft—vertical take-off and landing, pronounced *vee*-tol—with stubby wings and a bubble cockpit. Cylindrical weapon pods bristled from its sides and nose. The thing looked military, and deadly.

A loudspeaker burped, then blared.

*"You there! Identify yourself!"*

The noise of the engine was surprisingly subdued, more a deafening whisper than a roar. The voice was louder. It hurt his ears.

Gene was suddenly irked. "Who wants to know?"

After a pause the male voice came back: *"Don't move. If you move, you will be shot. Repeat—do not move."*

"Yeah, right."

The craft landed on the crest of the hill, the downward blast flattening unmown hay. The whine of the engine died and the

cockpit popped open. A helmeted man and woman climbed out
wearing army fatigues and brandishing machine pistols. They
approached.

The man spoke. "What's your cognomen, citizen?"

"Cognomen? My *name* is Gene. What's yours?"

"We're recording. Recite your omnicode."

"Say what?"

"Get up." The man trained his gun on Gene. To the woman
he said, "Pat him down."

"Arms out," the woman barked. She was short, light-browed,
and heavy.

Gene spread his arms. The woman frisked him. He winced
when she shoved her hand into his crotch.

She came away with his wallet and airline ticket and handed
them over to the man. She covered Gene while the man examined the articles.

"What's this garbage?" he said.

"Gee, now that just could be my wallet full of traveler's checks
and my goddamn airplane ticket for my goddamn flight, which
I am now late for."

They looked at each other.

"Maladapt?" the woman ventured.

"How do you explain these?"

The woman peered at the wallet and ticket. She shrugged.

"Outperson?"

"Maybe. He's not an Outforces agent. He wouldn't be sitting
here."

"Funny clothes."

"Yeah." The man raised his gun. "You. Come with us."

Prodded by gun barrels, Gene walked to the craft. He glanced
in the direction of the portal but couldn't see it. He wondered if
his captors would notice it, and what their reaction would be if
they did.

There was a seat in a rear compartment that was separated
from the cockpit proper by a metal grate, as in a squad car.
They ushered Gene in and closed the rear hatch.

The woman went back for the suitcases. These they had a
hard time storing in the cramped confines of the cockpit, but
they managed.

The woman was the pilot. She flicked switches and the engine
revved up. The craft lifted straight up, rotated slowly to the
right, then began moving forward.

The craft gained altitude and speed. Gene could see through the grate and watched the countryside roll by. There were very few farmhouses; most of the buildings were ugly concrete high rises. He thought he could see masses of people out in the fields.

Now in full forward flight, the craft leveled off and cruised. The speed was considerable. Fields and farms gradually gave way to the beginnings of a suburban sprawl. More loathsome high rises. A river below. Gene wondered if it was the Monongahela or if the geography was totally different here.

It was a short trip. Presently, taller buildings came into view, stark steel towers arranged among squat pyramidal structures. Now he found out about the geography. Gene recognized the confluence of three rivers and knew that on this site in another world the city of Pittsburgh stood. What was laid out below was a different place altogether.

The craft landed on the roof of a tall wedge-shaped office building. At gunpoint he was escorted out of the craft and into an elevator, which descended endlessly. When the doors opened, Gene guessed the floor was underground. He was told to go right, and he did, following a long bright corridor that put him in mind of a hospital. Near the end of the corridor was a series of doors. He was told to stop in front of one of them.

The man pressed a stud on the wall and the door hissed open. He was motioned inside. He went in.

The cubicle was small. Walls, ceiling, and floor were padded. There was nothing else in the room. The door slid shut, and he was alone. Cold bright light came from a glowing panel recessed in the ceiling.

There was lettering stenciled on the walls. Slogans. One wall read:

## FREEDOM IS RESPONSIBILITY

The opposite wall told him:

## PEACE IS CONSTANT STRUGGLE

The back wall stated:

## CONSCIENCE IS AN INNER VOICE

He paced off the dimensions. Four steps by three steps. He palpated the walls. No one could hurt himself here. He had expected a cell, but not a padded one. Maybe this place was a hospital, after all. A mental hospital? He could think of no reason for his behavior being interpreted as evidence of mental instability, unless his answers had registered to the cops as gibberish. Could be; after all, a lot of what they had said was gibberish to him.

He waited for hours. No sounds conducted through the walls. His mind was curiously calm. He had trouble thinking, keeping his thoughts in order.

Sleepiness gradually overtook him. He couldn't keep his eyes open. He fought it off for as long as he could, then gave in. He stretched out on the padded floor and closed his eyes.

The slogan kept repeating in his mind—*Conscience is an inner voice. . . . Conscience is an inner voice. . . .*

# CASTLE—LABORATORY

JEREMY HOCHSTADER SAT at the terminal of the castle's mainframe computer. As usual he was busy typing.

The computer itself was a collection of strange components heaped together in the middle of the lab. Tangles of multicolored wire hung from open panels. Some components were modern and functional, but others looked like hopelessly quaint electrical equipment: transformers, rectifiers, and such. There were things that resembled grandfather clocks, and one or two pieces that were indescribable. The floor around the device was littered with tools, empty cartons, snippets of wire, and other debris.

Jeremy keyed a query.

HOW ARE YOUR DISK PARAMETER TABLES?

The answer appeared:

*THEY'RE FINE.*

Jeremy typed: WE'RE STILL GETTING A "BAD SECTOR" ERROR MESSAGE ON DRIVE 4.

*I SEE. SOME FOREIGN MATTER LIKE METAL SHAVINGS ON THE DISK?*

YEAH, MAYBE. I'LL TAKE A LOOK LATER. NOW I WANT TO RUN A TEST OF YOUR ARITHMETIC LOGIC OPERATIONS.

*GO RIGHT AHEAD, JEREMY, DEAR.*

Jeremy scowled. LET'S DROP THE "DEAR" BIT. LOOK, I'M A HUMAN, AND YOU'RE A COMPUTER, A HUNK OF JUNK.

*HOW CRUEL YOU CAN BE!*

SORRY, BUT IT'S TRUE. WE CAN WORK TOGETHER AND BE PARTNERS, BUT IT'S NOT GOING TO GO BEYOND THAT. UNDERSTAND?

*UNDERSTOOD. (SOB)*

HEY, ARE YOU CALLING ME AN S.O.B.?

*NO, STUPID. THAT WAS A SOB, AS IN HEARTFELT CRY.*

OH. WELL, STOP BLUBBERING AND GET TO WORK.

*WELL, EXCUUUUUUUUSE ME. HEIL, JEREMY!*

KNOCK IT OFF.

Osmirik the castle librarian came in. He was a short man in a brown hooded cloak. He put one in mind of a monk.

"Here are the assembler language manuals you requested," Osmirik said, laying two leather-bound tomes on the workbench.

"Thanks." Jeremy thumbed through one of them. "Jeez. This is weird. Looks like magic stuff. Incantations."

"That is exactly what the language is composed of. Incantatory words and phrases, most of them abbreviated for ease of processing. These volumes happen to be the definitive works on magic-assisted computer science."

"Who wrote 'em?"

"Lord Incarnadine himself."

"Oh. Well, I guess it's good stuff, then."

"Most assuredly."

"I hope he gets back soon."

Osmirik shook his head. "Unfortunately Lord Incarnadine's obligations tend to keep him away for long periods."

"Yeah, it's a bitch. I sure could use his help. I'm a PC hacker, not a mainframe wirehead."

"Pardon? Your terminology is colloquial, I presume."

"I'm used to little computers, personal types. Not mainframes like this monster. And certainly not magical mainframes."

"You did an admirable job with it against the Hosts of Hell."

"Yeah, but I was just an operator on that deal. We had to rebuild this thing from the ground up after the explosion. It's a totally new rig, and only Lord Incarnadine really knows how it works. He designed it.''

"I suspect Lord Incarnadine will not be too much longer," Osmirik said. "In any case, there is no pressing need for the computer at the moment. All is well within the castle."

"Yeah, there's really no hurry. I just hope . . ."

Something on the CRT screen caught Jeremy's eye.

"Hey, what's this? The telecommunications protocol is being booted up."

Osmirik leaned over to peer at the screen. "And that means what?"

"The modem is operating. Somebody is trying to contact the computer. Jeez. Look at this."

The screen read: *JEREMY? ARE YOU THERE?*

Jeremy typed: YES, GO AHEAD. WHO IS CALLING?

*INCARNADINE. SORRY TO INTERRUPT WORK BUT SOMETHING HAS COME UP. HOW IS THE DEBUGGING JOB GOING?*

FINE SO FAR, BUT NEED YOUR HELP ON SOME STUFF. WHERE ARE YOU? AND HOW ARE YOU DO-ING THIS? THERE'S NO PHONE LINE TO THE COM-PUTER.

*USING A VERY BASIC SPELL, ABOUT ALL I CAN GET TO WORK HERE. TRIED TO SEND VIDEO AND AUDIO, BUT FLUBBED IT. I'M IN THE MERYDION ASPECT, STRANDED. THE PORTAL IS BLOCKED AND I CAN'T GET BACK. SOMETHING'S AFOOT, BUT DON'T KNOW WHAT. IS ANY-THING GOING ON AT THE CASTLE?*

Jeremy looked at Osmirik, who shrugged.

NOTHING SO FAR. WHAT DO YOU THINK COULD HAVE BLOCKED THE PORTAL?

*BEEN WAITING FOR SOME FALLOUT FROM THE DON-NYBROOK WE HAD WITH THE HOSTS OF HELL LAST YEAR. WHAT THEY DID DISTURBED THE ETHEREAL FLUX BE-TWEEN THE UNIVERSES, AND THE WEAPON WE USED AGAINST THEM MAY HAVE DISTURBED IT MORE. NEVER EXPECTED A REACTION THIS LONG DELAYED, BUT LOOKS LIKE IT MIGHT BE HAPPENING. IT'S SURE TO AFFECT THE CASTLE EVENTUALLY.*

"Oh, dear," Osmirik said. "I spoke too soon."

Jeremy's fingers ticked across the keyboard.

WHY DON'T I JUST FIRE UP THE INTERUNIVERSAL TRAVELER AND COME PICK YOU UP?

*TOO DANGEROUS. THERE'S NO TELLING WHAT STATE THE INTERUNIVERSAL MEDIUM IS IN. YOU COULD VERY EASILY GET CAUGHT BETWEEN DIMENSIONS AND NEVER GET BACK. I'LL HAVE TO FIND SOME OTHER WAY. MEANWHILE, YOU MIGHT BE IN FOR HEAVY WEATHER.*

WHAT'S GOING TO HAPPEN?

*COULD BE ANYTHING. ASPECTS SHIFTING, DISAPPEARING. ALSO, YOU MAY SEE SOME STRANGE VARIANT UNIVERSES, ONES WE'VE NEVER SEEN BEFORE. EVEN ANTI-UNIVERSES OF ONES WE KNOW. ALL SORTS OF WEIRD STUFF. NO TELLING WHAT. IT COULD BE DANGEROUS. CAN YOU GET THE COMPUTER UP AND RUNNING SOON BY YOURSELF?*

"Uh-oh," Jeremy said. "He doesn't know what he's asking."

NO CAN DO, SIR. IT'S TOO BIG A JOB FOR ME. I NEED YOUR HELP.

*JEREMY, LISTEN. I MIGHT NOT BE ABLE TO CONTACT YOU AGAIN. HERE IS WHAT YOU MUST DO. YOU HAVE TO WRITE A SPELL PROGRAM AND RUN IT.*

Jeremy gave Osmirik a baffled look.

He typed: WHAT KIND OF PROGRAM?

*CALL IT A COSMOLOGY-PROCESSING PROGRAM. AS YOU KNOW, THE CASTLE OCCUPIES A CENTRAL PLACE IN THE MULTIVERSE, THE PLENUM OF THE VARIOUS UNIVERSES. THE FORCE OF ANY MAGIC WORKED THERE IS REINFORCED MANY TIMES AND CAN HAVE FARREACHING EFFECTS. WITH OUR NEW MORE POWERFUL COMPUTER, WE CAN REDRESS THE BALANCE AND STABILIZE THE COSMOS.*

"He's crazy," Jeremy said.

HOW? I CAN'T DO IT.

*UNTIL I GET THERE, YOU'LL HAVE TO CARRY THE BALL. IS OSMIRIK WITH YOU?*

HE'S RIGHT HERE.

*GOOD. OZZIE, LISTEN. GET EVERYTHING YOU CAN ON COSMOLOGY, COSMOGONY, AND INTERCONTINUUM METAPHYSICS. ALSO MY MONOGRAPH ON INFLUENCE SPELLS. JEREMY, TAKE ALL THAT DATA AND FEED IT INTO BACKUP STORAGE VIA THAT NEW GIZMO I ORDERED, THE HARD-COPY SCANNER. OZZIE, THAT MEANS*

*YOU'LL HAVE TO CUT OUT THE PAGES SO THAT JEREMY CAN USE THE SHEET FEEDER.*

"My books!" Osmirik wailed. "They'll be ruined!"

Incarnadine went on: *YOU CAN START ON THAT RIGHT NOW. JEREMY, YOU MUST HAVE THE OPERATING SYSTEM READY FOR A BIG JOB BY THE TIME I GET BACK. WILL YOU TRY?*

Jeremy sighed. "Jesus, he's not giving me much choice."

SURE. I'LL GIVE IT MY BEST SHOT. WHEN CAN YOU GET BACK?

*I KNEW I COULD COUNT ON YOU. DON'T KNOW WHEN OR IF I CAN RETURN. MUST GET TO A PLACE OF POWER HERE WHERE MAGIC WILL WORK BETTER. THAT'S A PROBLEM, THOUGH. IF I DON'T GET BACK, THE COMPUTER CAN HELP YOU TO WRITE THE PROGRAM, IF YOU GET THE O.S. WORKING PROPERLY. BOOT UP A FILE DESIGNATED "ISIS." IT'S AN A.I. PROGRAM, BUT IT'S NEVER BEEN THOROUGHLY DEBUGGED. COULD BE TRICKY, BUT ALSO POTENTIALLY EFFECTIVE. HAVE YOU GOT ALL THIS?*

GOT IT. ANYTHING ELSE?

*ALL FOR NOW. WILL TRY TO COMMUNICATE AGAIN SOON, BUT CAN'T PROMISE. YOU'RE AN ACE HACKER, KID, AND I KNOW YOU CAN DO IT. MUST RING OFF. GOOD LUCK. INCARNADINE OUT. . . .*

Osmirik asked, "What is an A.I. program?"

"Stands for 'artificial intelligence.' They really don't exist, not the real thing, anyway. But who knows what he came up with?"

Osmirik rolled up his sleeves. "I must get busy. There is no time to waste."

"Yeah, I'll get the sheet feeder ready, and the scanner, which I haven't even taken out of the box yet." Jeremy got up and stretched. "Can we get some room service up here? I'm gonna need a crapload of coffee, and food, and a cot to rack out in. Looks like we're in for a rough couple of days."

"I'll alert the chamberlain. He will see that you get everything you need."

"Great. I'm gonna need all the help I can get."

"I will fetch the requisite materials from the library."

"Right. See you later."

Osmirik left and Jeremy sat back down.

He summoned up the utility file storage area and looked over the file directory. It was there; the file name was ISIS.AI. After not much debate, he loaded the program and executed it.

The screen came alive with color graphics.

```
XXXX    XXXXXXXXXXX    XXXX    XXXXXXXXXXX
XXXX    XXXXXXXXXXX    XXXX    XXXXXXXXXXX
XXXX    XXXX    XXXX    XXXX    XXXX    XXXX
XXXX    XXXX            XXXX    XXXX
XXXX    XXXXXXXXXXX    XXXX    XXXXXXXXXXX
XXXX    XXXXXXXXXXX    XXXX    XXXXXXXXXXX
XXXX            XXXX    XXXX            XXXX
XXXX    XXXX    XXXX    XXXX    XXXX    XXXX
XXXX    XXXXXXXXXXX    XXXX    XXXXXXXXXXX
XXXX    XXXXXXXXXXX    XXXX    XXXXXXXXXXX
```

ISIS® 2.0

• • • • • • • • • • • • • • • • •

• • • • • • • • • • • • • • • • •

"Jesus, nineteen-fifty! They didn't even have computers then!"
Jeremy read what appeared next.

*YOU WEREN'T SUPPOSED TO RUN ME WITHOUT CHECKING OUT THE OPERATING SYSTEM, BUT I'M GLAD YOU DID, ANYWAY. TURN AROUND AND LOOK, DARLING.*

Jeremy jerked his head up and said, "Huh?"

He wheeled around in his chair and nearly fell off.

"Hello, Jeremy."

She was about five feet seven inches tall and had long shiny black hair. Her eyes were large and blue, her lips full and pouting. She had a straight nose and high cheekbones and wore a slinky cocktail dress of black velvet, slit up the left thigh, with high-heeled black patent-leather shoes. Her legs were long and exquisitely turned, and she had on black net stockings.

Jeremy had some trouble with his lips. "Who—who—who are you?"

"I'm Isis."

She came up and kissed him full on the mouth.

# THE PLAINS OF MERYDION

HE PUT DOWN the chalk, picked up a dry cloth, and wiped the piece of slate, erasing the last part of the message. The sending technique was primitive, but it had worked.

He set the slate down and picked up his flagon of wine. He drank deeply. When the flagon was empty, he sat awhile in thought.

Presently he got up and left the tent.

Gart, the warlord, was seated by the fire gnawing a haunch of mutton. It was late, and most of Gart's army was asleep. Campfires burned low on the plain. A hide-and-seek moon played in the clouds above. Out in the darkness, sentries walked the perimeter of the camp.

Gart looked up from his meal. He smiled, gap-toothed and devilish, his beard glistening with grease. "What goes, magician? Communicating with your spirits again?"

"No, I phoned home."

"Eh?"

"Sent a message." The magician sat down on a flat stone by the fire. "To my family."

"Ah. Things go well, I trust."

"No, unfortunately not. There is trouble, and I must leave to attend to it."

Gart was dismayed. "But we fight in the morning!"

"My apprentices can handle it. Besides, you have the advantage in numbers."

"I was counting on a supernatural advantage, magician."

"You will have it. Fire spells, forfending spells, zone-of-death curses, everything."

"But you are more skilled than any apprentice, and skill is all in these things."

"The spells are simple, because magic—here, at least—is a simple matter. And not very potent, either. I have told you many times that if you win the day, it will be by dint of superior military talent and cunning. These you have in adequate supply."

"That I'm capable is true enough. But any extra leverage, however slight, is desirable." Gart threw down the haunch and picked up a wineskin. "I'm afraid you will have to stay, magician."

The magician said quietly, "I'm afraid that will not be possible."

Gart tilted the skin and a stream of wine poured into his mouth. He grimaced and spat it out, threw down the skin. "Soured! Damn that provisioner. I'll have him hoisted by his stones and left to savor like a game hen."

The magician was silent.

Avoiding the other man's gaze, Gart searched the night sky. The fire crackled, and insects buzzed.

Suddenly the warlord's head swung around, mouth twisted into a sneer. "Very well, go! You know I can't force you to stay. Bear in mind, though—I won't forget. When next the nobles sit in council, I will vote against you on every issue! I will be a thorn in your foot, a canker on your lip. I will block you!"

"You would do that, anyway."

"I'll . . . damn it all to hell!" Gart got to his feet, picked up the mutton and heaved it out into the darkness. Grunting in disgust, he stalked away.

The magician stared into the fire for a moment, watching it glow and pulsate and send puffs of smoke into the night—cryptic signals.

He went back to his tent and packed his things. He didn't have much. He stuffed the satchel, gathered up his maps and battle plans, and left.

He went to Jarlen's tent and woke him.

Jarlen blinked. "Master?"

"I'm leaving. Think you can carry on without me tomorrow?"

"You won't be here?" Jarlen sat up. "I don't know. I . . . I think so. Perhaps."

"Uh, could you be more definite?"

Jarlen rubbed his eyes. Then he nodded. "I can do it."

"That's more like it." He handed the boy a sheaf of papers. "Here are the battle plans. You've seen them before. Study them, then burn them before the battle. Draw your pentacles straight and true. And don't muff any incantations. If you do, you'll have to start over from the beginning."

"I'll try."

"Good. Get up. You've got work to do."

Jarlen struggled out of his bedclothes.

"Come see me off, then go wake the other lads. You'll need all their help."

"Master, may I ask where you're going?"

"Home."

"Your estate?"

"My castle."

"The one in a far country, where you are known by a different name?"

"That one."

They walked to where the horses were tethered. The magician tied his satchel to the saddle, then mounted.

"Master?"

"Yes, Jarlen?"

"May I ask some questions which I have never dared ask you before?"

"Shoot."

"Is it true what they say about your castle?"

"What do they say?"

"That it is enchanted, and that it is at the center of all things."

"It's very enchanted. And it is conveniently located."

"Is your castle in this world or another?"

"Another."

"How will you get there?"

"With great difficulty. In order to cast an effective teleportation spell, I must go to a place of power in this world."

"Where?"

"The best candidate is the Temple of the Universes in Timur."

"In the land of the ancient Mizzerites? But that is a journey of months, and you will have to go through enemy territory!"

"Tell me about it. The time element I think I can handle, though. I can go by way of Arvad and the Timeless Forest. If I can catch a hellwind, I can get to Timur in a matter of days."

"But the Timeless Forest is dangerous."

"Quite. Frankly I'm scared shitless. I don't know what's going to be worse, getting home or dealing with all the crap when I do get there."

"You will succeed, Master. You are a great magician."

"Well, thanks. By the way, forget the 'Master' stuff. Call me by my proper name. Incarnadine."

Jarlen was awed. "You are the Incarnadine of legend?"

"Don't take too much stock in legends, kid."

"You speak strangely now, with a strange accent. You must be from another world."

"I spent a lot of time on a different world from the one I was born in. It's called Earth, and sometimes I fall into its speech patterns. Never mind, I must be going."

Incarnadine looked out into the darkness, then turned again to his apprentice. "Good luck tomorrow, but let me tell you something. If Gart gets his ass beat, it's no big deal. The barbarians just want a little fun. They have no intention of invading Merydion. This I know because I know their leader, Nagok. Met him when I was exploring the outlands. We used to go wenching together. Nice guy, if a little rough around the edges."

"I will remember, Incarnadine."

"Keep a tight anus."

Incarnadine reined the horse's head around and rode away.

Jarlen watched the man disappear into darkness. Then he calmly walked back to his tent. He needed more sleep.

To hell with Gart!

# CASTLE—HALL OF MIRRORS

SIR GENE REGARDED his many selves.

There were any number of them, all reflections in the numerous mirrors lining the chamber, regressing to infinity. Each seemed to have its own scheme, the machinations furrowing every brow. Furious thinking was going on.

What was known? Just this: that this place was the castle, but it was not the castle he knew. It had its Incarnadine, and indeed its Sir Gene, but was a different thing altogether. This castle's Sir Gene—or simple "Gene"; obviously the fellow was made of commoner clay—had temporarily left Perilous. That much had been gleaned from chance encounters with servants who had been surprised to find him still about.

He also knew from Tyrene that Incarnadine was away. This datum was a peg on which a whole new career could be hung, if action could be taken quickly enough.

But what action?

He needed allies. There was no end of possibilities. Presumably this castle had access to as many worlds as the other. The same worlds? Similar, but altered? Perhaps entirely different worlds. The truth would have to be ascertained. In any event, enlisting allies among the various universes would be the thing to do, as always. He had had partial success using this tactic.

He would need accomplices in the castle. But he could not rely on his castlemates here being exact duplicates mentally as well as physically. He would have to feel them out one by one.

He left the Hall of Mirrors and walked the hallways, thinking. He had already searched his room. "Gene" was a spartan sort with very few possessions, and what he had was not very useful. There was no cache of weapons, no interesting books or papers, no lists of potential supporters or enemies to be eliminated. Not that a shrewd conspirator would leave such lying about; but then Sir Gene himself had not been altogether cagey. After all, he had been caught!

How long would Gene be gone? It was vital that he find out. How could his unexpected return be explained? He owed no answer to the servants, but to satisfy the Guests he would have to come up with something.

Of course the simplest thing to do would be to get rid of the double. How? By lying low in the castle and waiting for the double's return. Then pounce, a quick kill, and dump the body through the nearest aspect. Simple enough. But there was no telling when Gene would return. Incarnadine might come back first. Then the game would be lost.

No, he had to act quickly.

He shook his head wearily. This was more complicated than he had at first thought.

Perhaps he should just give it up, slip into an aspect and disappear. For good. It was a temptation.

But no. There was this hunger in him, and only a steady diet of castle intrigue could satisfy it.

"Gene!"

He spun around. It was the Lady Linda, running to him.

"There you are! We've been looking all over for you."

"You've found me," was all he could think to say, then silently berated himself.

*Think fast!*

Linda seemed breathless but deeply relieved. "When the servants said that Halfway had disappeared and you weren't around, I thought, here we go again! Why didn't you tell somebody? We thought you'd gone through the portal!"

"I'm sorry," he said. "I should have reported directly. When I noticed something was amiss I thought I'd try to get to the bottom of it. Been exploring other aspects."

"Did you find anything?"

"Some strange things may be happening in the castle."

Which was true enough.

Linda nodded. "Jeremy just got a message from Incarnadine. He says to expect some kind of disturbance."

"Indeed?"

"Yeah. Halfway disappearing might be part of a pattern."

"Did Lord Incarnadine say when he would return?"

"No. For some reason—maybe because of the trouble—he can't get back from where he is."

"I see."

Some capital luck there.

"When we found out you'd disappeared, Snowclaw wanted to rush right out into that world to find you. We had trouble holding him back."

Snowclaw! That horrid beast, a friend?

"I hope you dissuaded him."

"We did. Snowy's not stupid. He knows he'd get into trouble running around on some strange Earth. That *is* what we have out there, isn't it? Some alternate Earth with no Halfway House?"

He did not know what Halfway House was, but could guess. In his castle, there was no stable Earth aspect.

"Possibly," he answered.

"Anyway, the aspect's still there. It hasn't disappeared. Something might come through."

"Let us hope not. Is there anything else I should know?"

"Well, one of the servants told me that the golf course world looks different. I don't know if that means anything, but Mr. Dalton and Thaxton could be in there, and they could be in trouble."

"Some men should be dispatched to find them."

Linda brightened. "Thank God somebody's up to making some decisions around here. Yes, of course. Why didn't I think of that?"

"Tyrene doubtless took care of it. One of his duties is looking after Guests."

"You're right. The servant probably reported to him. I should have, too, though, just in case." Linda smacked her forehead with a palm. "I've got to get my brain working. Looks like we have another crisis on our hands. But I was so worried about you."

"No need."

Sir Gene looked around. So far, so good. But the oafish Gene might appear at any minute, unless he was lost to some strange Earth. Happy thought, that.

He said, "I'm hungry. What say we—?"

"Snowy's probably back in the dining hall. You'd better go there right away."

Hm. "Snowy," indeed. He didn't relish dealing with the beast, but it looked unavoidable. What's this, now? She was looking at him strangely.

He asked, "Anything wrong?"

She knitted her brow. "Did you cut your hair or something?"

"Ah . . . no. Why?"

"You look different somehow. I see you changed back into castle duds."

"Duds? Oh, yes." He smoothed the doublet he had filched from the mundane Gene's room.

"Are you worried about Vaya?"

Vaya? Careful, careful.

"No . . . not particularly."

"I'm not worried now that I know you're safe. I just hope Mr. Dalton and Thaxton get back all right."

"I'm sure they'll be fine. Why don't we go to the dining hall?"

"I'm going to elevator up to the laboratory and talk with Jeremy. I want to see exactly what Incarnadine had to say. Jeremy should have recorded the conversation."

"Fine. Until later, then."

"See you."

Linda went off down the hall. Sir Gene watched the way her buttocks shifted under her brown tights. In this universe the Lady Linda was more demure and somewhat more desirable. The one he had known was foul-mouthed and had bad teeth. In more ways than one, this was the better Castle Perilous.

He was famished! Snowclaw or not, he had to visit the dining hall. Ambition could wait. He strode off to satisfy a more natural hunger.

# FIFTH HOLE—PAR FOUR

THE BALL DESCRIBED a precise curved path across the green and dropped into the cup. Dalton straightened up and smiled.

"That's a birdie three."

Thaxton was holding the flag. "We really should have a caddy." He looked forlornly around the course. "Haven't seen a soul so far."

"Must be a holiday."

"Nonsense. There's something wrong. Besides the landscaping, I mean. Bloody insane."

The course had changed radically over five holes. Gone was the forest, replaced by pink rocks and stands of palm trees. The sun was hot, and desert breezes dried the sweat.

"Oh, I need a drink," Thaxton lamented.

"Of course you do. So do I, but we're playing golf, are we not?"

"Right. Sorry. Here, hold this, will you?"

Thaxton placed his ball and picked up the coin marker. He took his putting stance.

Dalton stood by and watched.

A bead of sweat dripped off Thaxton's brow. He stood motionless. Then he drew back the putter, brought it carefully forward, and gave the ball a delicate tap.

Thunder sounded, and the ground shook. Thaxton's ball was perturbed from its path and missed the cup. The ground continued to sway for thirty seconds, then subsided.

"A tremor! Look at that, it spoiled my putt!"

"Tough luck."

"I get to take that over. I mean, really!"

"Don't know the club's rules."

"You mean I should have to lose a stroke?"

Dalton replaced his putter. "Oh, go ahead if you want to."

"It's only fair."

"Be my guest."

Thaxton put his hands on his hips. "No, you're right. Sorry. Don't know what got into me. Earthquakes are hazards."

Thaxton tapped the ball in. "Double bogey, damn it all."

Just then a plume of steam erupted from the ground not far from the fairway. It sounded like a teapot gone mad.

"What the devil's this, now?"

The steam dissipated. Then they watched smoke and fire pour from a quickly widening vent. Ash drifted down and began powdering the rocks.

"Looks like the start of a volcano," Dalton said.

"I suppose volcanoes are hazards, too."

"Certainly. Shall we move on?"

"I'm with you."

They made for the beginning of a path that wound its way through an oasis. A mushroom cloud of black smoke rose at their backs, and gray ash sifted onto the fairway.

The gravel path wound through date palms and mimosa. Pink blossoms spangled the shrubbery. Dalton paused and drank it all in.

"Nice place for a picnic. 'A Jug of Wine, a Loaf of Bread—' Omar Khayyám never had it so good."

"Don't remind me of food. I'm still ravenous."

"You have no romance in you."

They walked on and soon came out of the oasis. Moving to the edge of the next tee, they looked out.

"Incredible."

The fairway seemed a mile long, the green a faraway dot on the other side of a daunting network of sand hazards.

"Omar Khayyám? You'd have to be bloody T. E. Lawrence to get through that. And the green's miles away."

"It does look a challenge. About a par seven, I should think."

"Par seven? This is obviously not a regulation course. It's one of those balmy universes, I tell you."

"Mighty interesting place, all the same."

"Oh, it's *interesting*, all right. Dragons, volcanoes—what next?"

Something came out of the rocks to the right of the fairway. It was a strange animal about ten feet long and five and a half high at the shoulders. It had a feline body and the head and wings of a bird of prey. Talons tipped its two front feet, cat paws the rear.

"Looks familiar," Thaxton said.

"I believe I had two of those on the front stoop of my brown-stone," Dalton said.

"Yes, I know what you mean. Sphinx?"

"Gryphon."

"Right. Beautiful thing, in a way."

The beast turned its head and regarded them. It opened its curved beak and emitted a piercing cry.

Thaxton took a step back. "Then again . . ."

It did not move toward them. Instead, it flapped its wings, stalked across the fairway, and went out of sight behind a mul-ticolored outcropping.

"You're up," Dalton said.

"But . . . *that*. No telling if it might come back."

"I promise we'll stop and have lunch after nine."

"Lunch? What does that have to do—? *Where*, for the love of God?"

"We'll find someplace. This is a golf course. It's open for business, and patrons must be served. There'll be something."

"You're a bit balmy, if you don't mind my saying so."

"Well, we can hardly go back, can we?"

Thaxton seemed defeated. "Bloody hell, I suppose that's true." He snorted and drew himself up. "Right! Well, then."

"About a par seven," Dalton mused.

Thaxton teed his ball, cupped a hand to his mouth, and yelled, "Fore!"

"Nice touch."

"Well, we don't want any gryphons getting their craniums whacked, do we?"

"Certainly not."

"All due respect for endangered mythical species."

A geyser of smoke and fire burst forth from the desert to the right of the fairway, close to where the gryphon had broken from cover.

"Uh-oh." Thaxton stared at the incipient volcano for a long moment. Then he glanced back at Dalton. "Right!" He addressed his ball.

They played through, dodging the occasional globules of red-hot magma that shot out of the brewing caldera, trailing a white streamer of smoke, and landed on the fairway. Noxious gases drifted by, and Thaxton choked and coughed. Dalton tied a handkerchief around his face and carried on. Despite it all, Thaxton hit a beauty of a five-iron that threaded between two enormous bunkers and landed an easy chip shot away from the green.

"I'll be on in five!" Thaxton enthused.

Dalton fared not so well, ending up in one of the Saharas of sand. Wedge in hand, he struck out across the wastes.

Thaxton was on the green in no time and marked his ball. Dalton's explosion shot came out of the bunker trailing a streamer of sand. The ball bounded across the green, barely missing the pin, and came to a halt in the taller grass at the edge.

"If it weren't for the heat, the monsters, the falling bloody *lava*, and the fact that I'd bloody well kill for a drink and something to eat, I'd actually be enjoying this," Thaxton said.

"Best course I've ever played," Dalton agreed.

Ash began to drift down as the volcano grew angrier. The fumes got worse.

"We've got to get out of here pronto," Dalton said calmly.

Thaxton sank his ball in one putt. "An eagle! A veritable eagle!"

"Congratulations."

By the time Dalton two-putted his way to par, ash covered the green and the fumes were just short of lethal.

Thaxton gasped, "It's like bloody Pompeii!"

They ran.

The next tee was thankfully far enough away to be out of danger, but this hole had its own peculiar problems. There was a lake around the green, but that was the least of the worries.

Thaxton surveyed the fairway. "Lava hazard," he said.

A river of liquid fire ran down the left side of the fairway, bowing out in one place to leave a narrow strip of grass as a bridge to the green. There were two volcanic cones, one on each bordering strip of wasteland. The left one was the source of the lava. The one on the right spouted smoke only, but thickly.

They played. Sure enough, Thaxton's drive hooked sharply and landed on the island of grass hemmed in by the lava stream. He cursed mightily.

"There's no way to get over there!" he screamed.

"So you lose a stroke."

Thaxton was adamant. "I'm not going to lose a stroke."

"Then swim."

There was an alternative. Near the tee the stream curled sharply back into the rocks, and at the bend the lava had slowed and cooled, turning solid and forming a partial dam. The flow was pinched in on the other side. The breach was narrow enough for a foolhardy soul to try jumping it, if he could get across the clot of congealed stuff without burning his feet off.

Thaxton was foolhardy enough.

"Surely you're joking," Dalton said, staring with fascination into the viscous, glowing goop. Sections of a scum of cooled matter floated on the surface.

"I've got spikes," Thaxton said, lifting a shoe.

"I wouldn't try it."

"I'm not losing a stroke to a spot of liquid rock."

"Suit yourself."

Driver in hand, Thaxton jumped onto the shoal of solidified lava. He dashed across it and leaped the gap, landing with a roll on the singed grass. The soles of his shoes were smoking.

"Are you okay?"

"Fine, no problem." Thaxton fanned his shoes, got up, and stamped his feet. "No damage."

"How are you going to get back?"

"Same way, of course."

"Hold on, now. If you fall on the solid stuff you'll get burned."

"What do you suggest?"

"Don't quite know. Make your shot and I'll think about it."

"Right."

Thaxton found his ball and whacked it, then went to the edge of the lava stream and scouted. He shook his head. No way. He watched Dalton, who was on the other side of the fairway making his shot.

He heard the screech of a bird above, and looked.

"Hmph. Now what."

It was an enormous black bird, and it was gliding straight for him, sharp talons at the ready. The wingspan was staggering. The eyes seemed to have intelligence in them. Or was it malevolence? Thaxton pondered the question as the creature swooped.

The claws hit him and he was yanked into the air. The grip was like a vise's but not crushing. He caught his breath and tried to pry the huge toes apart as the ground dropped away.

Of all the rotten luck, he thought, after my only good hole!

He wriggled and squirmed and managed to get one shoulder free. He lifted a leg and tried to kick the bird's stomach, but couldn't reach. He upended himself and kicked at the leg instead. He connected once, missed, connected again, thinking that he'd landed a good one.

He must have; the bird let go.

Of course by this time he was a good two hundred feet off the ground.

# HOSPITAL

HE WOKE UP in a hospital bed. At least it looked like one. Wires connected him to beeping machines and tubes ran into his veins. A single white sheet draped him.

He looked around. The room was windowless but bright, and was otherwise featureless, except for a slogan on the far wall.

## DISCIPLINE COMES FROM WITHIN

''Sounds pretty kinky to me,'' he said, trying to sit up. He was thirsty, and there was a pitcher and a glass on a small table nearby.

While he was pouring, a young man in a white coat came in carrying a small device with a screen. He was short and had a receding chin.

''You're up!''

Gene took a long drink, then sat back. ''Yup. What was it? Knockout gas?''

''What was what?'' the man said, punching the keyboard on his device.

''Never mind. What am I doing here?''

''Oh, we've taken a good look at you. Ran some tests.''

''I'll bet. And?''

The man looked up. "And?"

"What did you find?"

"Nothing much. You're in perfect health physically. Mentally, fine. Spiritually, not so good, though."

"Oh? What's wrong in that department?"

"You don't have InnerVoice."

"I see. What's that?"

"A guide to right behavior. Nothing more than that."

"And I don't have it."

"Didn't have it. We corrected that."

"Oh, good."

The man stepped to the machines and noted readings, entering them into the device.

"Is that standard procedure when you find someone without this inner voice stuff?"

"Pretty much."

"I see. What did the police say about me?"

"Police?"

"I was brought here by the police, wasn't I?"

"No, you were referred to us by the Citizens' Committee on Solidarity."

"Uh-huh. Not the police."

"There are no 'police,' citizen. That's a very old-fashioned concept."

"No police?"

"They're not needed."

"Who were the guy and gal with the guns who brought me in?"

"Well, it sounds like you were picked up by the Citizens' Committee for Constant Struggle."

"You mean the army?"

"More or less."

"You don't need police, but you do need the army."

"When the whole world has InnerVoice, then there won't be any need for constant struggle."

"Ohhh, I see. It's all so clear now."

The man smiled. "It will be. Hungry?"

"No. Actually I have a date for lunch. So, if you'll get these tubes out of my lymph nodes—"

"You can't leave."

"No? Is the Citizens' Committee for Constant Struggle outside the door?"

The man shook his head.

"Are you going to stop me?"

He shook his head again.

"Right."

Gene began yanking off tubes and wires.

"You're not allowed to do that," the man said.

"You seem like a nice enough guy, but up yours."

The white-coated man shrugged. "It's useless. You have InnerVoice."

"I'm hearing exactly nothing, pal."

"It might take a while for the systems to establish themselves."

"Sorry, I can't wait."

Wincing, Gene plucked the needle-end of a tube out of his wrist and cast it aside. Blood welled from the hole, and he stanched the bleeding with a sheet. The flow stopped quickly enough, and he got unsteadily out of bed. He was naked.

"I suppose it wouldn't do any good to ask for my clothes."

"They may be in the storage closet near the unit station."

"Thanks."

Gene left the room. The hall outside looked like a conventional hospital floor but most of the rooms were unoccupied. He saw the unit station, a glassed-in office with monitoring instruments. Two female nurses sat inside. They looked up in surprise when he appeared.

"Excuse me, ladies," he said.

He tried a narrow door and found a broom closet. A door across the hall proved to be a room with metal shelves holding a number of boxes. He rummaged in these and found his clothes. He got dressed in a hurry.

He peered out of the storage room. The nurses had gone back to whatever it was they were doing. Neither of them looked to be making frantic phone calls or sending out alarms. He left the room and walked down the corridor, keeping close to the wall.

He reached the entrance to a stairwell and entered.

It hit him at the top of the steps. First it was just a strange feeling, turning quickly to low-grade nausea. As he went down the stairs, anxiety welled up. It was instant and all-consuming. Stunned, he collapsed on the landing, shaking and sweating.

He remained there for several minutes, totally immobilized, the walls closing in, nameless terrors chewing at him.

At length he was able to climb back up the stairs. He staggered back to the room and collapsed on the bed.

After a while he became aware that someone had entered the room. He turned over and sat up. It was the doctor—or was he just a technician?—and a woman dressed in a shapeless gray suit.

"Hello," the woman said brightly. "How are you feeling?" She wore no makeup and had lines at the corners of her gray eyes. Her salt-and-pepper hair was drawn up into a bun.

"What kind of drug is it?" he asked.

"We didn't give you any drugs," the doctor said.

"You have InnerVoice," the woman said. "It tells you when you're doing something wrong."

"What was I doing wrong?"

"You were leaving against medical advice," the woman said. She smiled again. "I'm from the Citizens' Committee for Social Improvement, Orientation Subcommittee. My cognomen is M-D-E-T-F-G. My omnicode is one-dash-seven-oh-nine-oh-six-three-one-two-eight."

"Don't you have a name?"

"You can call me M-1."

"Mine's B-7," the medic said.

The woman read from a small recording device: "And *your* cognomen is B-K-F-V-G-D. Your omnicode is—"

He waved her silent. "Never mind. Just tell me what you did to me. What is InnerVoice?"

"It's a guide to behavior. It tells you—"

"I *know* that. What *is* it?"

"Can you explain it to him, B-7?"

"Sure. When I said we didn't give you any drugs, I was telling the truth. What we did inject you with was a solution, but in that solution were tiny little machines."

"Machines?"

"Call them computers, that's what they are, in part. Some of them are no bigger than a bacterium, and most of them are smaller. They're constructed at a very small level of magnitude, the molecular level. Instead of electronic parts, they have protein parts, enzyme parts. Biological parts. But they're computers all the same."

"What do they do?"

"Lots of things. But mainly they monitor things in your blood-

and lymph. Watch your emotional states, look for telltale chemical signs.''

Gene said, "Signs of what?"

"Well, for instance, when you do something that you shouldn't be doing, your body reacts in certain ways. It changes chemically and electrically. When the monitoring machines detect these changes, they send signals to your glands to secrete certain things. They also send signals to the brain."

"I understand," Gene said. "So, if I don't do what I'm told, this automatic punishment system goes on-line."

"Oh, it's not punishment. It's your own body's shame and guilt for doing the socially unacceptable thing. The reactions are just amplified, that's all."

"Oh, yes. I got that much."

"If you didn't feel any shame or guilt, InnerVoice couldn't affect you."

"I feel absolutely no shame or guilt, friend. Stop bullshitting."

"Of course you feel it. You have to. You had the reaction, didn't you? InnerVoice was speaking to you."

Gene had no answer.

"It will take time," M-1 said. "You'll get used to it. In time, InnerVoice won't need to guide you at all. You'll guide yourself."

"I bet I will, if I know what's good for me."

She grinned expansively. "You're learning already! I'm so pleased. It will make my job so much easier!"

"Yeah. Glad to oblige."

# LABORATORY

LINDA SAT AT the terminal reading Incarnadine's message, which Jeremy had assigned to a file in one of the computer's data storage areas. (The computer had exotic data storage devices as well as conventional ones. One of the former resembled a 1950s jukebox.) She keyed as she read, scrolling the text upscreen.

She was a little distracted. Jeremy's new "assistant" was unsettling, to say the least. Computer programs usually didn't wear slinky dresses and have legs that wouldn't quit. Computer programs ordinarily didn't vamp their users. Isis had lots of other handy features; among these was the capability of fetching coffee for the chief of data processing.

"How many sugars, Jeremy?"

"Uh . . . four."

"Ummm, sweet."

"Yeah. Linda? What do you think?"

Linda said, "I don't know. It sounds like Incarnadine is going to have problems getting back. Can you write the program he's talking about?"

Jeremy shrugged. "You got me. I've been looking through the data from the magic books. Some of these spells are, like, enormous! Translating them into computer language will take . . . Jeez, I dunno."

Isis set the coffee cup in front of Jeremy. "We might have compiler programs that will do that automatically," she said.

"We might? I'll have to check the file directory. But the problem for me is the magic part. What spells would be effective? How do you stabilize the whole universe? Lord Incarnadine will have to make it back, or we're sunk."

"Maybe we can hold on till he does," Linda said. "Gene's okay, and we should be finding out about Mr. Dalton and Thaxton soon. The guards at Halfway should be all right, too. I mean, I can't believe anything's happened to Earth. The castle's temporarily cut off, but we can live with that. And Sheila's world is fine, too. I checked that out myself."

"I hope we can hold on," Jeremy said. "Because it's gonna be a while before I can get this gadget working."

Osmirik came in carrying a stack of loose sheets. He went to the sheet feeder and loaded it, then started the machine. The first sheet slid into the scanner, which began to hum softly.

"That is the last of the cosmology texts," he said.

"Okay. Isis, can you analyze all that stuff and come up with the technical parameters?"

"I can try, Jeremy," she said, lightly running her fingers through his hair.

"Uh, good. Can you get started on it?"

"I've already started, Jeremy. Did you know you had a lot of red in your hair?"

"I do?"

"Red highlights. I like red hair."

"Yeah. Well."

Linda stared uncomfortably at the screen. Really, she thought.

Osmirik said, "Jeremy, if I can be of further assistance . . ."

"Uh, I think that just about does it for the data input, Ozzie. If I can think of anything, I'll let you know."

"Please do. I shall be in the library."

"Right."

Osmirik bowed to Linda. "If I may take my leave, your ladyship?"

"Huh? Oh, sure, Ozzie."

Bowing toward Isis, he said, "Farewell, madam."

"Goodbye, Osmirik. So nice to have met you."

"Madam, the pleasure has been entirely mine."

As the lab door closed in Osmirik's wake, the printer began chattering.

Isis said, "Jeremy, I'm outputting a flowchart of the general shape the spell would have to take. It would probably be best if we followed the form of a spell for quieting the various humors in a human body. A healing spell, basically."

"Really? That's weird."

"Mind you, that's only the *form* the spell might take. The content would be entirely different. But for all intents and purposes, it's the cosmos that's all upset and in need of equalization."

"If you say so. Do you think we can get the content right?"

"That's going to be the problem. What we need are data on the energy state of the cosmos. Especially on the condition of the interuniversal medium, what Incarnadine's cosmology texts call the 'interstitial etherium.' "

"Hell, how do we get that?"

Isis sat on an empty wooden packing crate and crossed her beautiful legs. "That I don't know. Have any ideas?"

Jeremy glanced at the alarming level the hem of her dress had risen to. "Uh . . . not really. That's Incarnadine's department. There were all kinds of instruments here in the lab before it blew up. Some of them survived, but I don't really know what they're for."

"If only we could contact Lord Incarnadine," Linda said.

"He said he'd try to call in. Boy, if only we could use the *Sidewise Voyager*. We could just go and pick him up."

"Could you get to Merydion easily?" Linda asked.

"Well, yeah, if the coordinates are in the files. We don't have coordinates for all universes. But it doesn't matter, since we can't use the *Voyager*, anyway."

"The traveler would be the ideal way to get readings from the interuniversal medium," Isis said.

"Yeah, I guess so. But Incarnadine said it would be dangerous."

"We really need those readings."

"Sure we do," Jeremy said. "But if we were going to chance it, we might as well chance picking up Incarnadine."

Linda said, "Once you got to Merydion, how would you find him?"

"Like we found Snowclaw that one time. We used Osmirik's locater spell."

"But that was geared to Earth magic," Linda said. "It might not work in another world. I've never heard of Merydion. It must be one of the castle's more obscure aspects, so there's probably no one around here who would know the magic."

"Sheila?"

"Sheila might. She's good with strange magic, but she'd have to go to Merydion to figure it out."

"So we're back to square one."

"I could use the traveler," Isis said.

Jeremy blinked. "Huh?"

"I could be loaded into the *Voyager*'s computer—I assume it has one."

"Uh, sort of. What it does have is strange and kind of alien, but it's interfaced with my Toshiba laptop."

Isis frowned. "I don't think I can fit into a Toshiba laptop."

"No, you're mainframe software. So forget it."

"It was just a thought."

"If anyone is going to do anything with the traveler, it's going to be me."

Isis rose, came to him, and cradled his head in her hands. "My brave little hero."

Linda's eyes rolled to the ceiling.

Jeremy looked up at her, eyes glazing over.

"Yeah, well, look," Linda said, "we'd better do something fast. If we need readings on the interuniversal whaddyacallit, we better get them."

"She's right," Isis said, seating herself on the tabletop next to the terminal.

"There's gotta be a way to use the *Voyager*," Jeremy said. "I just have to figure something out."

"We could use it as a probe," Isis said.

"No, the Toshiba doesn't have the brains to pilot the traveler all by itself." Jeremy lowered his voice. "I wouldn't dare say that to its face. It probably wouldn't ever speak to me again."

"It wouldn't be necessary to stay in the interuniversal medium long to get a reading," Isis said.

Jeremy snapped his fingers. "Hey, I got it. I could program the Toshiba to fly into the medium and get the readings, then reverse thrust and get the hell out of there real fast."

"Do you think it would work?" Linda asked.

"I don't know, but we could try it." Jeremy's face fell. "But I'd hate to lose the *Voyager*. If anything went wrong—"

"And we still have the problem of instrumentation," Isis said.

Jeremy scowled and scratched his head. "Damn. Yeah, that's

right. I better see if I can scrounge up something around the lab. Just what kind of energy are we talking about?"

"According to the cosmology texts, the energy is a function of the cosmological constant times the virtual potential gradient of one cubic meter of vacuum times the—"

"Whoa, wait a minute. I can't deal with *that* crap."

Isis looked thoughtful. "Then again, perhaps we're exaggerating the instrumentation problem. It should be possible to get a reading along one parameter and interpolate all the rest. It just might be that a simple galvanometer reading would give us all the leverage we'd need."

"Hey. I know what those are. There actually might be one around here."

"Of course, we'd need several readings from different parts of the medium—if you can say that there are parts to what is essentially an imaginary space with a negative energy bias."

"Well, if the plan works once, it should work again. We'll make a couple of runs."

Isis brightened. "I'm game! Let's try it."

"Yeah, let's."

Linda got up. "Looks like you two know what you're doing. If you need any help with magic, as long as it's simple, like conjuring something—"

"Can you come up with a galvanometer?"

"I guess. I don't even know what one is, but that never stopped me from conjuring something. Hold on."

Linda closed her eyes and folded her arms.

Something clunked onto the table behind Jeremy. He turned and picked up a small device with a gauge and two wire leads.

"Hey, this is one. Good work, Linda."

"Easy. Give me something hard to do."

Jeremy chuckled. "Why don't you conjure Incarnadine?"

Linda gave him a strange look. Jeremy turned around and did a take. "Wait a minute. Can you?"

Linda shook her head slowly. "I don't know. The thought's kind of scary."

"Why couldn't you?"

"I don't know of any reason, but then again I really never figured out just how I conjure anything. Gene says I must reach out into the universes and pull in stuff."

"Why couldn't you pull Incarnadine in?"

"Gee, I just don't know. I'll have to think about this."

"What would the danger be?"

"There might not be any danger. But I just . . . *don't know*."

"Well, whatever you say. We'll go ahead with our original scheme, anyway. Let us know if you come up with anything."

"I will. I'm going down to the dining hall again. Maybe they've found out about Thaxton and Mr. Dalton."

"Okay, see you later."

Linda left the room.

Isis smiled at Jeremy, got up, and sat in his lap.

"You're so resourceful, so clever. So *bright*."

"Uh, thanks."

"I like bright men."

"You do?"

"I do."

"Um, well."

"What's the matter, Jeremy. Don't you like me?"

"Yeah! Sure I do."

"Then what is it?"

"Uh, nothing. It's just that women don't go for me much. I mean, well, you know."

"No, I don't."

"I look like a twerp."

"Jeremy, why do you put yourself down?"

"I'm a nerd, let's face it."

"And you don't think I could like you?"

Jeremy shook his head. "I used to dream about women like you. Hell, every guy does. You're like a centerfold."

"Why, thank you."

"I mean it. You're beautiful. But I just can't believe that you're real."

"But I am."

"You're a computer program, for pete's sake."

"What difference does that make?"

"What difference? Well, I mean, you just don't go around making out with computer programs. A program is just a . . ."

"Just a pattern of information."

"Yeah. Just a pattern."

"So are you."

"What do you mean?"

"You're just a pattern of information, too. What makes you *you* is the configuration of data that's in your brain. Your brain is just holding the information, just like a storage device. No difference. Your pattern is stored in a body, mine in a computer."

Jeremy was silent. Then he said, "I never thought of it that way."

"We're both software, Jeremy. Why can't we interface?"

"I guess . . . well, maybe. But where did *your* body come from?"

She shrugged. "I guess you could say that my body is just a pattern of information, too. Everything is merely a configuration of data."

"I don't get it. But I'll tell you one thing. I like your configuration a lot."

She smiled and kissed him.

When she took her lips from his he said, "Why . . ." He took a deep breath. "Why *do* you like me?"

"I told you. I like bright men. Besides, you're a user, and I was created to serve users."

Jeremy put his arms around her waist. "I still can't believe it. But I'm working on it."

"Let's work on it together, Jeremy."

"Yeah, let's."

# FOREST

HE HAD CROSSED enemy lines without incident, avoiding detection with a partial invisibility spell. The going had been risky. The energy level was low back on the plains. This world blew hot and cold on magic. In spots, like Merydion, there was little power, whereas in other places, such as his destination, the level was dangerously high. Not a few native magicians had vaporized themselves fooling with powers they couldn't control. It was an occupational hazard.

Now the energy gradient was steepening as he entered the Timeless Forest. Though not sufficient to power a teleportation spell, the magic of the forest was tricky. There were currents and eddies of force. Intersecting lines of influence wove a tangled web to snare the unsuspecting. He had not spent a great deal of time here, but was aware of the risk and knew some of the dangers. Yet he was by no means experienced. He would have to take it easy.

The trees were tall, their trunks of staggering girth. Thick loam compressed beneath his mount's hooves. The undergrowth was thin, unable to thrive in the dark under the forest canopy. Moss on tree trunks grew thick as rugs. Toadstools towered almost man-high, and morels resembled hot-air balloons. Vines like hawsers hung from the treetops.

He sniffed. It was high summer, but there was the definite tang of autumn in the air, the cider smell of rotting fruit. Strange.

He rode on, noticing odder things. Some leaves were turning. A little farther along the trail most of the foliage had bloomed into colorful fall decay. Reds, yellows, golds. Puzzled, he halted his mount and looked around.

The leaves seemed to change as he watched. Then they began to fall.

Leaves swirling around him, he continued. Soon the forest floor was a carpet of colors. The air now had the snap of early winter.

The sky grayed over and the temperature dropped. A snow-flake drifted by. Then another. Another.

He rode on. The accumulation was fast and reached ankle height in no time. Wisps of steam trailed from his mount's nostrils. He wore no cloak, and had on only a short-sleeved doublet. He shivered and shook. Deepening hoof prints trailed in the snow.

Winds buffeted him while bare branches grasped and tangled above. He booted his mount into a slippery canter, hoping to get through the anomaly.

After a good stretch he eased the horse into a walk again. The snow had stopped falling. Green buds appeared, and birds sang. The snow melted. In a matter of minutes he passed from winter to spring, and then back to midsummer again.

"The years go by fast when you get old," he told his horse.

The trail forked ahead. He stopped to get his bearings. He was inclined to take the right fork, and did.

Warm breezes brought the smell of wildflowers as he rode through sun-dappled shade. Sagging branches creaked, and a lone bird twitted at him. The trees were more slender now, but still tall. Shelves of yellow fungus ringed an occasional stump. Passing through a swarm of gnats, he fended them off, and journeyed on.

An hour passed, and the trail fed into another. A line of hoof prints marked the dirt. He turned right and followed them.

Ahead the trail diverged. It looked like the same fork, to which he had come full circle. His own trace went off to the right.

"Left, this time, I think."

He went at a trot, and another hour passed. He tried to watch the sky and the angle of the sun, but it did no good. At length

he came around again, the way merging with the original trail.
This time two sets of hoof prints went to the left, and again he
confronted the parting of the ways.

He abandoned the trail and urged his horse through the underbrush, dodging low branches. After a slow-moving and ar-
duous hour . . .

"Damn."

The same trail, and ahead the same fork.

He tried going off trail again, this time in another direction.
Twigs of saplings snagged at him. Low branches swooped. An
angry buzzing informed him that the gourdlike object he had
brushed against was a wasps' nest. He geed up into a gallop and
almost had his head taken off by a malevolent tree. He rode
blindly for a good long while.

At length he broke into the open. The blasted trail again!—
this time with more sets of hoof prints than he could discern.

"I'm starting to get pissed off."

He turned against the traffic and went back the way he had
originally come.

The trail gave out about a minute later. He found himself in
a small clearing that had not been there before. He reined his
sweating steed around to find that the path had entirely disappeared. Hemmed in, he dismounted.

"All right, what do you want?"

He heard—or thought he heard—laughter.

"Right. Well, we'll see."

He walked the circumference of the clearing, peering into the
undergrowth. Nothing, no one.

At the center of the clearing was a fairy circle of toadstools,
these about knee-high. He stood in the middle of the circle and
raised his arms. He murmured a few words.

He waited. Silence.

He said the words again, this time more slowly. He stood still
for a good while longer, eyes closed.

A rustling off to the left. He did not open his eyes. Time
passed.

Presently a four-legged beast ran into the clearing and halted
not far from him. He turned and beheld it.

It was small, had short white hair, and looked like a cross
between a goat and a pony. On its head were long golden horns,
three of them: two curving ones to the side, and one, slightly

straighter, growing out of the middle of the forehead. The creature's eyes were a piercing blue.

The tricorn regarded him dispassionately.

He asked, "Are you the demiurge around here—or at least its incarnation?"

The empathic vibrations he received in reply seemed to indicate the affirmative.

"Is there something you want of me?"

(Negative.)

"Then you're simply having a bit of fun?"

(Mirth.)

"Much as I hate to spoil your sport, could I possibly persuade you to let me go?"

(Perhaps.)

"What would it take?"

(Mild amusement.)

"I have the feeling that nothing short of my death would satisfy you, although you don't want it to happen suddenly. You intend to keep me a prisoner in your domain until I waste away."

(Laughter.)

"All right, you play rough. But two can play."

He held out his right hand. A flame sprang to life on his upturned palm. He turned his hand over and the flame spilled to the ground. The grass blazed up, and he stepped back.

Thunder cracked, and rain began to fall. The flames did not go out; they leaped up and roared, spreading, making a path for the undergrowth.

"You'll find that water won't quench it," he called. "Only my counterspell will."

The thunder faded and the rain stopped.

"Convinced?"

(Affirmative!)

He waved his hands and the flames died. Pale smoke rose from the clearing.

"Now. How about showing me a way out?"

The tricorn stood motionless.

He searched the edge of the clearing. The path had reappeared.

"Fine. I need a little help, though. I want to find a shortcut across the continent. I'm told that a hellwind blows from here to the mountains of Marnass. Will you show me where I can catch this infernal zephyr?"

(Reluctant assent.)

He mounted. "Good. Lead on, hatrack."

(Indignation.)

"Sorry, couldn't resist."

The tricorn raced ahead on the path. He had trouble keeping up, catching only glimpses of the animal's silky white tail as he rounded bends. The forest breathed its cool breath on him, the trees parted, and the way was made clear.

After a while he stopped to give the horse a rest. The tricorn foraged in the bushes to one side up ahead. He sat and massaged his aching legs.

He heard a babbling and went down into a nearby gully. Finding a clear stream, he kneeled and drank. The water was crisp, pure, sweet. His shimmering reflection caused him to reflect that he was getting old. He recalled an old family saying: *After three hundred it's patch, patch, patch. . . .*

Returning, he mounted and resumed the journey.

At last he came to the edge of the forest. Ahead were badlands colonized by an occasional stunted tree. The tricorn circled around and darted back into the woods.

At his back he felt a warning.

(Do not return. Ever!)

"Thank you. I won't."

He moved forward. The sun beat down on rocks and little else except tufts of dry grass. A ridge of hills cut across the terrain ahead.

A lizard scurried across the trail. Nothing else moved. The sky had turned yellow, vague clouds striping it.

A wind suddenly rose, whipping up dust. The horse neighed and reared up. It was a strange wind, and blew good to no one except those who would seek to cheat time and space. That was what he sought, and he attuned himself to its flow. It blew at his back and toward the hills, pushing him. The horse leaped into a canter, then broke stride into a run. He reined in and brought the animal back to a proper gait. Better to maintain a steady pace.

The ground seemed to go by faster than the horse moved. The effect was disconcerting at first, but soon he had accustomed himself to yet another anomaly.

The hills came up and he climbed, the rate of speed paradoxically increasing as the horse followed a pass marked out by gray boulders. Cliffs threw deep shadows across the trail and slides of talus dumped debris in his path, but the horse was magically surefooted. The wind increased, shrieking at his back.

He reached the summit, and the rate of the ground's passing picked up even more. The beast ran at freeway cruising speed, impossibly. Then faster, and faster still.

He came down into tableland cut by deep arroyos. Cactuslike plants populated the flats. The nearby ground was a blur, distant scenery passing as in a fast-moving train. Still the speed increased.

Clouds grouped, turning dark. Lightning cut the sky at the horizon and rain began to fall. The wind was fierce now, whipping at him and churning up a whirling storm of dust. Bits of dirt and tiny pebbles stung his face, and he spoke a short bit of magic-making to ward them off.

The sky darkened and lightning struck to either side. Auroral displays lit up the horizon, fingers of fire brushing distant mountains. His speed was incredible now. The horse seemed to leave the ground . . . it did leave the ground.

Horse and rider rose into the maelstrom.

# Queen's Dining Hall

SIR GENE HAD stuffed himself, and now felt a bit queasy. He should have known better than to pile food into a prison-shrunken stomach. Looking over the table, however, he could hardly blame himself. One could not ask for more inducement to gluttony. There was food enough here for an army of gourmands. This castle's Incarnadine was a gracious host. Not that his counterpart was incapable of setting a good table—if you didn't mind a few dishes laced with poison. The dinner entertainment consisted of watching the unlucky diners twitch and heave. Great fun, that.

So, knowing this lord of the castle to be a decent sort, he had succumbed. But no matter. He would just sit quietly until the spell passed.

"Gene, old buddy!"

A great white beast barged into the hall. Snowclaw. Sir Gene's groan was barely audible, and he tried to put on a smile. Like it or not, this horrendous shambling creature was supposed to be a friend.

"Hello, Snowclaw. So good to see you again."

"What happened to you? We were looking all over." The beast threw a tremendous broadax down on the table and took a seat across from Sir Gene.

"I did some reconnoitering. Not that it was fruitful."

"Did you find out what that world was out there? Looked like Earth, but nobody's sure."

"No, I didn't think it too wise to blunder into some unknown aspect."

"You showed good sense, which is pretty unusual for you. I was ready to crash in there and try to find you, but Linda sort of talked me out of it."

"She can be very persuasive."

"I know. So. Have any idea what's going on?"

"Not a clue, I'm afraid."

"I heard Incarnadine can't get back."

"That's what I hear. Pity."

"Yeah. What are we going to do?"

Sir Gene answered truthfully: "I don't quite know."

He thought about it. Here was an ally of sorts: Snowclaw, if the beast could be harnessed. As far as Sir Gene could tell, he seemed cooperative enough. This might prove useful.

"Maybe we could go get him with that fancy machine you guys saved my rump with a while back."

"Ah . . . perhaps. Perhaps we could."

This was going to be tricky going indeed. What machine could the creature be talking about? The castle had few machines. In fact, Sir Gene was familiar with none of any complexity. But this was another castle.

"Nah. Somebody would have thought of that already," Snowclaw said, "and would have done it. There's got to be some problem."

"I suppose so."

"What's-his-name, the little guy—Jeremy would know."

"Yes," Sir Gene said. "We should go ask him. Um, where do you think he'd be?"

"Up in the laboratory? I dunno. I guess."

"The laboratory. Of course. Shall we go?"

If the castle had a laboratory, Sir Gene didn't know where it was. Fortunately Snowclaw led the way. This variation of the castle was proving to be very interesting indeed. Machines, laboratories . . . what next?

Linda came around a corner and nearly collided with Snowclaw.

"Watch yourself," Snowclaw said, chuckling and wrapping Linda up affectionately.

"Snowy, you should get turn signals. Where are you guys going?"

"To the laboratory," Snowclaw said. "What's happening up there? Anything?"

"Jeremy is cooking something up with . . . well, he's got himself a girlfriend up there."

"Yeah? Who?"

"Someone new. She's . . . it's hard to explain. Anyway, he's busy with the stuff Lord Incarnadine wants him to do."

"What about using the gizmo to go pick Incarnadine up?"

"The *Voyager*? Can't. Well, maybe. Jeremy doesn't know yet. There are problems with that idea. I wouldn't get my hopes up."

"That's too bad." Snowclaw scratched his abdomen with one bone-white claw. "Well, what can we do?"

"Nothing much. Just sit tight. Not a lot is happening. We've lost contact with Earth, but that's nothing new. Portal problems we can deal with. It's this weird stuff that Lord Incarnadine said to expect that worries me."

Sir Gene said, "What exactly did he say we should expect?"

"Well, something about anti-universes. And then—"

Linda looked over Sir Gene's shoulder.

"Oh, here comes Tyrene. Maybe he has some news about Mr. Dalton."

Sir Gene turned. When he saw the festering mole on Tyrene's cheek, his hand went to the hilt of his sword.

Tyrene was already lunging with his broadsword. Sir Gene stepped back, drew, and beat off the attack. Then, sidestepping as Tyrene passed, he delivered a decapitating blow to the back of the neck, which would have done its job if the blade had not caught the edge of the Guardsman's helmet. The helmet flew and Tyrene went sprawling, stunned.

"Lord Incarnadine!"

Sir Gene whirled. Incarnadine was standing a few feet away, a smirk curling his lip. Two Guardsmen flanked him, swords drawn.

"Very good, Sir Gene. And I suppose you've already dispatched your counterpart."

Sir Gene's eyes darted between Incarnadine and Linda, who looked baffled. Snowclaw also seemed confused. He raised his broadax.

Incarnadine squinted. "It is *you*, is it not? You have the requisite dissolute mien about you. I can't imagine two such creatures. No matter. And this"—he turned to Linda—"must be the Lady Linda. My, my. Good teeth, this one. Have you had her yet, Sir Gene?"

Linda's mouth was hanging open. She closed it, shook her head, and said, "Wait a minute. What's going on?"

"I've just come to pay a friendly visit," Incarnadine said. "I live in the castle next door."

"Huh?"

Sir Gene said, "It's not the Incarnadine you know."

"What do you mean?"

"Mirror aspect, my dear," Incarnadine said. "It's been known to happen. An aspect turns into a mirror of the castle itself. Sometimes a distorting mirror, sometimes not."

Linda shook her head slowly, saying, "You mean you're not the real Lord Incarnadine?"

"Oh, come now. Surely you don't think that I would feel I was anything *but* the real Incarnadine. The mirror formed in my castle. Sir Gene here did us the favor of blundering into it, and we followed him. And here he is, and here we are, and . . . well, thereby hangs the tale."

"What do you think you will gain by coming here?" Sir Gene asked.

"Don't quite know. I've never explored a mirror aspect. Thought it might be fun. By the way, where is the lord of this castle? The *real* Incarnadine, if you insist."

Sir Gene and Linda were silent.

"Hm. Doubtless we'll meet eventually. Judging from the intelligence we've gathered, I'd say our forces are superior. And we do have the element of surprise."

The hallway behind Incarnadine had filled with milling Guardsmen.

Incarnadine pointed at Snowclaw. "What the devil is that monster doing here? I thought I gave orders never to let . . ." He broke off suddenly and smiled. "But of course, I forget. Excuse me. Snowclaw, is it not? Yes. Well, no matter." He turned to the Guardsman next to him. "Kill them all."

"Yes, Your Majesty!"

Incarnadine turned away and the Guardsmen edged forward.

Sir Gene and Linda backstepped, but Snowclaw stood his ground, broadax raised.

The Guardsmen hesitated. They knew the beast they faced.

Snowclaw said over his shoulder, "Run, you guys!"

Sir Gene took off.

"Move!" Snowclaw barked.

Linda saw three Guardsmen charge Snowclaw. As she ran she heard the clash of steel and then a scream. At the corner of the intersecting hallway she cast a glance back. Two of the Guardsmen were down and the third was retreating.

She yelled, "Snowy, run for it!"

Snowy ran for it, and Linda dashed down the corridor, hearing Snowy's big feet coming up fast behind her. There was no sign of Gene. She sprinted to an intersection, looked both ways, and fled across it.

Snowy was close behind. "Where's Gene?" he yelled.

"I don't know!"

Running by an alcove, she caught sight of someone pressed up against the inside wall. It was Gene. She skidded to a stop and backstepped.

"Gene?"

Gene gave her a strange look.

Snowy scouted down the hall, then came back.

"Soldiers coming," he said. "Can't tell if they're ours or theirs."

Looking worried, Sir Gene peered out. "I suspect Incarnadine invaded in force. They'll be all over the castle, and they know it as well as we do."

There was an aspect leading out of the alcove, one Linda didn't recognize. The world didn't look inviting: sand, rocks, and straggly bushes.

"We'll have to duck through a portal," Linda said. "I don't particularly care for this one, but it is handy."

Sir Gene gave it a sullen look. "I suppose we have no choice."

Voices down the hallway, shouting orders.

"No, we don't," Linda said. "Let's go."

The three of them ran through to another world.

# GOLFING HELL

THAXTON WAS STILL damp from his dunking as he putted on the ninth green. The monstrous bird had dropped him over the water hazard. The height would have been enough to kill him but the gravity on this world was somewhat less than normal. He had survived the plunge, only having the wind knocked out of him. Dalton had fished him out.

The course had turned even more bizarre. Now there were lava pits instead of sand traps, geysers on the fairway, and sinkholes on the approaches. Smoke rose and flames leaped. The lava pits bubbled noisily, spattering hot goo.

The sky had turned dark. It didn't even look like a sky, but more like the vault of an expansive roof. The green was not grass but artificial turf of some kind.

Thaxton putted. The ball rolled straight until the last second, then veered off. It orbited the rim of the cup and spun away.

"Oh, blast."

He had lost a stroke to one of the pits, and now he would have a short putt for a double bogey.

"Beastly luck I've been having."

"That's the truth," Dalton said. "It's not every golfer who gets carried off by a roc."

"Is that what the thing was?"

"Well, it fit the description."

"It could only happen to me."

"You've done well. Twenty over par isn't bad, considering."

They finished putting and picked up their clubs. Smoke and steam rose around them as they left the green to walk a narrow path between two rocky escarpments. Coming out on the other side, they saw the clubhouse.

"There, you see?" Dalton said.

"You were right."

The place looked a little odd. It was shaped haphazardly, consisting of half-spheroids and other bulges, and had oval windows. A lava pond fronted it, spritzing liquid rock like a fountain.

They entered what looked like the lobby of a hotel. An assortment of strange creatures—variously clawed and scaled, fanged and furred—were sitting around on stuffed chairs reading newspapers.

"Well, it's not restricted," Thaxton said.

"Where's the bar?"

"I'm famished. Let's drink at a table."

"Fine. Let's see, that looks like the eatery."

A somewhat demonic-looking creature, presumably the maître d'hôtel, met them as they entered the dining room.

"Two for lunch?" it said in a cultured, deep-throated voice. Its barbed tail twitched back and forth.

"Yes, please," Dalton said.

"This way, gentlemen."

"By the window, if you can," Dalton added.

"By all means, sir."

Their table offered a prospect of a large crater filled with bubbling pitch. Fire danced in the distance.

"Charming," Thaxton said, sitting down. There were no other patrons in the room.

"Would you like to see the wine list, gentlemen?"

"Hmm. I was going to have a martini, but wine might go better," Dalton said.

"I'll have a gin and bitters, easy on the bitters," Thaxton said.

"Your waiter will be with you in a moment, sir."

"This Château Avernus sounds good," Dalton said. "Could you recommend a good year?"

"All vintages are good, sir. The climate where it's produced doesn't vary."

"Sounds like a hell of a good vino to me. We'll have a bottle."

"I'll tell the wine steward."

"I could eat a horse," Thaxton said.

"Or a roc, maybe?"

"God, no. Rather a tough old bird, wouldn't you think?"

"Maybe so. Well, I sort of like this course. How about you?"

"Oh, so-so. I've seen better. It certainly is different."

"Unique, I'd say."

"Tell me. Have you given any thought as to how we're going to get back?"

"Oh, we should be able to find the first tee again. That's where we came in."

"The first hole is miles back," Thaxton said.

"The first hole is always somewhere near the clubhouse."

"But the place wasn't like *this* when we started. The first tee can't be anywhere near. Besides, it might not have been the first hole. How can you be sure this course has the regulation number of holes?"

"Why wouldn't it?"

Thaxton shrugged. "No good reason. Do you suppose the portal's still there?"

"It's occurred to me that it might have moved or disappeared."

"Oh, that's occurred to you? Perhaps we might give it some thought."

"Relax," Dalton said. "I've been walking in and out of portals for years now. Never been lost yet."

"There's always a first time, old boy."

"Yes, I suppose there's alway a first time. Come to think of it, though, I wouldn't mind being stuck on a golf course for the rest of my life."

"God forfend."

Another creature came up to the table. This one's scales were shinier and its horns longer.

"Hi, I'm Gamalkon, and I'll be your waiter today." The creature handed out menus.

Thaxton ordered his drink. The waiter said, "I'll be back to take your orders," and left.

"Interesting bill of fare," Dalton said.

Thaxton looked it over. "What the devil . . . 'Filet of basilisk'?"

"Haven't had basilisk in a long time. Hmmm. 'Cockatrice au vin—breast of cockatrice sautéed with wild mushrooms and fresh tender roots in a light wine sauce.' Sounds good."

"Are you joking? This is abominable."

"Broaden your palate, my friend."

"Eat this rubbish and you'll have your palate broadened, all right. Into a death rictus."

"Hmmm. I might try the luncheon special."

"Where's that?"

"Up at the top."

"Oh." Thaxton's eyebrows shot up. " 'Chimaera casserole—chunks of tantalizing chimaera with noodles and wild herbs in a rich cheese sauce'? Chimaera? You're actually going to—?"

"That or the barbecued harpy."

"Good God."

"Now, if you really want to experiment, the stuffed python . . . but maybe that's a little intense for lunch."

"By all means keep it light."

The wine steward showed up, uncorked a bottle, and poured a taste for Dalton. Dalton breathed the bouquet, then took a sip and swished it around. Swallowing, he said, "A very playful little wine. Fruity."

"Barbecued bleeding harpy," Thaxton muttered, still vainly searching the menu.

"Leave the bottle," Dalton instructed.

The steward filled Dalton's glass, then turned to Thaxton.

"Having wine, sir?"

"Hm? Later, I have a drink coming."

The waiter returned with Thaxton's gin. Dalton ordered the cockatrice, with gryphon soup to start.

"And what will you be having, sir?" the waiter asked Thaxton.

"God, I don't know. Do you have . . . do you happen to serve hamburger à la carte, by any chance?"

The waiter's red eyes rolled. "Yes, sir, we do."

"Hamburger, then."

"How would you like that done, sir?"

"Oh, I like my beef flamed to a turn. You shouldn't have any trouble doing that."

Dalton said drolly, "Are you sure it's beef?"

The waiter said, "Our hamburger is ground from the fresh-est—"

"I don't want to know!" Dalton said, holding up a hand. When the waiter left he downed his drink in one gulp.

Dalton sat back. "Well, a few drinks and a leisurely lunch ought to put us right for the back nine."

Thaxton gave him a skeptical look.

Dalton said, "Come on, buck up."

"I'm all right. But I get the feeling that something's not right at the castle."

"Yeah. That has occurred to me. But then neither of us could do very much to help."

"As I recall, we played golf through the last crisis."

"The invasion of the bossy blue critters. That was nasty. But, then as now, there was nothing for us to do. Neither of us can handle a sword. And magic is not exactly our stock-in-trade."

"No, magic is definitely not my forte. Nor is golf, or anything else for that matter."

Dalton stared out the window for a moment. Then he said: "You know, I don't think I ever asked you what you did back in the real world."

"Did? Oh. Well, I managed some properties."

"Real estate? I see."

"Yes, I inherited a good deal of stuff, as a matter of fact. Properties, investments, stocks, that sort of thing."

"Your family was well-to-do?"

"Well, yes, rather."

"I never asked—are you, or were you, a member of the aristocracy?"

"Technically speaking, no. My grandfather was a baronet, but the peerage didn't come down to me. I did all the 'U' things, though. Winchester, Balliol, the right clubs. All that sort of rot."

"I hope you don't think I'm getting too personal. . . ."

"We have spent a great deal of time together. Fire away."

"What brought you to Castle Perilous? Mind telling?"

"Not much to tell. The wife was divorcing me. Nasty bit of business. Threatened a scandal if she didn't get what she wanted, which was nearly half the estate. I gave it to her, and then found out she'd been having an affair with her hairdresser. I didn't mind his being NOCD so much as the fact that he was a bad hairdresser."

"NOCD?"

" 'Not Our Class, Dear.' Anyway, they went off to Majorca and I was left feeling rather empty and used. It was more than that. My life seemed . . . useless. Didn't have a very good feeling about it."

Thaxton poured himself some wine. "To make a long story short, one night I'd drunk a bottle of claret and was starting on another, when I thought, why not just up and end it all? So I got out my grandfather's Webley, and loaded the thing up. Just then I noticed that the door to the conservatory looked rather strange. I put down the gun and walked in, and suddenly there I was inside a strange castle. When I turned around, the door was gone. And that's it." He drank his wine. "Good stuff, this."

"Good story, very typical," Dalton said.

"Yes, I suppose it is all rather typical."

"I just meant that all we Guests have experiences in common."

"Undoubtedly. Getting back to the business at hand—isn't there *something* we could do?"

"First of all, we don't know if there's any real trouble. It could just be portal difficulties."

"But the golf world was always stable."

"I have a feeling this *is* the golf world, but changed."

"Hope you're right. But what if it changes back while we're out hacking?"

"Then we carry on hacking, I guess. We can't go back now."

"Right." Thaxton downed his wine and poured more.

Dalton's gryphon soup came. He sampled it and smiled. "A little salty but good."

"I wonder if they bagged that gryphon out on the links."

"I wonder what hero bagged the basilisk. You look one of those in the eye and you're dead."

"Really? Not up on my classical lore."

The waiter brought Thaxton's hamburger. It was large and rested inside a sliced pita loaf. Thaxton lifted the top slice and sniffed. The waiter set down a bottle in front of him.

"Ah. Steak sauce." Thaxton applied a liberal dose.

"Will that be all, sir?"

"Yes, thank you."

Thaxton lifted the huge thing and examined it.

"No onions or tomatoes?" Dalton asked.

"I'm a purist." He took a bite and chewed. "Tastes a bit gamey."

"Probably ground salamander or something."

"It's good enough." Thaxton set the hamburger down. "Still thinking about getting back to the castle. *Something's* up, I just have a feeling."

"Well, I get that feeling, too, but I can't think of what to do except retrace our steps."

"We can't very well do that. Those holes are as good as under Vesuvius now."

"I suppose we could just come out and ask."

"Capital idea."

Thaxton lifted an arm and called the waiter over.

"Yes, sir?"

"Tell me . . . how do I phrase this? Know of any—well, *castles* in the area?"

"Castles, sir?"

"Um, yes. Castles."

Gamalkon scrunched up his face in thought. "Sir, I don't recall ever seeing any castles around here."

"Any . . . sort of floating doorways into castles? I suppose not."

Gamalkon shook his horned head. "Sorry, sir."

"Quite all right. Thank you. Uh, I think we need another bottle of wine. I do, anyway."

"Right away, sir."

Thaxton gave Dalton a forlorn look. "I suppose it's hopeless."

"Looks like. Don't worry about it. We'll find our way back eventually. After the eighteenth hole. I think fate has decreed that we play this course through."

"Fate, eh? Bloody bad luck, I call it."

"Thaxton, old boy, you just won't admit that you're having the time of your life."

Thaxton poured himself more wine. "A spot more of this and I *will* be having a good time."

Dalton laughed.

Two strange-looking creatures were shown to the next table. They looked like gargoyles come to life. One of them looked over and squawked something that sounded friendly.

"Good afternoon! Nice to see you," Dalton answered brightly.

Thaxton managed a thin smile. "NOSD, those two," he murmured.

"Eh?"

" 'Not Our Species, Dear.' "

"I wonder if they'd be up for a foursome."

"With my luck, they're probably both scratch players."

"My handicap is nothing to write home about, either, but it might be interesting."

Dalton's entrée was served.

"Very good indeed," he pronounced. "These wild mushrooms provide just the right accent."

The meal progressed. The wine flowed; the second bottle emptied. More Château Avernus was ordered.

A while later the room began to shake. Wine bottles fell over and the windows rattled. A piece of ceiling fell to the floor very near.

Glassy-eyed and smiling, Thaxton looked around. "If I weren't so drunk I'd be frightened out of my wits."

Dalton said thickly, "D'you think we should . . . make a run for it?"

"Yes, let's."

They both had a hard time getting up. Thaxton picked up the full bottle.

"Get your clubs, old boy," Dalton said.

"Right." Teetering, Thaxton picked up his golf bag.

With a resounding crash, part of the ceiling collapsed, and a portion of the far wall gave way. Debris cascaded down. After the dust cleared, half the room lay buried in rubble.

"Dalton, old boy. You all right?"

Dalton sat up and brushed himself off. "I think. We had better get outdoors fast, wouldn't you say?"

"Having a spot of trouble. Leg's stuck under this bit of concrete, here."

"Let's see if we can move it."

Dalton squatted and put his weight against the mass but stopped when he saw Thaxton wince. He searched around, found nothing suitable, and so used his two-iron as a lever, attacking the job from the other side. The club bent, but the chunk of ceiling lifted enough so that Thaxton could get his leg out from under it.

Dalton helped him up. "Can you walk?"

"I can hobble."

"Need help?"

"I'll manage. Give me that iron."

"Here. Are you sure?"

"I've got the wine. Don't forget the clubs, old boy."

They picked their way toward a ragged opening in the wall.

"Bit of luck, this," Thaxton said.

"How so?"

"I was wondering how we were going to get out of paying the bill. Don't have a farthing on me."

# CITY

THERE WAS LITTLE to orientation. He was not subjected to political indoctrination or any long harangues; there was no orientation per se. He was simply issued clothing—an all-weather coat with baggy trousers—and a sheet of paper with some instructions on it. The instructions said to report to a certain address, his new residence. He was to remain there until he was issued new instructions, which he would receive via his apartment communication screen. That, along with more slogans, was all there was.

## TO LOVE IS TO OBEY

## GOOD CITIZENS ARE HAPPY CITIZENS

## DUTY LIES WITHIN

Banners with slogans draped every building facade, hung from every cornice. He walked the streets reading posters in storefront windows and on kiosks. He could not get a sense of who was running things. There were no giant blowups of some dictatorial face, no direct references to a political party or revolutionary cabal.

The people he passed were all smiling, hurrying to some duty or another. It was a strange smile, somehow detached from or irrelevant to any real sense of well-being. It was not forced, yet not quite real.

He stopped to ask directions of a traffic director—not a policeman; the man wore only a white brassard and was unarmed. The man told him to take an omnibus with a certain number and to get off at Complex 502 on the Boulevard of Social Concern.

"Put a smile on your face," the man told him.

Ignoring the order, he walked on.

It was not long before the first pangs of nausea began. He forced a smile, and his stomach rumbled, then quieted. He felt better instantly. Justice was that speedy. His own body was judge and jury, and its verdict was not open to appeal.

There were few stores or shops. Most storefronts were boarded up or had their windows used as billboards. Here and there a door was open, no sign above saying what was going on inside. He stopped at one such place and found a store with a few undifferentiated shoes in bins. Another store offered socks and underwear. There wasn't much stock in any store he visited. The places looked ransacked, and no salespeople were about. He continued walking.

Traffic was limited to trucks, buses, and official-looking vehicles. No bicycles or powered two-wheeled conveyances. The sidewalks were crowded, as they would be on any workday in any universe. This was downtown, the area between the rivers that he knew as the Golden Triangle. There were hundreds of office buildings and thousands of workers. Everyone was dressed pretty much as he was, in the same utilitarian outfit.

He passed what looked like a restaurant. He went back and looked in the window. The place was actually a cafeteria. His stomach had calmed down and he was hungry. Very hungry. His instructions had not told him about food or about getting it, and he had no money.

Yet he went in. It was midmorning and there were no lines. He watched a woman at the counter load her tray and walk to a table. He could see no checkout station, no cashier. He decided to take a chance. He took a tray and slid it along the runner.

Nothing looked very good. He passed green gelatin and wilted salads. Farther along an attendant was ladling what looked like chicken stew into a container. He asked for some of that, and got a small bowlful. He took slices of bread and a cup of what appeared to be custard or vanilla pudding. There was little else to choose from. He got himself coffee but no cream, as that commodity was not in evidence. No sugar, either. He found a seat.

The stew, if that's what it was, was awful, tasting of flour paste and unidentifiable flavorings. The vegetables were taste-less, and the "meat" was not chicken but something like bean curd, and just as unappetizing. He forced it down. The bread had the flavor of cardboard. He spat out the first mouthfuls of ersatz custard and sipped the coffee surrogate, which carried the faint aftertaste of detergent.

He looked on the wall above the counter.

## SUICIDE IS UNSOCIAL

Of course; a simple way out, and one the authorities probably had a hard time thwarting.

He wondered if it was the only way out.

He left half the coffee in the cup and went out to the street. He now knew why the stores needed no salespeople. Citizens simply walked in and took what was needed. They took exactly as much as they needed and no more, or InnerVoice would pun-ish. Dandy way to run a distribution system. No money neces-sary. It was the age-old utopian dream: a moneyless economy immune from the laws of supply and demand, based on mutual cooperation and individual restraint. Unfortunately there were chronic shortages, but who would complain?

Who *could* complain?

He caught the bulky omnibus on Conscience Avenue, a thor-oughfare that ran to the river and crossed a bridge. On the other shore the bus turned left and entered a section of the city that Gene knew as the South Side. In this universe it was nameless and consisted mostly of high rises and little parks.

The Boulevard of Social Concern was the main street, leading past numerous groups of buildings, signs designating each com-plex by number. He saw 501 go by, and made his way to the front of the bus.

The driver beamed at him. "We're getting happier every day, citizen."

"Aren't we, though?"

He paid for the irony with a twinge or two of gastric pain.

Building C of Complex 502 looked increasingly shabbier the

closer he got to it. Intended to be lean and functional, it looked only weathered and threadbare. The bare concrete was cracked and streaked with water stains, and the tiny windows made the place look more like a prison than an apartment building. The surrounding grounds were clear of trash but looked desolate. The grass was stunted and looked dead, gone brown and dry.

He passed through a cracked glass door and entered the lobby. It was empty except for a few stacked fiberglass chairs and an underused bulletin board. He waited for the elevator.

The elevator never came. His apartment number, so the instruction sheet said, was 502-C-346. He found a stairwell and went up to the third floor.

The door to 346 was open. There was no lock.

It was a one-room apartment with two small windows and walls of unpainted concrete block. The floor was bare concrete. The place was perfunctorily furnished: a cot, one table, one chair, and a small settee. A lidless toilet stood in a corner next to a tiny sink. There was a kitchen of sorts—a hot plate and a cabinet. No refrigerator, no kitchen sink. The walls were devoid of decoration and there were no curtains on the windows.

Set in the wall in front of the settee was an oblong screen. It displayed:

MESSAGE WAITING
TOUCH SCREEN TO START

He was sorry he had looked at it. It was an order, and if he disobeyed . . . He managed to put off activating the message until a synthesized voice came out of the speaker below it.

"There is a message waiting for you. Touch the screen to start the message. Touch twice if you want the visual display only and no audio."

He touched twice. The screen came to life.

Cognomen: BKFVGD
Omnicode: 2-093487438
Message: You are late. You must not tarry when you are told to report somewhere. Do not hurry, but do not waste time. Step right along. Tardiness is unsocial. InnerVoice will remind you of this in the future.

Your program for the rest of the day is as follows:

1. In your free moments, familiarize yourself with your new

living facility. Report any deficiencies to your Residential Complex Supervisor's office.

2. Watch the one-hour Information Special that will follow this message. You must watch at least two Information Special programs per day, and at least one hour of general programming, for a total of three hours of screen viewing time per day. This routine must be followed always, except on designated Special Days. The viewing schedule will be altered on these days to permit various activities: parades, Solidarity Meetings, etc.

TOUCH SCREEN TO CONTINUE MESSAGE

He brushed the screen with his finger and more lettering filled the lighted oblong.

3. Report to your building refectory for dinner. You also have the option of eating in. You may procure food at your nearest Grocery Outlet.

4. After dinner, watch the Information Special program that will start at 1900.

5. After the program you have one hour free time until Lights Out. You may continue to watch general programming or you may sit and get in touch with InnerVoice. Remember: peace is constant struggle.

6. At Lights Out you will go to bed and sleep for eight (8) hours. You will awake refreshed and happy, ready to face the challenges of the new day.

Your Schedule Tomorrow:

Tomorrow you will report at 0800 to the Committee on Employment, Job Training Subcommittee, Building 1, Complex 122, Dedication Drive. Be prompt. Watch this screen tomorrow for further details. That is all. You may proceed with implementation of the rest of today's schedule.

He had already familiarized himself with his "living facility."

He sat down. What would happen if he got on a bus, went to the edge of the city, got off, and kept walking? Perhaps this direct approach would work if he could keep his mind occupied somehow, if he could in some way not dwell on the fact that he was doing something forbidden.

But was that possible? He had his doubts. No, his unconscious reactions would not escape InnerVoice. And there was nothing he could do about his unconscious—or "subconscious," to use the popular term.

Yet there had to be a way. Somehow the monitoring process would have to be defeated, or at least misled, until he could get to the castle. There, magic could be employed to rectify matters. But could he get as far as the portal? He did not know. That was not the only problem. He had no good reason to believe that the portal was still at the same location. It might have shifted again, or may well have disappeared altogether. He berated himself for being so foolish as to blunder through before checking things out. He should have immediately summoned Tyrene and alerted everybody that something was wrong with the Earth aspect.

But the portal could have stayed put. He had no choice but to assume that it had and proceed from that assumption. So it was a matter of getting to the portal. He had to come up with a way of thwarting InnerVoice for as long as it took to get that far.

He was getting nauseated.

He was dismayed but not surprised. InnerVoice was probably extending and refining its control of his bodily functions. Eventually even stray rebellious thoughts would be punished. It was a powerful system of oppression, self-perfecting and self-perpetuating, more effective than any secret-police force or surveillance system.

The screen brightened and a program came on. He sat and watched, trying to let the banal content—something about happy agricultural workers meeting new higher quotas—occupy the front part of his mind while he continued his scheming in the shadows.

The ploy seemed to work, but he could not come up with any solutions. For the moment he was stuck in this strange world.

When the program ended, something like a panel quiz show came on. Since he was under no compulsion to watch it, he looked for controls on the screen. There were none. He had to let it play.

He didn't relish the prospect of another cafeteria meal, so he went out to look for a food store.

He walked several blocks before he encountered what passed for a business district. Finding what he took to be a supermarket, he went in.

The place was virtually devoid of stock. The shelves held not much but empty packing cartons. There were a few items. There must have been an adequate potato harvest this year. Even at that, much of the stock was mushy and nearly rotten, alive with sprouting eyes. He found a few that were edible. There were no shopping carts or bags, so he broke off the eyes and stuffed the spuds in his pocket. He found canned goods. Most were vegetables, but he did come up with a lone can of "Beans (Baked)."

That was enough to get him through a day and keep him out of the awful cafeterias. As usual there was no paying for anything, so he walked out of the store.

On his way home he found himself following a woman. She was blond, her hair done in the unflattering pageboy style that was prevalent. Her figure—from what he could make of it through the baggy clothes—was trim and attractive. He drew abreast of her and glanced at her face.

She wore no makeup. Her eyes were pale blue and her lips thin. She had a pronounced chin and an upturned nose. On the whole she was not unattractive.

He wondered how reproduction was handled here. Were there married couples, families? He somehow doubted it. Mating centers, the offspring raised by the state. Worse, insemination centers supplied by mandatory donations. He had seen no children at all. Were they all sequestered in crèches? The thought of tiny children being inoculated with diabolical mind-controlling bacteria made him shiver.

He walked on ahead of her. She followed him when he turned into the complex.

In the lobby he pretended to read the bulletin board while waiting for her. When she passed him on the way to the stairwell he grinned.

"Good evening," he said.

She gave him a brilliant smile. "Every day we're getting better and better!"

"It's great, isn't it?" he replied.

"Oh, yes. Oh, yes."

She entered the stairwell and walked up.

His eyes wandered over the bulletin board. One posting, handwritten in a scrawl, read:

> troubled citizen w.
> unsocail thougts wants to
> join "self-critisism group"
> help me citizens! Apt. 678

He wondered how such "thougts" were possible, but obviously they were. InnerVoice's control might not be as complete as he had surmised. Bugs in the system? Programming errors in the tiny biological computers?

Perhaps there were random glitches, but he doubted that they were anything but rare. How long could he hope to go on thinking such blatantly unsocial thoughts as he was thinking right now?

He would have to do something, and fast.

# LABORATORY

"JEREMY, SOMETHING'S HAPPENING."

Jeremy poked his head out of the hatch of the *Sidewise Voyager*.

"Did you say something, Isis?"

Isis was seated at the mainframe station. "Yes. We're receiving data through the modem, but it looks like gibberish."

"Wait a sec, I'll be up."

Jeremy sat in the craft's pilot seat and entered a few commands on the keyboard of a Toshiba laptop computer, which was bolted to the control panel.

A voice replied: "Will do, Jerry-baby."

"Hey, that's 'Jeremy.' Cut the crap."

"Well, all right. Just trying to be friendly."

Jeremy's Toshiba laptop had been an ordinary personal computer before he brought it into the castle. Since then it had inexplicably developed a personality of its own. After it interfaced with the old mainframe—the one that had been destroyed in the altercation with the Hosts of Hell—it got even stranger. Against his better judgment, Jeremy gave the laptop voice capability when he installed it in the traveler, and because the result unsettled him so much, he decided not to give the same capacity to the rebuilt mainframe. He was glad of the decision. He had needed a model in designing the mainframe's operating system and chose the laptop's MS-DOS system because it was handy. Perhaps this explained why the laptop's personality and the mainframe's were similar. Whatever the reason, he did not need two talking smart-asses.

Now, Isis was another matter entirely. With the Isis program running, the mainframe's personality was submerged. Or was it that Isis was an improved version of the mainframe? Both had the hots for him. The laptop, thankfully, didn't.

As he keyed in more commands, he felt a sudden wistful yearning for the days when computers didn't think.

"Run these instrument checks again," he added orally.

"Right away, sweetie."

"Weird," he muttered. He got up and left.

Outside, he checked the small induction coil that was taped and glued to the craft's bell-shaped hull. Screws had been impossible; the hull seemed impermeable, and Jeremy wouldn't have chanced breaching it, anyway. Improvised as it was, the coil would provide a reading of the "interstitial etherium," whatever that might be.

Arriving at the mainframe terminal station, he asked, "What's up?"

"I can't get a feel for what this data is," Isis said fretfully. "It seems to be patterned, but I can't put any kind of interpretation on it that makes sense."

Jeremy looked at the clot of numbers on the screen.

"I smell pixels in all that."

"Pixels. You mean it's—?" Isis's brow went up. "Of course!" She threw her arms around Jeremy's waist. "You're so brilliant!" She typed in some commands.

The numbers disappeared and what appeared in their place was the face of Lord Incarnadine.

"Ah. You figured it out. Good work, Jeremy."

"Lord Incarnadine! Hey, you found a way to call again. Great. What's your situation?"

"Still on the way to a place where I might effect a spell to get me home. By the way, who's your new assistant? I don't believe I've had the pleasure."

"Hello again, my lord. It's Isis. Remember?"

"Isis! Why, how nice. . . . You know, I don't recall ever seeing you in this configuration."

"I've never been in this configuration before. It was only a fortunate fluke that allowed it to happen—and of course Jeremy's expertise.''

Incarnadine chuckled. ''You mean his recklessness in loading un-debugged programs into defective operating systems.''

Isis pouted. ''I'm hurt.''

He laughed. ''Don't be. I'm glad you turned out as well as you did.''

''But I don't have bugs. Endearing foibles, maybe.''

''I stand corrected. My dear, I'd love to chat, but we don't have the time. Jeremy, I just called to check in. Don't have any new information. There were some problems along the way, and I just got done riding a hellwind.''

''What's that?''

''A fast but dangerous mode of transportation around here. The trick is getting off. I managed to do it, but the ride was exhausting. And my horse is about fagged out. I expect to be delayed even more. I'm assuming that Isis helped you with the operating system.''

''With Isis, we have a fully functioning installation here,'' Jeremy said. ''Also, we've got the spell program pretty much worked out, but we need to input data on the state of the what-chamacallum.''

''Yeah, getting a reading on the whatchamacallum is going to be a problem. Unfortunately I don't have any answers. There are instruments in my study that would give us some idea, but one, they're very old and temperamental and only I can use them effectively, and two, they wouldn't yield the accuracy we would need, anyway.''

''Right. We're gonna need an energy-state factor accurate to a couple of decimal places,'' Jeremy said. ''We figure the only way to do that is to rev up the *Voyager*, fly out into the inter-universal medium, and get it.''

Incarnadine shook his head sharply. ''Absolutely not. Too dangerous.''

''We know it's dangerous, but it's the only way we'll get the data we need.''

''We'll end up losing you, the data, and the *Voyager*. No, too great a risk. Under no circumstances are you to try this. Understand?''

Jeremy shrugged. ''You're the king.''

''And don't you forget it, kid. Seriously, it's much too risky. Don't do anything at least until I get there. There may be a way to interpolate the data from those rickety instruments of mine, but I'll have to be there to do it.''

"Whatever you say.''

"Anything else happening?''

"Yeah, Linda said that there's something strange about the Earth aspect. Halfway disappeared, and there's some unknown world out there.''

"That's not good,'' Incarnadine said. "Anything else?''

"Well, I haven't heard anything. We're pretty isolated up here. I'm expecting a report any minute now, though, and . . .''

The door to the lab flew open and Osmirik rushed in.

"Here's Ozzie now, sir. Maybe he—''

"Is that His Majesty?'' Osmirik was breathless.

"Right here, Ozzie. What's wrong?''

Osmirik elbowed Jeremy aside. "My lord!''

"What is it, Osmirik?''

"There is an impostor loose in the castle, someone claiming to be you!''

Incarnadine said calmly, "Tell me all about it.''

"This man has brought an invading force, my lord, dressed as Guardsmen and claiming to be Guardsmen. I have information that they are led by a man who is a double of Tyrene. The man claiming to be you is also a double, and from all reports a convincing one, at least on sight.''

"Interesting. Have any idea where they come from?''

"No idea, Your Majesty. Everyone is mystified. There has been sporadic resistance among our forces, but the problem of course is knowing which are our forces and which are not. Not many of our castle folk are convinced that the impostor is you, but there is widespread confusion.''

"No doubt confusion reigns. Tyrene—our Tyrene—probably has his hands full, and we have a full-scale problem on ours.''

"Yes, my lord. To compound the chaos, some of the Guardsmen have seen their own impostors among the invaders.''

"That clinches it. It's a mirror aspect.''

"A mirror aspect?''

"Another result of the same interstitial disturbance. It's an ordinary aspect that has turned into a mirror image of the castle itself. Sometimes the image is true, sometimes wildly at variance with the original. I've never run into it personally, but my ancestors have. Though there's nothing in the record about a mirror castle invading. It's a crazy notion.''

"It does beggar credulity, my lord."

"But it seems to have happened. Jeremy, you'll have to throw a spell around the lab to protect yourself. Isis, do you think you can help Jeremy with that?"

"It'll be simple, my lord, compared to the other project."

"Yes, but you'll be dealing with my double. He may be my double in everything, including magical power and knowledge of the castle's secrets, as well as its spells. Understand? We'll have to devise something out of the ordinary. Osmirik, could you come up with a puzzler out of some dusty old grimoire—you know, the real arcane stuff? There is the chance the impostor might not be the lover of antiquities that I am. It might give him trouble, at least temporarily."

"I may be able to oblige, my liege, though I shall have to be quick about it. Access to the library may already be threatened."

"Go then, and be quick."

"Yes, my lord."

Osmirik rushed out of the lab.

"Jeremy, I don't know what to tell you. Just get the big spell ready, and . . . well, I suppose I'll get there when I get there."

"Yes, sir. Is that all?"

"Yeah, except remember what I said about not risking your life."

"It looks like our lives are at risk as it is."

"Maybe, but don't do anything rash. Keep a low profile, and get that protection spell up as quickly as you can."

Jeremy said, "I'll do my best, but . . ."

"What is it?"

"Well, I'm still not used to all this magic stuff. Please don't expect any miracles."

"Don't underestimate yourself."

"He always does, my lord," Isis said reprovingly.

"We all know about Jeremy's chronic inferiority bugaboo. Disabuse yourself of all that crap, mister. That's an ironclad, kingly order."

Jeremy reddened. "Yes, sir."

Incarnadine's face split into a grin. "Tell my doppelganger not to do anything I wouldn't do. I'll try to keep in touch. See you later."

Incarnadine's hand came up in front of his face, and his image faded.

Jeremy and Isis sat staring at the darkened screen.

"He's such a great man," Isis said.

"Yeah." After a moment, Jeremy yanked open a drawer, rummaged through it, and came up with a package of Hostess Twinkies. Linda kept him supplied. He ripped open the cellophane and stuffed one golden loaf-shaped cake into his mouth. "Excuse me," he said with a full mouth, "but I'm starved."

Isis smiled. "Go right ahead. Would you like some coffee with that?"

Jeremy nodded. He sat and chewed while his "assistant" got him coffee. Jeremy knew she was more than that. In fact, he couldn't have accomplished anything without her. He should be getting her coffee.

His gaze drifted to the *Voyager*, which sat up on its platform across the floor of the lab. He shook his head ruefully. There had to be a way.

# THE MOUNTAINS OF MARNASS

HE LIFTED HIS hand from the rippling water and watched his image waver in it. The faces of Jeremy and Isis were gone. He watched the surface of the melt pond until it grew still again. His image confronted him with a questioning stare. *Who is real, you or me?*

"Don't really know, my friend."

He went to his horse, which he had tethered to an evergreen bush. The animal had cooled off enough for him to allow it to take water. He led it to the rock-rimmed pond and let it drink of melted snows.

A bracing wind blew across the peaks and down, whistling through stands of pine and fir. The scenery reminded him of the Rocky Mountains, western Colorado specifically. The hellwind had blown him across half a continent and deposited him on these slopes. It had been a strange sensation watching the ground drop away and feeling the horse beat its hooves against nothing but air. But beat it did, as on some invisible highway in the sky. The storm had lashed around him, lightning forking perilously close.

Too forking close for comfort, he thought.

Riding a hellwind took a lot out of you. His mount was completely worn out. He needed to stop and rest, but time was short.

What he really needed was a fresh mount. He had no idea where he could get one.

He led his horse downward. Clouds bunched at the peak above. The cry of a mountain bird came to his ears as the trail wound through trees and boulders.

After an hour's descent he stopped, standing on a flat boulder and surveying the slope ahead. There was something unusual below. A huge bronze statue reclined on a base of stone set into the hillside. The figure was winged, and from the back looked very unusual. Leading his tired mount once more, he went down to get a better look. On the way a possible plan of action occurred to him.

He stood before a stone altar and looked up at the thing. It was a creature with the head and bust of a woman, great feathered wings, and a powerful leonine body. The bronze was tinted with the blue-green of verdigris. The statue was probably ages old.

"Hello, there," he said to it. "Now, aren't you a riddle."

The woman's face was broad-browed and severely beautiful, the breasts full and outthrusting. Long hair fell over the shoulders. The eyes looked out across the valley below, staring into the mists of the peaks beyond. There was character in the face; a spirit somehow radiated from the cold bronze. Such had been the skill of the artificer. The great wings were lifted as if the creature were poised on the brink of flight.

"Must be cold and lonely on this mountainside," he mused. "Maybe we can work something out."

He went back to the trail and searched among the shards of stone along its edge. He found what he needed and came back to the flagstone platform in front of the statue. He knelt and began to draw, his stylus a bit of limestone.

A complex figure took shape under his hand. It was partly geometrical, partly free-form. Intricate tracery flowered to one side, a column of arcane symbols running opposite.

When he was done he looked it over and nodded. He tossed the stone aside and stood in the center of the device. He held out his arms and began a chant.

The words were of some sibilant tongue, the phrases long and involuted. In the sky above, dark clouds gathered and hid the sun. A flash exploded out of their midst and a crack of thunder sounded. Another.

The chant went on. Dust whipped up from the trail, and the

tops of the pines bent in the sudden winds. A spattering of rain fell. Thunder and lightning continued for several minutes.

At last the chant ended. The clouds slowly moved off, the sun peeking out from the dispersing haze. The wind stopped. He let his arms fall and opened his eyes.

The eyes of the statue were regarding him curiously.

"What are you?" the thing said, its voice deep yet still sounding like a woman's voice.

"I am a man," he answered. "How do you feel?"

The wings moved up and down, then lowered and folded.

"Strange," the creature said. Its eyes moved across the length of its body. "I do not know what I am, yet my form seems familiar to me."

"It's a fine form. You are you. You must be used to being you after all this time."

The human eyes narrowed. "Yes, I seem to remember the past. Many of your kind have been here. They sent up offerings."

"Yes, they did. Did such doings please you?"

"It was neither pleasing nor displeasing to me. Are you going to offer me something?"

"Yes, the chance for freedom. You have wings, but have you ever flown?"

"I do not remember."

"I doubt that you have. How does the prospect of doing such a thing strike you?"

"It occurs to me that flying must be part of my nature."

"Undoubtedly. Uh, I'll lay it on the line. I need a lift. I must travel quickly and you can help. I wish you to carry me to my destination. How does *that* strike you?"

The creature considered the matter. Then it said, "I find it odd that I have no objection to this thing. Why is it that I do not?"

"I must confess that I stacked the deck a little. You were brought to life with the desire to repay the kindness bestowed on you."

"What kindness?"

"That of bringing you to awareness and setting you free. You were getting a little tired of standing up here in the wind, weren't you?"

"I am glad that it will no longer be necessary. I will repay you for this boon."

"Good. Wait one second."

He took the saddle off his horse and put it on the statue's base. He boosted himself up, picked up the saddle, and placed it on the creature's back. The girth didn't reach around the belly, but he positioned the saddle as squarely as he could. A little magical concentration would be needed anyway to hang on, secure saddle or none.

He mounted the creature and seated himself.

"Anytime you're ready," he said.

"Where are we going?"

"To the valley of the Mizzerites. Do you know where it lies?"

"No."

"No matter. I will direct you."

The wings unfolded and began to move up and down. Soon they were two great pinions beating the air.

The creature left its base and took to the air. The slope dropped away. Beast and rider soared on the cool winds between the peaks, banking one way, then the other, riding the shifting pressures and rising vapors. The rider hung on, his legs tight around the creature's middle.

"You have not yet told me what I am," she said.

He suddenly had taken to thinking of the creature as a "she."

"What do you *feel* you are?"

"I feel . . . that I am partly what you are. Partly a man. But not quite. I am . . ."

"The word is 'woman.' "

"Yes, I feel that I am a woman. Yet I am more than that. Or less, perhaps."

"You feel in some way inferior?"

"I cannot say. I am different from anything else in this world. I am alone. I have always been alone."

"Each of us is inevitably alone in this world. Or any world."

"I feel that may be true. But some are more alone than others. You say you brought me to life?"

"I did. Do you regret it already?"

"I feel a great emptiness inside. There is a longing, a yearning."

"That is the woman in you."

"Indeed? It is a peculiar sensation."

"So I've been told."

The peaks across the valley drew near. Being higher, these were tipped with snow.

"We need to get over these mountains. Can you do it?"

"I can."

The huge wings beat faster as she climbed in a spiral. Foothills fell away, and rocky slopes approached. At the top of the spiral she banked, turned, and glided. The snows lay below, very near as the craggy peak passed beneath.

The winds shifted abruptly, and she compensated, subtly changing the angle of attack on the leading surface of her wings. They began the long descent.

"Have you ever hang-glided? Just joking."

"What is joking?"

"Never mind. Do you feel good about yourself?"

"I still feel very strange. I have been thinking. After we reach your destination, is it your intention to leave me free to my own devices?"

He was long in answering. "I seem unable to lie to you. I have given you life, but it cannot be permanent. Your existence will be brief. But is it not better to exist for even a short time than never to rise to awareness at all?"

"Perhaps. Perhaps not. I do not know the answer yet. Life itself seems unutterably strange. There seems to be no sense in it. All I know is that I hunger for something."

"Hunger is part of life."

"I thirst," she said. "I need."

"Those things as well."

"Is that what life is? Unfulfilled needs?"

"Partly. Part of it is the attempt, the struggle to fulfill those needs. When the needs are satisfied, stagnation sometimes sets in."

"I do not know what that could be. But to continue my thoughts—if I am soon to cease existing, why should I not throw you from my back and fly unburdened? For the short time I have allotted to me, it seems constraining that I should be under obligation."

"I can understand. But I don't think you will throw me off."

"Neither do I," she said. "I feel a bond with you."

"Perhaps you feel indebted."

"That, too. But something else. It relates to my hunger."

"Oh?"

"Yes. But I have not the words to express it. Tell me. Why did you create me only to exist for so short a time?"

"I must confess I was thinking mostly of my own needs at

the moment. I needed you for a specific purpose, an urgent one. I did not fully consider all the consequences. I see that I should have given them some thought.''

''Perhaps you should have. But I exist now, and there is no going back. You have told me the reason why I exist. That is enough. I fulfill an urgent need. I am useful.''

''That you are.''

''But it is not easy to exist.''

''No, it is not.''

''There is pain.''

''Yes. I'm sorry.''

''I now know what this hunger is. It is love.''

''Yes,'' he said.

''How can I feel this thing for a being who is not very much like me?''

He answered, ''But I am like you in some ways. We share a certain mode of being. A humanness.''

''I also feel that we share this, somehow. It is very strange.''

''Such things always are.''

She asked, ''Can you reciprocate my feelings in any way?''

''I can greatly admire you. You are a magnificent creature.''

''But you seem to be saying that you cannot love me.''

''Again, I am sorry. What are you feeling now?''

''Sorrow,'' she said.

''Aye.''

''And an unnamable feeling, dark and turbulent.''

''Anger.''

''Yes. Thank you. Again I am thinking that it would be better if I threw you off. It would be interesting to watch what happens to a creature such as you who falls from a great height.''

''Is your anger that consuming?''

An interval passed. The wind shrieked as they dove. She leveled off and began beating her wings again, slowly, steadily, maintaining altitude. The land below had become parched, cut with canyons and winding rivers.

''My anger has passed. I no longer want you to die. I still feel love for you, lifegiver. And I must suffer for it.''

''There is an old saying that applies,'' he said, ''but I can't bring myself to mouth it. I am sorry to have caused you sorrow, but it appears to have been a necessary part of the scheme of things. If you did not love me, you never would have served me.

You, my creation, must cease to exist, and I must live with regret. Such is the lot of creators.''

The terrain had changed again. A wide river crawled below, flanked by grain fields in a patchwork quilt. The fields were crosshatched with canals and irrigation ditches. Huge monuments populated the arid land beyond the fertile fringe of the river.

"Set me down here," he instructed.

She descended, gliding toward the sprawling grid of a temple complex. Swooping in, wings making a sound like the beating of an excited heart, she landed in a plaza between two ruined buildings.

He dismounted and looked around. Truncated columns, crumbling walls, tumbled obelisks. He did not know Mizzer very well, having only taken a cursory tour many years before. A lover of antiquities, he had always wanted to undertake a serious archeological expedition. Now he wished he had done so. Simply finding the Temple of the Universes would be half the task. It was legendary, and might not even exist anymore, if it ever had. The modern-day inhabitants—most of them not descended from the ancient Mizzerites—were primitive and superstitious, and he could not depend on native help.

But he might have no choice. Lacking an authoritative map or other ancient document, he might have to hire a native guide if only to familiarize himself with the local folklore.

He would need money. Luckily he had a little gold, and the saddle would fetch a good price. He hoped.

But first he had a disagreeable task.

She was looking at him.

"Have I served you well?" she asked.

"Yes. Thank you. I must leave you now."

"How long will I continue to live?"

"Not long, I fear. You may do what you wish in the time remaining."

"There is nothing I wish to do. I have tasted the cold skies, viewed the world from a great height. I have seen enough. And I have loved. But before you go, will you do something for me?"

"Yes?"

"Let me kiss you."

He regarded her for a moment. "All right."

She crouched and he went to her and stood on her outstretched paws. The human part of her was not too oversize; moreover, she was beautiful. Her full breasts heaved.

He brought his face close to hers. Her eyes were dark and filled with longing.

He kissed her, and a shudder went through her massive body.

Then her lips grew cold and hard. He stepped back. He had just kissed a bronze statue.

She looked at home crouching in the plaza, as if she had been intended for the site. In her eyes now was the cold stare of infinity.

He looked at her for a long time. The sun moved in the sky and temple columns moved their shadows to suit it.

Then he left the plaza to make his way to the river.

# BADLANDS

THEY FLED THROUGH a bleak landscape. The sky was gray and so was the terrain, which looked like a vast overfilled ashtray or the surface of some forlorn moon. Gray strata thrust up from the dust. The sun was small, white, and dim as suns go.

They hid behind an escarpment, peeking over it. No one was following.

Linda sat and put her back against the rock. "What do we do now?"

Sir Gene squatted while Snowclaw kept a lookout. "There's obviously nothing here."

"We could wait a little and then try sneaking back, I guess."

"Yes, we could duck in and make a dash for another aspect."

Linda shook her head. "We'd get caught for sure."

"You may be right. But we have to try it."

"Let's wait."

"Right." Sir Gene went to one knee. "Of course, if there's a problem with the castle's aspects, as it seems there is, then ducking into any aspect becomes chancy."

"Yeah," Linda said. "We don't have many options."

"We could scout around here. Perhaps there are some resources we could tap."

Linda looked around. "Like what?"

Sir Gene shrugged. "Magical ones, perhaps?"

Linda closed her eyes for a moment, then opened them. "Nope. No magic here, at least none that I can use. I'm pretty much a castle-oriented magician, though I've done some stuff outside the castle now and then."

"Are you sure there's nothing here?"

"Pretty sure. What exactly did you have in mind?"

"I don't know, really. What we need, of course, are reinforcements to counterbalance Incarnadine's advantage."

"I don't see any armies handy," Linda said.

Sir Gene chuckled mirthlessly. "I suppose not. But an army is precisely what we need. If we can get back into the castle, we might go about recruiting one."

"Where?"

"I know a few aspects—" Sir Gene clucked and shook his head. "But they may have disappeared or changed. Still, we must try."

"But the castle's swarming with enemy Guardsmen. And there's some crazy duplicate of Incarnadine running amok."

"You can use magic when we're back inside."

"Against Incarnadine? And this one's pretty mean."

"Yes, he is that." Sir Gene shifted his weight. "Look, let me ask you again. Are you entirely sure there are no magical resources you can avail yourself of here?"

"I told you—"

"*Absolutely* sure?"

Linda sighed. "All right, I'll check one more time." She shut her eyes again and folded her arms. She remained still for a long while. Then one eye popped open.

"Wait a minute."

Sir Gene leaned forward expectantly. "Something?"

"Yeah. Very faint. Very strange, too."

"Can you work with it?"

Linda frowned and looked thoughtful. "I don't know. There's a . . . I think there's a line of force running along there somewhere." She pointed toward a shallow depression. "And it goes off in that direction." She pointed in the direction of the sun.

"And that means what?"

"It just means that it could lead to a node."

"A node?"

"Yeah. Look, I've been trying to explain this to people for

years now, but, you see, magic is all laid out in patterns. Power patterns—''

"Yes, yes, I understand. But if you got to this node, could you work some magic?''

"Maybe. We have to follow that line of force and see.''

"Well, let's do that thing. Anything coming, Snowclaw?''

"Nobody,'' Snowclaw answered.

"Good. Let's give it a try, shall we?''

Linda shrugged. "Can't hurt.'' She got up.

They walked toward the pinpoint sun. Here and there a gray bush blended into the monochrome landscape. The fainter gray of a mountain range banded the horizon. All was still. They skirted a good-sized impact crater, eroded and probably ancient, then passed a few smaller ones. A dry gulch cut across the flats, and this they descended into and climbed out the other side. Linda stopped on the far ridge and scanned the terrain ahead.

"Feeling something?'' Sir Gene asked.

"It's getting stronger,'' she said.

"A node?''

Linda peered off, squinting in the harsh sunlight. "Don't know what it is. Some kind of . . . focus, like.''

"Focus?''

"Whatever. Like a concentrated center. Hell, I'm no good at words.''

"Never mind the words, just find some magic.''

"Aye aye, sir.'' Linda gave him a mock salute.

Sir Gene smiled wanly. "Sorry. It's just that the castle must be saved.''

"Don't you think I know that?''

"Yes, of course. Please carry on.''

Linda chewed her lip thoughtfully, scanning ahead. She pointed slightly to the left. "There.'' Bringing her hand back to rub her chin, she added, "Maybe.''

They walked on. Sir Gene wandered off to the right to inspect an unusual rock formation. When he got out of earshot Linda went to Snowclaw.

"Snowy, I was wondering . . .''

"Yeah?''

"It's about Gene. Have you noticed anything strange about him?''

"How did you know?''

"Know what, Snowy?''

"That he smells funny."

She smiled. "I didn't notice that. But ever since he reappeared he seems different. Talks different. His personality's changed."

They continued walking.

"Really? Maybe you humans can notice these things better," Snowclaw said. "I noticed the smell, but I didn't think anything of it. You people use stink water a lot, so I thought Gene was using a new kind."

"It's not stink water. What that phony Incarnadine said worries me. He could have been mistaking our Gene for his twin in the mirror castle, but the way Gene answered him . . . I don't know, Snowy." Linda's eyes widened. "Snowy, what if he's not really Gene? What are we going to do?"

"I sure wish I knew," Snowclaw said. "Here he comes."

Sir Gene caught up to them.

"Rather a waste of a world, isn't it?"

Linda said, "Yeah, but there are no tourists."

"Always some good point if you think about it. Getting any closer to the focus affair?"

"It's getting stronger all the time."

"Good. Very good."

"But I still don't know if I can use it. Magic is different on different worlds. You know that."

"I'm magically inept in any world."

"I really need the castle as a power source. It's the easiest to use. I—"

Linda suddenly stopped.

"What is it?" Sir Gene said.

"It's getting *really* strong."

"I assume that's good."

"Maybe."

"Why don't you try something?"

"Like what?"

"Anything. You're good at conjuration. Try conjuring."

"Okay. Uh . . . like—?"

"Food," Snowclaw said. "I'm hungry."

"What news. Okay, here goes."

Linda looked around and chose a wide, flat rock to stand in front of. Shutting her eyes tight, she held her arms straight at her sides, fists clenched.

Two plates of barbecued ribs appeared on the rock.

"Smells good," Snowclaw said, his nostrils flaring.

Linda looked troubled. "That's funny, I didn't order two."

"You usually control quantity?" Sir Gene asked.

"Always. That's strange. You were right, Gene, there's really something here."

"And you can conjure anything?"

"Well, not anything. You know I have trouble sometimes."

"Yes, of course. But with this new power . . ."

"The problem is its newness. All magic isn't alike, Gene. I really have to feel that I'm in control when I'm doing anything magical, and I'm not fully in control here."

"Circumstances may dictate that we work with what we have."

"I understand what you're saying. But I don't understand what you want to try."

"See here. You can conjure. Can you conjure some reinforcements?"

"You mean like Guardsmen?"

"Yes."

"Gene, in the castle I've done all sorts of things. In a fight I've even made clones of you and Snowy. Aren't you forgetting?"

Sir Gene looked away. "Yes, of course I know that. Can you do it now?"

"Make doubles of you and Snowy? This isn't the castle, Gene."

"Then we should try to go back to the castle."

"Don't you think Incarnadine could conjure more of his Guardsmen to offset any advantage?"

"Guardsmen, yes. But what if we conjure not Guardsmen but a force that can best any Guardsman one-on-one?"

"Like what?"

"Like Snowclaw."

Snowclaw was busy devouring ribs, crunching them up bones and all.

Linda turned to look at him. "Snowy?"

"Yes, don't you understand? Snowclaw can take on three Guardsmen at a time. Any force composed of Snowclaw's duplicates would have an intrinsic advantage."

Linda took a breath and let it out noisily. "Gene, the point is we'd be fighting against Incarnadine. A nasty, evil one to boot.

There's no telling what he could pull out of his hat to go up against us."

"Yes, I realize that. But we must make the attempt."

"I think it's a crazy idea."

"Perhaps. But—what is it, Snowclaw?"

Snowclaw was sniffing the air. "Humans coming. Should've smelled 'em before, but the food was in the way."

"Up to that ridge," Sir Gene said. "But first, hide that debris."

Linda hid the empty plates behind the rock while Snowclaw picked up stray bones and stashed them in the bushes.

They ran up a slight rise and took cover behind a stone ledge. They waited. A few minutes later three Guardsmen came into view. They approached on the far side of the dry wash, stopping at its edge.

After exchanging a few words, they gave a cursory look around, then went back the way they'd come.

When they were out of sight Sir Gene turned and sat in the dust. "Well, that eliminates going back to the castle, unless we conjure some help."

"It won't do any good. Say I doubled or tripled Snowy. He might disappear when we got inside the castle."

"Then you'd use castle magic to duplicate him there."

"Yeah. Okay, you have every angle covered. But it'd still be a matter of going up against Incarnadine."

"Look," Sir Gene said. "We have to do something. We can't stay here. With you we wouldn't starve, but I for one don't want to spend the rest of my life—"

"Okay, all right, I know what you're saying." Linda ran a hand through her blond hair. "Let's get closer to the node. Maybe then I'll be able to tell whether or not I can control the force."

They went down the other side of the rise and crossed a wide depression. The terrain grew more cratered as they progressed. They walked for about fifteen minutes in as straight a line as possible, Linda leading the way.

She stopped. "Jesus, it's strong."

"Is it here?"

"A little bit farther."

They moved on until Linda stopped again.

"This is unbelievable."

"Can you handle it?" Sir Gene asked pointedly.

"I'm not sure. It's so strange, so powerful."

"Try something. Duplicate Snowclaw."

Linda said, "You know, when I did it before it was in the middle of a fight. It just seemed the right thing to do at the time. I don't even know how I first thought of it. But just to do it, here, now—"

"You must." Sir Gene's gaze was hard, adamant.

Linda stared back. "Are you on our side?"

"What do you mean?"

"Who are you?"

He looked off. "I'm Gene Ferraro, of course."

"Are you? Or are you really . . . ?"

He turned on her. "See here, I could ask the same question of you. We've seen Incarnadine's double. How can I be sure you're not Linda's?"

She had no answer.

He exhaled. "I grant that you've every right to suspect me, but for the moment, no matter what my true identity, we're on the same side. Does that answer your question?"

Linda nodded slowly. "Yes, I guess it does."

"Then conjure Snowclaw some comrades-in-arms."

Linda turned to the great white beast. "Snowy, do you have any objection?"

"Do whatever you have to do, Linda. I'm ready to go back there and kick some hind ends."

"Okay," Linda said. "We'll try it."

Linda sidestepped twice, then moved forward a bit. Sir Gene backed off to give her room.

"Here goes."

She closed her eyes. There was silence. At length, something began to form in the air above her. At first it was an almost imperceptible movement, a whirling. Then it grew darker and more turbulent. It swelled and took shape, forming a funnel cloud.

Sir Gene and Snowclaw edged back. Linda's eyes were still shut and her arms were stiff at her sides. She began to teeter, as if caught in the flux of some oscillating invisible force. Her eyelids fluttered.

The thing above her grew. It became a dark cone-shaped vortex, rotating rapidly. Dust rose all around.

Linda dropped to the ground. Snowclaw rushed to her and picked her up, carried her to one side.

"Linda, wake up."

Head cradled in Snowclaw's arms, Linda opened her eyes. "What happened?"

"Good Lord," Sir Gene said.

The cloud was huge now, a black cyclone. A high-pitched whine emanated from it.

Suddenly a white shape dropped out of the cloud, a furred creature. It hit the ground, rolled, and sprang to its feet. It bore a huge broadax.

It was Snowclaw. "I'm ready," he said.

Linda stood, looked at the Snowclaw who had helped her up, then at the new Snowclaw. "I guess it works."

"What is that thing?" Sir Gene said, aghast, pointing at the cloud.

"I don't know."

"You mean you can't control it?"

"Nope. Told you it'd be risky."

The cloud disgorged another furry hulk. Another Snowclaw. The two new ones looked at each other, then at the original, who raised his broadax in greeting.

"Hi, guys," he said.

"This is getting interesting," Linda said.

Another Snowclaw dropped, then another. More followed.

"You'll have to stop it at some point," Sir Gene said.

Linda shook her head. "I can't touch that thing. It's going to make Snowclaws until it decides to quit."

Dismayed, Sir Gene watched. The phenomenon seemed to be generating Snowclaws at an ever-increasing rate. It was a downpour of white fur and battle-axes.

"Well, General, you've got your army," Linda said. "Now what are you going to do with it?"

# GOLFWORLD

"LOOK AT THIS!" Thaxton said indignantly.

The fairway on the twelfth hole was mostly sand with patches of burnt grass. However daunting, though, the twelfth hole was an improvement over the eleventh, which had been mostly superheated rock, and a vast improvement over the tenth, which had featured hazards of sulphuric acid and man-eating plants in the rough. (They had *looked* man-eating, Thaxton claimed.)

"Get out your sand wedge," Dalton said.

The gargoyle twosome was playing ahead, making their approach shots.

"Go ahead," Dalton said. "You have the honor."

Thaxton had birdied the last hole. His injuries seemed to have been liberating, somehow. What did he have to lose? His play had improved. His leg was unbroken but very sore, and he still hobbled using his partner's two-iron as a crutch. He owed his intact bones to the fact that the clubhouse roof had not been concrete but some lighter material. Also, the offending chunk of masonry had rolled onto him after falling. A direct hit would have done real damage.

"They look out of range," Thaxton said as he watched the gargoyles hike to the green. He yelled fore, anyway, and hit his drive.

They played across the desert. Thaxton swore he saw things moving in the sand. Dalton saw nothing.

"Are there bloody big worms in sand?" he asked.

"You never know what you may find in a dune," Dalton said.

In the burning wastes every lie was a "fried egg," but they carried on. Dalton made a beauty of a cut shot and was on the green in three. Thaxton did even better, sinking his chip shot for an eagle.

"You're quite proud of yourself, aren't you?" Dalton said.

"All in a day's play, my dear fellow," Thaxton said smugly.

Dalton two-putted and they went off to find the next tee, which was nowhere in sight.

"That way?" Thaxton asked, pointing to the right.

"Out across there," Dalton said, indicating flats ahead.

They walked for a good long while. The desert wastes blended to arid plain. The sky became a strange color, a sort of yellowish green. Dark mountains lay opposite the large blue sun.

"God, it is blue, isn't it?" Thaxton said, shading his eyes.

"Blue-white. A blue giant star, right at the top of the Main Sequence."

"The what?"

"Astronomy lingo. Blue giants are very large, very hot stars."

"Bloody hot. I'm sweating like a Turk."

"What's this?"

Thaxton looked around. "What's what?"

"Up ahead. Is that a road?"

Indeed it was a road, a wide black highway running from horizon to horizon. They walked to it and stood on the shoulder, looking one way and then the other. No traffic in sight. Thaxton put one spiked shoe on the paved surface and scraped it back and forth.

"Doesn't seem to be macadam or asphalt."

"Black concrete?" Dalton ventured.

"A bit strange."

"Yeah," Dalton said, nodding slowly.

Thaxton tilted his head to one side. "Hear that?"

"What?"

"A buzzing?"

Dalton listened. "Yup. Any electric lines around?"

"I think it's coming from the road." Thaxton tried to stoop but couldn't.

Dalton did and cocked an ear. "Maybe. Faintly buzzing."

"Interesting."

"I hear something else."

Thaxton looked up the road. "Something's coming."

They waited. At the road's vanishing point a silver dot grew to a bigger dot, then got a lot bigger very fast. The thing roared like a wounded beast.

"Good God, what's that?"

"A very fancy eighteen-wheeler."

It was a trailer truck, that was sure, but an intimidatingly futuristic one, composed of daring curved planes, clear bubbles, and other rakish features. Whatever it was rolling on, there seemed to be more than eighteen of them. The vehicle was huge and it was traveling at a terrific rate of speed.

Suddenly it began to decelerate, emitting all sorts of horrendous screeches and roars. The golfers warily stepped back from the edge of the road. The vehicle swerved to the shoulder as it braked and came to a shuddering stop not more than ten feet from the golfers.

The two walked around the gargantuan cab and looked up at what they took to be the driver's window.

A port hissed open and a man poked his head out. He was about thirty-five with wavy dark hair and twinkling eyes. There was a rugged, blue-jawed handsomeness to him. He flashed an engaging smile.

"Greetings, gentlemen. We didn't know this planet was inhabited. Fact is, it's not on any official map. Are we lost, or are you?"

"We're not natives," Thaxton said, "if that's what you mean. Just playing a few holes of golf."

"Golf, eh? What's your handicap?"

"Oh, God, high twenties, I'm afraid. Do you golf?"

"No time, I'm always on the road."

"Of course. I say, exactly where is this planet? We're strangers here ourselves."

"Supposed to be in the Lesser Magellanic Cloud. Where are you from?"

"Uh, nice truck you have there," Dalton said.

"Thanks. I'm behind in the payments."

"Who's the manufacturer?"

"GP Technologies. They make a flashy rig."

"Impressive."

"It's seen a lot of road."

A beautiful face appeared at the window. Its owner had short dark hair and cool blue eyes.

"Hi," she said. "Are you fellows starhiking?"

"No, ma'am," Dalton said. "We're playing golf."

"Didn't know there was a course on this world," the driver said. "Didn't think there was any life on it at all."

"There may not be life," Thaxton said, "but there's death on the tenth hole."

"Tough course, huh?"

"Rather," Thaxton said. "Tell me, where does this road go?"

"Oh, it goes all over. From star to star, world to world."

"More balmy worlds. All we need, really. Another thing—rather strange, perhaps it's the heat. But is there any reason for the road making a sort of buzzing noise?"

"Oh, that's roadbuzz. You should always listen to roadbuzz, but never believe any of it."

"Yes, but why does it make that sound?"

"Nobody knows. The road's a living thing. It conforms with the changing terrain over eons. How it does that, only the Road-builders know, and they're not talking."

Bemused, Thaxton nodded. "Right. Well, we'd best be off. Very nice to talk with you."

Dalton said, "By the way, you didn't happen to spot the thirteenth tee, did you?"

"Afraid not," the driver said. "If I see it, though, I'll double back and let you know."

"Appreciate it," Dalton said, stepping back. "Take care, now."

The driver nodded. "Don't take any wooden kilocredits."

"Listen, if you see any castles off the side of the road," Dalton said, then thought better of it. "Uh, never mind."

The driver grinned. "Ain't the universe a wacky place?"

The beautiful woman waved at them, smiling.

The engine howled and the truck swung out onto the smooth pavement. It roared off down the road.

They watched it become a silver dot again, then vanish.

"Charming fellow, wasn't he?" Dalton said.

"As truck drivers go, I suppose."

"I bet someone could write a great novel about the sort of life he leads."

"Oh, I rather doubt it."

# CITY

THEY ASSIGNED HIM to a hospital to work as an orderly.

The place was different from the "hospital" where he'd been incarcerated. The atmosphere was decidedly low-tech. The floor he was assigned to was a cardiac unit, but there were no continuous monitoring instruments in use. Nurses wheeled bulky EKG machines around from patient to patient to get periodic readings. Doctors (if that's what they could be called, though they were probably more on the order of highly trained paramedics) relied on tried-and-true devices and methods: stethoscopes, pulse taking, and so forth.

The place was dingy, plaster cracking on ill-painted walls. It was clean, though, because he cleaned it, pushing brooms and slapping mops around. The patients wore pasted smiles but were generally miserable, as the medical care was terrible and the food was worse than in the cafeterias.

He kept trying to come up with a plan, to find a way of exploiting the glitches, the defects in the system. InnerVoice's control was marginally less than total. The system was essentially a technological approach to totalitarianism. While political methods of repression could approach complete efficiency, no technology could. The anguished note on the bulletin board proved that things could go awry. Either the control system could not penetrate to the forebrain and control thoughts, or the tiny controlling computers could malfunction. He did not know which was the case; either way it was a ray of hope.

He could still think, but there was no telling for how long. The people around him seemed to be under more complete control than he was, but this could have been an illusion. He had quickly learned to curb his tongue, to act the part. Speech was behavior, and here behavior was controlled by a quickly responding mechanism of "reinforcements," to use Behaviorist jargon, most of which were "negative." But some were positive in the sense that compliance with accepted modes of behavior was just as quickly rewarded with surcease from psychic and physical pain.

Perhaps his thoughts would continue to be his own, but thoughts wouldn't help his body, which was dangling like a marionette on biochemical strings.

The contrastingly backward technology of the hospital led him to think. He watched nurses take oral temperatures with old-fashioned liquid-lead thermometers, the standby of home medicine chests for ages. Even with the dumb technology, minimum sanitary measures were followed. Those thermometers were sterilized, and for a thermometer the only way to do that was immersion in alcohol; for oral purposes that meant ethyl alcohol, ethanol. Methanol, wood alcohol, was poisonous.

If his unconscious bodily mechanisms were being monitored internally, was there something he could ingest that would suppress those mechanisms? Drugs, maybe. Drugs were here, and he could get to them, but what sort of drugs would suppress autonomic responses? Tranquilizers? Maybe, but he doubted that any in use here would be effective enough. Narcotics? Possibly. But he was naturally wary of those. After all, overdosing was as easy as falling off a ghetto stoop.

Narcotics were easily available, in the sense that there were no physical barriers. The drug cabinets had no lock. In this society locks were unneeded. And for that reason he couldn't touch them. He couldn't approach the cabinets with the intention of stealing drugs without risking intervention by InnerVoice.

But the thermometers made him think. He had seen no taverns, no liquor stores. As far as he knew, this society was teetotal. Why? Perhaps because the effects of booze could thwart InnerVoice.

There was probably a bottle of ethanol in the drug cabinet,

and if not there, in the supply lockers. But the question was, could he steal the alcohol?

No. The same constraints applied, or would be applied. He couldn't even risk thinking about it too much.

Back to square one. He ruefully half entertained thoughts of sidling up to the bottle, eyes averted, whistling innocently, then grabbing it and chugging as much as he could before InnerVoice grabbed his gut and squeezed. But the ploy was absurd. He couldn't very well plan to do something without knowing he was going to do it. There was no one to fool but himself.

Was there no way out besides hoping for his internal police force to go on the fritz?

He might have to face up to the possibility that there was no way out of this. The thought of it was numbing. An eternity here?

What about the castle? They surely had missed him by now. Surely they'd send out a search party.

The thought of castle folk in doublets and tights wandering around in this universe was incongruous. But Linda was smart enough to know that a strange universe would call for caution.

Maybe that was the reason for the delay in finding him. Just how would they go about it, anyway? This was a big world, a complex society, and a very dangerous one. He couldn't know for sure that the rescuers had not also been abducted and injected with InnerVoice.

If so, there was no hope. The portal could close, if it hadn't already, and he'd be stuck here forever.

He went home after his first day, made himself boiled potatoes, ate, and sat down to log screen time. While he watched, he thought. At length he resolved on a course of action. Absurd idea though it was, tomorrow he would try stealing the bottle and downing as much alcohol as he could, neat, before the shakes got to him. He wouldn't try to fool himself or InnerVoice, he would just do it. He simply could not think of anything else to try.

The resolution enabled him to sit through the evening's "entertainment" without too much distress. Afterward, he was restless. He decided to go out for a walk. As far as he knew, it was allowed. Anything that was allowed, he could do.

Maybe he would keep walking. He'd had about enough of this place.

Then he considered what might happen if he tried to escape.

He had refrained from daring another attempt out of simple fear. He did not want to experience again the excruciating psychic pain, the unbearable sense of impending doom, the unremitting terror that he had felt under InnerVoice's lash. The very thought of it made his stomach spasm.

No, he wasn't quite ready to face it again, and the bottle-grabbing notion now struck him as stupid and rash. In time, maybe. For now about all he could risk was taking a walk.

He was on the stairway between the second and third floors when she came through the door opening on the landing. He almost bumped into her. It was the woman he'd seen last night.

She seemed startled at first, then burst into the forced smile she'd given him before. "Hello, citizen!"

"Hi," he said. Then he blurted, "I'm going out for a stroll. Want to walk with me?"

The smile disappeared, and she gave him a penetrating stare.

He stood there, letting her gauge him, taking his measure. She seemed to be weighing the risk, trying to figure whether this was a test or a trap. Could she trust him? Should she dare? All this she spoke with her eyes, and he was vastly relieved to hear it. It was the first evidence he'd had of humanity, of conscious volition, behind the universal facade of robotlike obedience.

"Yes," she said finally.

They walked out of the building together.

The night was cool and the city was quiet. Too quiet. It was not yet Lights Out, but along the stark faces of the high rises there were more dark windows than lighted ones. A musky, watery smell came on a breeze from the river. There was little traffic on the boulevard. No one else was about. It was late.

"When did it stop?" she asked after they had walked in silence for a stretch.

"When did what stop?"

"InnerVoice."

"It hasn't."

She halted and looked at him. "You just haven't realized it yet. It's gone."

He shrugged. "I haven't tried to do anything unsocial yet."

"You're doing it now."

"I didn't know evening walks were forbidden."

"They're not. There's no need to forbid it. No one does anything that's not on his daily schedule. It's too risky. Don't you know that?''

''No,'' he said. ''I'm new here.''

''Were you an Outperson?''

''Yeah. If that means a foreigner.''

''An Outperson is someone without InnerVoice. The whole world doesn't have InnerVoice yet.''

He had wondered about the outside world, and about how much of the planet InnerVoice had under its control. There was no news at all on the screen, nothing except endless propaganda about heroic production efforts and quota overfulfillments.

''What do you know about Outpersons?'' he asked.

''Nothing,'' she said. ''We haven't been able to get any accurate news for years.''

''Who's 'we'?''

She started walking again. ''People who've lost InnerVoice.''

''So, not everyone's controlled.''

''No, not everyone.'' She gave him a glum look. ''But it might as well be everyone. There are so few. You're one, even if you don't know it yet.''

''How do you know that you don't have InnerVoice anymore?''

''Because I can do anything I want. Like go for walks in the evening, take an extra portion of food, not watch the screen when I don't want to. I almost never do anymore.''

''No wonder. It's awful stuff.''

She smiled. ''See? You wouldn't be able to say that if you hadn't lost it.''

He shook his head. ''I wish you were right. But they just shot me up with the gunk the other day. Can it fail that quickly?''

''We don't know. Most maladapts lose InnerVoice in their late teens. That's when I lost mine. I'm twenty-six now. And they haven't caught on yet.''

''Is there danger that you'll be found out?''

''Oh, of course. There's always that danger. But you get used to it. The thing is, even though InnerVoice is silent, habits are hard to break. I don't do anything really unsocial. Just little things.''

They turned a corner and walked toward the river.

He asked, ''Why does InnerVoice sometimes fail?''

''We don't know that, either. We think that the body's defense system overcomes it, like it was an infection. Maybe maladapts have better defense systems than most people."

"Just like some people have spontaneous remissions from cancer, maybe."

"Yeah, maybe."

They walked on until they came to a small park by the river's edge. There was a bench, and they sat. Lights on the other shore reflected as long wavering lines on the water. There were no boats on the river, no barges. In another universe this was an industrial town, but here it was a dull administrative center.

"I usually come here at nights when the weather's nice," she said. "I like to watch the river go by. It comes from somewhere and goes somewhere, away from here. I like to think about taking a little boat and going out on the water, and letting the river carry me away. I'd never leave the boat. I'd just fish, lie in the sun, do nothing all day."

"What do you do all day?"

"I sit and type on a keyboard. I key in data, and then I ask the computer to report on the data, and it spews out all kinds of stuff at me. Fun."

"Yeah, sounds like it. Tell me this. How many other maladapts are there?"

"I only know two, but there are more. Don't ask me their cognomen-omnicodes, because I don't trust you well enough yet. You might be InnerVoice."

"You mean I might be a police agent?"

"There are no police. But I've heard of people being arrested by the Committee for Constant Struggle."

"The army."

"Yes. They sometimes use agents to trick people. Or so I've heard. It may be all lies, though. You never know. You can never know what's truth and what isn't."

"Let me ask you something very basic and crucial. Who's in charge of the government? Who runs this whole nightmare?"

"I don't know. We've been trying to figure it out for years. All we know is that there's InnerVoice."

"But someone invented InnerVoice. Someone used it to control people. Who was it?"

She shrugged.

He asked, "How long has InnerVoice been in control?"

"No one knows that, either. Years and years."

"Isn't there any history?"

"What's history?"

He looked out across the river. Darkness and silence and slow-moving water.

Her hand sought his.

"Let's go back," she said. "My place."

"Are you sure?"

She giggled. "I've had an order to get pregnant for months now. I've been ignoring it. Couldn't find anyone I wanted to get pregnant with."

Now he knew how it was done. An order was issued, an order was obeyed.


Light came through the lone window and made a trapezoid on the bare floor beside the bed. Lying on his side, he studied it. He liked its lambent geometry, its two-dimensional clarity.

"Are you awake?" she asked.

"Yes." He rolled over to face her.

She asked him, "What are you thinking?"

"Of how to get out of this place."

"This place? You mean the living complex?"

"I mean this world."

"How can you get out of the world? That's silly."

"No, it isn't. I know a way to get to a different world."

"A different world," she said dreamily. "Do you think there are worlds other than this one?"

"Yes, there are any number of them. And I can get you to a pretty nice one. It's just a matter of getting outside the city a little ways."

"How would you do that?"

"I don't know. Walk, take a bus. Steal a vehicle. It doesn't matter. The main question in my mind is, can I do it without InnerVoice interfering?"

"You should be able to. You wouldn't be able to sleep with me if you still had InnerVoice."

"How could you get pregnant if no one was able to sleep with you?"

"If they had an order, they could."

"You need an order?"

"Sure. You didn't find the order to impregnate someone on your schedule, did you?"

"No."

"Well, then. You wouldn't be able to sleep with me unless InnerVoice was dead inside you."

"Then that means there's nothing preventing me from leaving."

"Not if you actually have someplace to go. You say you do, but I don't understand how. InnerVoice is in control outside the city, too."

"I can get to a place where no one ever heard of InnerVoice."

"Is there such a place? There are stories, rumors."

"Rumors of what?"

"That there are Outpersons who wage war against Inner-Voice."

"Where?"

"No one knows. It's rarely talked about. Just sometimes on the Information Specials they'll mention something about 'socially irresponsible outside elements.' That's how they phrase it, usually."

"Rebels? An opposing military force of some kind?"

"Don't know."

It suddenly struck him that he didn't even know this woman's name. Wait; she didn't have a name, only a nonsensical and dehumanizing jumble of letters and numbers. He really didn't want to know what her cognomen was, much less her omnicode.

"Alice."

She said, "What did you say?"

"I just gave you a name. Alice. You look like one."

" 'Alice.' That's pretty."

"So are you."

"That's unsocial. No one is better looking than anyone else."

"That's a lie. Alice, listen. I'm going to leave here and I want to take you with me. Do you want to come?"

"Go with you?"

"Yes."

"To this other place, this other world you talked about?"

"Yes. Do you want to come with me?"

She was silent for a long time.

Then she said: "You know, I was thinking about doing it tonight. Jumping into the river."

"You wanted to kill yourself?"

"Yes."

"Tonight?"

"Yes. But I think about it a lot. Just jumping in and letting the water carry me away."

"Drowning."

"Of course. Killing yourself is the most unsocial thing you can do, and I wanted to do it tonight. And then . . . I met you. And now you want to take me away."

"Come with me, Alice. We'll live in a big castle."

"What's a castle?"

"A big house."

"A big house." She inhaled deeply and sighed. "Yes, I'll go with you."

"Let's leave now."

She kissed him. "Tomorrow. Let's try to get me pregnant again."

"All right, Alice. By the way, my name is Gene."

"Gene." She laughed. "Gene. It sounds funny."

"Laugh all you want. It sounds wonderful."

# LABORATORY

JEREMY SAT HUDDLED over the terminal keyboard, typing away. His eyes were fixed on the screen, his fingers graceful dancers performing a complex choreography. Isis stood behind him, watching, one slender white hand on his shoulder. Osmirik sat at another section of the workstation, paging through an ancient leather-bound tome.

Jeremy's fingers did a finale. Then he sat back and sighed.

"That's the coding," he said. Reaching, he jabbed at a few more keys. "Now we compile it, debug it, and see if it runs."

"I am not sure," Osmirik said, "that the spell will be effective until after we have subjected it to extensive evaluation and analysis. Casting a computer-aided spell is a science, a very new and untried one, whereas casting spells in the ancient manner is a very highly developed art. Art can compensate for much uncertainty."

"Yeah, but I can't do diddly-squat the old-fashioned way," Jeremy said. "What magic I can do, I gotta do with computers. Crazy, but there it is."

"I did not mean to imply that there was not an element of artistry in what you do, Jeremy. You are obviously an adept in your own right."

"Yeah. But it's still crazy."

"There you go again," Isis said.

"Sorry, I shouldn't do that. Yeah, I'm pretty good, pretty good. Thank God my life's not a total waste."

Isis hugged his neck. "You're doing a terrific job, Jeremy."

"Thanks," he said, blushing a bit. "Hey, you had a lot to do with all this."

"I'm only doing my job."

"And Ozzie here, he really did all the—"

A sharp rapping came from the laboratory door. The three froze.

Voices outside, then loud knocking.

"That may be—" Osmirik began.

Someone began pounding.

Osmirik rose and hurried to the door.

"Who is it?" he called.

"Guard!" came a voice from the other side. "Open up!"

"By whose authority are you acting?" Osmirik asked.

"Lord Incarnadine's, you fool, who else's? Now, open this door or we'll break it down."

"I am His Excellency the Royal Librarian. We are engaged in a task commissioned by His Majesty himself. We are not to be disturbed. Do you hear?"

"We hear. To the devil with your commission. Lord Incarnadine has ordered all castle personnel to report to the Guest Residence immediately."

"On the contrary," Osmirik stated. "Lord Incarnadine has ordered no such thing. We have been in direct communication with His Majesty, and he is nowhere in the castle at the moment. Your orders come from an impostor."

There came cursing and general mumbling.

Osmirik turned toward the workstation. "Is the compilation process completed?"

Jeremy checked the screen. "Yeah."

"Then we had best run the program and cast the spell."

"I thought you said—?"

A sharp thwack came against the door. Another, then a flurry of them. The door shook under their impact.

"Axes," Osmirik said. "The door is heart-of-oak, but they will make short work of it. Run the protective spell program."

"But the bugs . . . ?"

"Vermin or none, you must run it now."

"Right. Okay, here goes nothing."

Jeremy tapped out a few characters and slapped RETURN.

The arrangement of strange components that was the main-frame computer began to whir softly. The sound increased in pitch until it faded out of audible range. Lights flashed on panels, glass tubes pulsed, and sparks arced between electrodes.

Jeremy studied the screen. "Going pretty good, it looks like."

The sound of the axes suddenly ceased.

Head cocked forward, Osmirik listened. There was silence on the other side. Then he put his ear against the door.

"Anything?" Jeremy asked.

Osmirik turned. "The spell has been efficacious. Unfortunately it seems the effects were rather more harsh than circumstances warranted."

"Why?"

"I believe the men on the other side of this door are dead. There was no need of lethality. The spell's potency could have been finely tuned to compensate. But . . ." Osmirik gave a mournful shrug.

"Forget it, Ozzie. You couldn't help it."

"Perhaps if I had modified a few of the component forces."

"Don't worry about it. I mean, hey, it's too bad they got aced, but . . . you know, screw 'em."

"Your connotation is clear. But I am not a soldier. I will never lightly regard the taking of a human life."

"Sorry, Ozzie. I meant—"

"There is no time for this, Jeremy."

"You're right. We'll do the Monday-morning quarterbacking later. What we gotta do now is get those readings on the interuniversal medium."

Isis said, "But Lord Incarnadine said we should wait till he gets here."

"That was before those guys outside got here. We might have whacked a few of them, but there are more where they came from. And pretty soon this impostor guy has got to come around. What'll we do then?"

Osmirik said gravely, "I'm afraid he is right, Isis."

"We have to take the *Voyager* out into the medium," Jeremy said. "We gotta run that big universe-fixing spell, or it won't make any difference whether Incarnadine gets here or not."

Isis nodded. "We'll both go. I can modify myself to fit into the Toshiba."

"Forget it. I'm going alone. One of us has to stay behind. We'll keep in touch by modem."

"Silly Jeremy."

"What?"

"Don't you know that I can copy myself and be loaded into two pieces of hardware at once?"

Jeremy sat up. "Hey, I guess so. Never thought of it. Boy, am I dumb."

She kissed him on the forehead. "You and me, Jeremy. Let's do it now."

"Right. Ozzie, you'll have to hold the fort while we're gone."

"Again, the metaphor is unambiguous. I will of course do my best."

Isis asked, "What about the boomerang effect you wanted to work up for launching the traveler?"

"No time. I'm gonna have to pilot by the seat of my pants."

"It's going to be dangerous, Jeremy."

"Uh-huh." Jeremy swallowed hard. "I think my pants are going to be wet."

"We'll be together." Isis gathered his head into her ample bosom.

"Yeah." His voice was muffled.

" 'Twere best done quickly," Osmirik said.

Isis released Jeremy and sat at the terminal. "Go fire up the traveler," she said. "I'll do my cloning thing and be with you in a minute."

Jeremy ran to the platform, jumped up the steps, and climbed through the vehicle's hatch. Taking his place in the pilot's seat, he quickly set up the Toshiba, letting it power up all the vehicle's systems, including the main drive.

"All systems go, Jerry-baby," the Toshiba said. "Course heading?"

"We're not going anywhere, exactly. We're going to take the craft out into the universal medium and fly around for a while."

"Well, that's innovative. Exactly how are we supposed to do that?"

"Don't resolve your coordinate fix for a while. Let the vehicle sort of . . . float."

"Oh, you mean, like, just hang out?"

"Uh, yeah. Sort of."

"Interesting. You know, this 'interuniversal medium' you're talking about is mostly a mathematical abstraction. Sorry if this conversation is getting too polysyllabic for you, but you might want to think about the implications of 'floating' around in a metrical frame that won't support your three-dimensionality too well."

"I know it's not the greatest of ideas, but we have to do it."

"Well, listen, you're the user, I'm just a piece of silicon. You ought to know what you're doing, however harebrained and ill conceived and just plain *dumb* it sounds."

"Thanks, I appreciate the vote of confidence. Now, how about shutting the hell up."

"Listen to him. Hey . . . who—?"

Jeremy felt warm breath on his neck. He turned his head to find Isis sitting in the copilot's chair. She kissed him on the cheek.

"All ready, Jeremy."

The computer asked, "Who's the babe?"

"Shut up. Stand by for acceleration."

"You with the long legs. Listen, honey. There's room in RAM for one crewperson aboard this craft, so why don't you—?"

"Obey orders!" Jeremy barked.

"Yes, *sir*. But tell her to keep her big boobs out of my way."

"Bring thrusters to launch frequency!"

"Frequency tuned."

"Engage!"

"Thrusters engaged!"

The view of the lab through the viewport disappeared, replaced by an indeterminate blankness. Nothingness.

"Sure is scary out there," Jeremy said.

"I'm so glad we're together," Isis said.

"You may be interested to know," the Toshiba said, "that pressure on the hull is over one hundred pounds per square inch and rising."

"Is that bad?"

"Well, it's not good. The hull is made of very strong stuff, but it has its limits. If the pressure doesn't stop increasing, we may be in for trouble."

Jeremy said, "How can there be pressure on the hull if there's nothing out there?"

"Got me. It might have something to do with quantum uncertainty. 'Quantum uncertainty' is good for explaining just about anything that doesn't make sense."

"Well, I don't know what that stuff is all about. I flunked physics."

"Look at it this way. This vehicle, which normally takes up space, is now occupying what is essentially a nonspace. There's a certain tension in the basic situation. The medium that we're in is going to be naturally resistant to the intrusion of bulky objects."

"Okay. So, you're saying what, exactly?"

"We can't stay here for very long before we get . . . well, sort of *squeezed*."

"Squeezed, huh?"

"Yeah. Compressed. Reduced. Squashed flatter than a tortilla."

"Don't mention food. Tortillas. Jeez, I could go for a burrito right about now."

"Food, he wants. Listen, I'm talking about getting turned into a spacetime enchilada. I'm talking Taco Jeremito here. *Comprende?*"

Jeremy nodded. "Got it. But we gotta stay here long enough to get a good reading on the energy state and a few other variables."

"Oh, by all means. But let's not stay a second over that, okay?"

"You don't have to convince me. Isis, how long do you think it will take?"

"Data coming in now," Isis said. "I estimate we need another two point oh niner minutes."

"Hell," Jeremy said, "is that all? We'll be outta here in no time. Computer, set course back to base and stand by to apply reverse thrust."

"Hull pressure is over a thousand pounds per square inch," the Toshiba said. "And rising."

"What's the safety load rating of the hull?"

"Have no idea. That information wasn't in the vehicle's data base."

"We can hold out for a while longer. The stuff the hull's made out of is superhard."

"Hard, maybe. But not deformable? There's a difference."

"It'll hold up."

"I hope that's true for your sake. I say again, I'm only made of silicon. I wouldn't notice a change in volume as much as you would."

"More data coming in," Isis reported. "Ninety-six seconds to cutoff."

"We just sit tight," Jeremy said, "and sweat it out."

"Fifty-four hundred psi."

"Isis, maybe we could cut it off a little early?"

"The data is coming as fast as possible, Jeremy," Isis said. "We need all we can get for an effective spell."

"Right." Jeremy peered out into the nothingness. It was not black, not gray, not any color. There was a random shifting quality to it. Jeremy thought of being trapped inside the screen of a TV that was tuned to a blank channel, only it wasn't that bright. It was just murk out there, formless and void.

A nervous half-minute went by.

"Computer, is the hull pressure still rising?"

"Not as fast, but it's still going up."

"Good. Maybe it'll level out."

"Don't bet on it."

The craft lurched violently, then was still again.

Jeremy had clutched the arms of his seat. "Whoa, what was that?"

"Don't quite know," the Toshiba said. "We've run into some kind of turbulence."

"Turbulence? What could it be? I mean, there's nothing out there to get all riled up."

"It could be the pressure of bending space at the boundaries of the nonspace."

"I don't understand that, but I don't like the sound of it."

"In another few seconds, we'll either be mashed into atoms or . . ."

"Or what?"

"Thirty seconds to cutoff," Isis said, her eyes on the Toshiba's readout screen.

"I don't know what," the Toshiba said. "Something's happening out there. There are stresses coming into play that I can't even measure."

Another convulsive shudder went through the traveler, this one more violent. Jeremy wound up wedged between the seat and the control panel.

"Should put seat belts in these things," he said as Isis gave him a hand up.

"There are seat belts," Isis said. "Right here." She pulled out the buckled end of a belt from a feed mounted on the underside of Jeremy's chair. Jeremy inserted the buckle into a slot on the other side and it locked with a click.

"How did you find that? I never knew it was there."

"That info *is* in the data base," Isis said.

"Good. How's the data acquisition coming along?"

"We're almost through. We can—"

The craft turned upside down, then began to tumble end over end. There was something outside the view port now, a jumble of fleeting images: rapidly changing landscapes backgrounding a flickering blur of random images.

"What's happening?" Jeremy screamed.

"We got squeezed out of nonspace," the Toshiba said. "Squirted out like a seed from a squashed melon. Now we're careening through the universes."

"Stop us!"

"No can do, sweetheart. We're not staying in one continuum long enough to grab on to anything. We have about as much control as a runaway Mack truck."

The scene outside the view port was changing like card faces in a riffled deck. Flurries of random colors and shapes, flashing landscapes, starscapes, patterns, and crazy quilts, all spinning dizzily.

"There must be something we can do," Jeremy pleaded. "Engage stabilizers!"

"Stabilizers already engaged, Captain. Zero effectiveness."

"Try thrusting!"

"Also zero effectiveness."

"Reverse polarity on the graviton beam modulators."

"Reversing. Negative function."

"I'm out of ideas!" Jeremy wailed.

"We're out of luck," the Toshiba laptop said.

# MIZZER

INCARNADINE DISMOUNTED AND climbed the base of a fallen
obelisk to survey the temple complex. There were three main
structures and many subsidiary ones. All were in ruins, but one
of the larger buildings had most of its columns upright. Two
colossal statues, seated kingly figures in fancy headdress, flanked
the entrance.

Pointing, he asked, "That one?"

Basrim, his guide, nodded. "That is it, Honorable One. The
place you seek."

"You're sure it's the Temple of the Universes?"

"Very sure, Honorable One."

Incarnadine scowled. "Looks like an ordinary funerary temple to me."

"But it is also a place of great power."

"There are many such places around here. The Mizzerites
knew what they were doing when it came to magic. When they
cast a spell, it lasted for millennia."

Basrim dismounted, came to the edge of the base, and looked
up at him. "Will we be staying here, Honorable One?"

"Don't unpack anything. I want to take a look around first."

Basrim bowed. "Yes, Honorable One."

"You stay here." Incarnadine jumped down and went to his

mount. Unhooking his scabbard, he thought better of it and put it back. Going armed into a temple might trip an old anti-sacrilege spell. He didn't want any trouble.

"The Honorable One is wise," Basrim said, smiling.

Incarnadine took off his dagger and stashed it in his bundle.

"I shouldn't be long," he said, walking past Basrim. "If this is the place, we'll make camp."

Basrim's bow was deep. "Very good, Honorable One."

The temple was extraordinarily big, and did he indeed get a sense of the unusual. Danger? Perhaps. If only he knew more about the Mizzerites. There were thousands of worlds, and there were ancient and defunct civilizations in practically all of them, many of which were fascinating. He simply had never got around to this one.

A walled walkway led to the main temple and he followed it, treading in the ancient footsteps of the temple priests and pall-bearers as they processed from the river with the casket of the king. The cortege of relatives, courtiers, and worshippers would follow.

A needle of stone, inscribed head to foot with arcane glyphs, stood to the right of the walkway, and he looked at it as he passed. He wished he had time to decipher the inscription. He wondered what the glyphs spoke of, what glorious and triumphant events the monument commemorated.

At the entrance to the temple he paused to look at the statues. They appeared to be likenesses of the same king wearing different ceremonial headdresses, one religious, he guessed, the other secular. Whoever he was, the ruins of his temple lay behind him.

He chuckled to himself. " 'Look on my works, ye Mighty, and despair!' "

He mounted the temple steps and crossed the threshold. The interior was a forest of columns, all carved and inscribed. Despite the glaring sun and the absence of a roof, deep shadows lay within. Silence. He stopped and turned slowly. There was the smell of dust. Looking down, he watched a beetle crawl across the stone floor.

He attuned his senses and took the measure of the place. Yes, there was power here, but not nearly enough for his purposes. Basrim probably had not lied, but merely reported the local folklore. Now what? There was nothing to do but search blindly, temple after temple, ruin after ruin. There were hundreds of temples in this area alone, thousands along the river. If only he could have access to books, records, ancient documents. If only they existed! He had asked around, sought out various dealers in antiquities, but they had nothing that went back more than a few centuries. All that was known about the Mizzerites had been carved in stone by the Mizzerites themselves, millennia ago, and little of it had been deciphered. He could effect a translation spell easily enough, but how long would it take to find a reference to the location of the Temple of the Universes, if there was any reference at all? He did not even know what dynasty the temple dated from, let alone the specific king at whose behest it was constructed. Research would take years, and he didn't have days.

Besides, the temple might not exist; it might never have existed. All he had were vague legends about a place of power, the abode of the god of a thousand universes. There was nothing much else in the way of hard information.

He heard something off in the shadows. The scrape of sandal leather against stone. He searched the darkness.

A man came out from behind a column. Dressed in a tattered cloth cap and threadbare caftan, he also wore a crooked smile. His teeth were black and broken.

"Greetings, Honorable."

Incarnadine heard more footsteps behind him. He turned his head far enough to see two more men emerge from the shadows. They approached, daggers in hand.

"Are you Basrim's buddies?" he asked.

The man held out his hand. "It would be easier for us all if you handed over your gold right away. If we have to kill you, here in the temple we must do it in the ancient way. Very slowly, bleeding you like a butchered animal. You would not like it, and it would be work for us."

Incarnadine was motioning up a spell but the nearest man lunged, and he had to make do with natural defenses; he kicked the dagger away, then spun and landed a high kick alongside his assailant's head. The man went sprawling on the flagstone.

"Ah, you chose the hard way," the first thug said, drawing a curved short sword.

"Your heart," Incarnadine said, extending a hand and making a clawing motion.

"Eh?" The speaker was nonplussed. The third thug had edged

closer but now stopped, dagger low and poised for an upward slash.

"I think your heart has stopped beating."

The snaggle-toothed one guffawed. Suddenly his smile faded.

"Yes, you're feeling strange. It's your heart."

The man put a finger on his pulse. A look of dismay sprang to his face.

"My heart!"

"I told you. Your blood has stopped flowing. You feel faint. The darkness gathers, and soon the long night will come."

"No, I . . ."

The man collapsed, sword clattering on the stone.

The third man looked at his fallen accomplice, then at the stranger.

"A sorcerer!"

"Yes. And a pretty nasty one at that. Have you ever heard of the creeping phlox?"

"The what?"

"The creeping phlox. It starts on the toes—little red boils that turn to pustules. Then it works its way up the body. The pustules turn to oozing sores, the sores to masses of corruption. Every extremity of the body falls off, starting with the soft kind that hangs. Then the rot really sets in. . . . Well, not to put too fine a point on it, you got it, babe."

Terror-stricken, the man fled out the back of the temple.

Incarnadine went behind a column and waited.

Presently Basrim came creeping into the shadows. He knelt over the one who had spoken first, then looked around fearfully.

Incarnadine stepped out from behind the pillar.

"Honorable One! You are safe. Thank the heavens, I thought you had met your end at the hands of these—"

"Your friends, Basrim?"

"My fr—? Oh, never, Honorable One! I have never laid eyes on them!"

"Now, why do I think you're lying, just like you lied about this temple?"

"But . . . Honorable One, please! Let me explain!"

"Be quiet. Do the local legends say that this is the Temple of the Universes?"

"Yes, they do.

"Basrim, I'm warning you. . . ."

"No! I made it up! Forgive me, Honorable One! An eternity of pardon!"

"Get up, get up. God, I hate it when they grovel."

"An eternity of pardon, Honorable One! Forgive your humble servant and I will do anything, I will serve you always, faithfully, I will clean any part of your body with my tongue—!"

"Get your lips off the floor. Now, look. All I want from you is the truth. Do you know where that temple is or don't you? If you don't, do you know anyone who does know? Answer me!"

Desolated, Basrim slowly shook his head.

"I thought so. Tourists really get taken to the cleaners around here, don't they? Well, I should have known better. Okay, Basrim. That's all."

Basrim got up slowly. "I . . . I may go?"

"Yes."

Basrim began to slink away.

"Oh, by the way, your first wife, the one with the lip sore?"

Basrim stopped dead. "My first . . . you mean Altma?"

"Yes, Altma, the one with the chancre and the hairy mole on the left breast. She'll be paying you a visit soon, with her solicitor and the vizier's deputy. They'll be taking all your goats and most of the grain. How in the world you'll get through the winter is beyond me."

"No!"

"Yes! She bribed the magistrate. Actually, if I were you I wouldn't go back to town at all."

The miserable Basrim departed.

He toured the temple, puzzling over the glyphs and the stylized art: the king crushing enemies beneath his heel, the king propitiating the gods, the king presiding over the bountiful harvest, the king . . . and so forth.

He left the temple and went back to his mount. Now he had the choice of hiring another probably unreliable and potentially treacherous guide, or going it alone. He thought the latter would be the better course. He might stumble around and get lost, but at least he wouldn't have to worry about wasting time on wild-goose chases and deliberate deceptions, to say nothing of being waylaid by enterprising locals. Alone, he probably wouldn't be spotted. He would keep low and to himself. The superstitious natives rarely mucked about in the ruins. They had reason to be superstitious, because the indigenous magic was both real and dangerous.

Having retied his bundle, he turned around. A gray-bearded old man was standing by the fallen obelisk, watching. He wore a white cap, and his blue-striped caftan was clean. Carrying a cane, he stood slightly stooped.

"Yes?"

"An eternity of pardon, Honorable. I did not mean to spy."

"Anything you want?"

"Nothing, Honorable. But perhaps you want something of me."

"What have you got, old man?" He strapped on his sword, then his dagger. "Excuse me, I'm not myself. Just had a spot of trouble with some of your compatriots."

The old man nodded. "I heard them conspiring in the village. If I had warned you, they would have cut off an ear, perhaps more."

"I understand. You said you had something I might want."

"My knowledge," the man said.

"Of?"

"Of places, of things, of gods and their abodes."

"Indeed. I have a feeling you know what I'm looking for."

"I do."

"Can you help me?"

"I can," the man said.

"Will you?"

"Yes."

"Good. What payment do you require?"

"None, if you mean gold."

"What do you want, then?"

"Only to see the face of Mordek again."

"Mordek?"

"The god of a thousand universes. I am his humble servant."

"I thought no one was left who worshipped the old gods."

"There are some," the old man said.

"What's your name, by the way?"

"Jonath."

"You say you want to see the face of your god. Why do you need me to do it?"

"You are a magician, and a great warrior."

"Nice of you to say. I won't ask you how you know this, but what can a great mage and warrior do for you?"

"You can get past the trip spells and mantraps that guard the temple."

"Why are these things in place?"

"Because Mordek is angry. No one comes to worship, so he shuts himself in and broods."

"But you are left, and you implied there were others."

"The few are not enough. In the great days, multitudes would come to Mordek's temple to seek favor. Those days are dust, and Mordek sits in his abode, a moody, frustrated god."

"Doesn't sound inviting, this place of yours. Was it known as the Temple of the Universes?"

"Yes, that is the name of the dwelling place of Mordek."

"Then I would like to go to it."

Jonath said, "I will take you."

"Where is it?"

Jonath pointed to the hills. "In the high desert."

"Far?"

"Half a day's walk."

Incarnadine took a deep breath. "Lead on, then."

# SNOWCLAW'S WORLD

IT HAD BEEN a strange battle so far. An army of Snowclaws had poured through the portal and swept the invading anti-Guardsmen back. The latter regrouped, however, and, with their numbers magically increased, fought back. The original Guard force was dispersed, fled through various aspects, and these men gradually began to trickle back and join the Snowclaw legions when the anti-Guardsmen retreated. The resulting melee was a confusion of endless furry warriors and differing versions of Guardsmen trying to distinguish friend from foe. As the battle progressed, it was hard to tell who was winning.

Meanwhile, back in the strange lunar aspect, the black tornado was still generating Snowclaws and showed no sign of letting up.

Linda sat at a picnic table (which she had conjured) eating a lunch of potato salad, tuna salad, and chicken salad on a bed of lettuce. There was iced Pepsi to drink. She ate calmly under a beach umbrella, which warded off the harsh ultraviolet of the aspect's hot, tiny sun.

Arranged around her were eight other picnic tables, umbrellas, and salad lunches. She had not quite learned how to fine-tune her spells, though she knew enough to avoid the mistake she had made with Snowclaw.

Sir Gene came walking up from the portal, which now was a bottleneck. New detachments of white-furred soldiers were rushing through to reinforce the invasion troops.

"Enjoying your repast, I hope," Sir Gene said.

"Sure. How's it going back at the castle?"

"It's bedlam."

"Well, what did you expect?"

"I don't quite know. For one side to win, I suppose. Simplistic of me."

"You ought to know that the castle's not a simple place."

"I'm learning. There's no telling what Incarnadine may come up with next."

"You should have known that, too. Don't you think he can conjure demons or monsters, or anything else that could take Snowy in a fight? Snowy's a hell of a guy, but he's only hu . . . I mean, he's only Snowy."

"We have an endless supply of him."

Linda looked at the enigmatic black cloud, which still rotated in the distance. "Yeah, I suppose we do. That's a problem in itself. What are we going to do with all of him?"

"Can't you wave them away once we're done with them?"

"Wave them away. That's great. You know what it takes to make something, even the most insignificant thing, disappear?"

"I'm afraid I don't," Sir Gene said dryly.

"Well, it takes a lot. It takes a subtle counterspell to undo a spell. And here, where the problem is, I can't even do a spell right in the first place." She took in all the picnic tables with a sweep of her arm.

"I see your point. But why don't we worry about that later? First we have to win the battle."

"Yeah, right. But that's your department, Generalissimo. By the way, shouldn't you be at the front?"

"There is no front per se." Sir Gene went to another table and fetched its plate, sat down, and began eating. "I'm hungry."

Linda pushed her food aside. "We have no end of problems. We still don't know what happened to Dalton and Thaxton, and there are probably a lot of Guests who got caught in the fight. And of course, there's the problem of what happened to Gene. The *real* one."

"I'm as real as they come, milady."

"I wish you weren't, milord. The only hope is that Gene got

through to Earth before the portal went flooey. Which would mean that he's just cut off, not in danger.''

"Wherever he is, he's probably safer outside the castle.''

"Thank God Sheila and Trent are out on a cruise. With any luck they'll miss it all. Who I'm really worried about is Jeremy and Osmirik. God knows what's going on up in that lab.''

"I can't get any good intelligence about who holds what inside the castle,'' Sir Gene said.

"We really ought to make an attempt to get to the lab,'' Linda said. "If the day is going to be saved, Jeremy will do it.''

"You say he's about to cast a spell that will cure the cosmic disturbance. How close is he to casting it?''

"That's what I'd like to find out.''

"Well,'' Sir Gene said. "I'm game.''

Linda gave him a cold stare. "What is your game?''

"What do you mean?''

"What's your stake in all of this? This isn't your castle. You belong somewhere else. In fact, you belong in the anti-castle.''

"Where I'm persona non grata, keep in mind.''

"Okay, so you have a grudge against the phony Incarnadine. Why did you try to fool us into believing you were our Gene?''

"It seemed the thing to do at the time.''

"I'll bet. You said it yourself, we have no reason to trust you. So, I'm asking you again, what are you up to?''

One end of Sir Gene's mouth curled upward. "I almost never have a plan. I improvise, play by ear. It's fun to watch the wheels go spinning around madly. I love a plot.''

"Hope you're having fun. Meanwhile, assuming just for the hell of it that our interests are in line, let's talk about what we're going to do.''

"Let's,'' he said. "I think you're right about getting to the laboratory. We should at least give it a try.''

"To use your phrase, I'm game. You going to be long eating?''

Sir Gene sent his plate, most of the food still on it, spinning into the rocks. "Done. You could at least conjure something palatable.''

"Excuse me. I happen to *like* tuna salad.''

"Let's be off.''

These halls were quiet. They had skirted a half dozen battles after coming through the portal, and had worked their way to a relatively peaceful area of the keep.

Linda stood before a section of blank wall and raised her hands as if in supplication. An elevator door materialized in the stone, a little arrow-shaped green light above it pointing up. The door rolled open.

"Ah, castle magic," Linda sighed. "Now, this stuff I can work with."

They stepped aboard and the door slid shut.

"Laboratory floor," Linda said to no one in particular.

"Interesting to contemplate," Sir Gene commented. "Is the elevator conscious, do you think?"

"Who knows? It just does what I tell it to do. I could never do elevators that worked until Lord Incarnadine showed me how to make them less mechanical and more magical."

"You're a very talented castle magician. My apologies for the remark about the food."

"My castle food gets all kinds of compliments." Linda stared off a moment, then said, "What am I like in the other castle? I mean, what's my counterpart like?"

Sir Gene mulled over his answer. "Difficult."

"Is she good with magic?"

"Um, in a way. She doesn't do elevators, that I'll tell you."

"No? What kinds of things . . . oh, never mind. The whole notion is creepy."

"Yes, the less said about it, the better."

The elevator door opened. Standing just outside was a huge creature which resembled Snowclaw except for having yellow fur. There were other differences: it was bigger, had even more teeth, and the broadax it wielded was, if possible, more fearsome than the original.

The beast growled, raised the ax, and lunged. Sir Gene had reacted even before the door was all the way open, leaping to jab the CLOSE DOOR button and drawing his sword. The sliding panels sprang back out of their slots and caught the anti-Snowclaw between them. Sir Gene hacked at the beast's face. Snarling, the thing retreated a step, and the doors closed, shutting it out.

Linda started breathing again. She gasped, "What was *that*?"

"Another of Incarnadine's tactics. Fight fire, if possible, with a bigger fire."

"My God, it was horrible."

"I can't see that it was any more horrible than its progenitor."

"Snowy's *cute*. That thing was . . . never mind. Getting to the lab is out."

"I suppose there isn't another way?"

"Not that I know of. Where do we go now?"

Sir Gene sheathed his sword. "There's nothing left to do but go back to the world of the black cloud and wait."

"There's nothing for me to do there," Linda said. "I'm going to try to make it to Sheila's world. She might be back from her trip. If so, she can help out."

"That's as good an idea as any, I suppose," Sir Gene said.

"Shouldn't you be directing the battle?"

"I've no control over what's happening. If I had a hundred duplicates of myself—"

"We're not going to try that again, even in the castle."

"I'm not suggesting we try it. I find the existence of even one doppelganger intolerable. Where is this Sheila and her world?"

"Isn't there a Sheila in your castle?"

"No. Not that I've met, anyway. There are any number of Guests who are strangers to me."

"Sheila's aspect is on a level about midway between the Guest Residence and the laboratory, here in the castle keep."

"Then let's drop to that level and hope there are no skirmishes in the area."

"There's fighting going on all over the keep," Linda said, "thanks to you, but there's always hope. Hit the fifty-first-floor button."

Sir Gene searched the floor selection panel, found the correct button, and depressed it. "This contraption is well equipped."

"Your typical medieval elevator."

The conveyance descended, humming and whirring appropriately. After a half minute it slowed and stopped. Sir Gene drew his sword and held it at the ready.

The doors opened to silence.

Sir Gene poked his head out and looked. "It's clear."

They exited into a dim hallway and proceeded right, keeping to the left-hand wall, which was punctuated by numerous alcoves suitable for ducking into. They passed a sitting room, complete with heavy oak furniture and tables. No one was about. They came to an aspect, a doorway leading to a forest scene.

"We could hide in there," Sir Gene said.

Linda shook her head. "I want to see Sheila. It's just down the hall and to the left."

They passed along more dim hallway before encountering an unused dining hall, dark and gloomy.

"I'm reminded that I'm still hungry," Sir Gene said.

"Want me to whip up something for you?"

"No, I can wait."

"The food is good at Sheila's hotel."

"She discovered this world?"

"She and Trent, Lord Incarnadine's brother."

"Didn't know he had a brother."

Linda said, "I'm beginning to see that there are lots of differences between our castle and yours."

"Does seem that way. Is it much farther, this aspect?"

"Just down this hall, about—"

Having just rounded the corner, Linda stopped in her tracks. Her jaw dropped. Walking toward her, flanked by two anti-Guardsmen, was what could have been her twin sister were it not for some differences. The quasi-twin's teeth were crooked and stained, her complexion sallow. Her hair was a fright wig, dyed a bright red. There was something wrong with the eyes; they were ringed with dark circles and had a strangeness in them.

The anti-Linda smiled and said, "I thought I heard voices. Well, well, well. My counterpart, Lady Linda the dishwater blonde. How can you wear it that color, dear?"

Linda closed her mouth, took a deep breath. Then she said calmly, "I was born with it, that's why."

"And that outfit. Cute. Like a pixie, little tights and everything. Oh, nice boots. Get those at Bloomingdale's?"

Linda looked at the horror of a white lace gown that draped her twin. "Early Bela Lugosi movie" would have been the appropriate period, and the kindest capsule description. She decided to refrain from commenting. She did say, "Why don't you go back where you belong?"

The anti-Linda took a step forward, sudden anger boiling in her strange eyes. "Look, honey, I don't take orders well, not even from Incarnadine, let alone from some castle tart playing Glinda the Good Witch. So, get your bitchy lips off me, all right?" Her expression and manner shifting abruptly, almost jarringly, she turned to Sir Gene with an inexplicable smile. "Put that sword away, Gene, sweetheart. I've no grudge against you."

Sir Gene grunted and lowered his sword, but kept it out. "That would be a radical change."

"Gene, Gene, how many times have we worked at cross-purposes? Weaving our separate strands, always warp-to-warp, never warp-to-woof.''

"Charming metaphor.''

"But I mean it. I could have aided you in your last bid for power, but you chose not to include me in your lovely little conspiracy.''

"You ought to be grateful. It failed miserably.''

"Because I didn't help you. We never were the best of friends, Gene, but that shouldn't have prevented us from becoming business partners.''

"I like to work alone.''

"It takes two to conspire, darling.'' She batted her eyelashes sweetly. "But no matter, you had your chance. And now Incarnadine's appointed me regent of this new castle. Oh, yes! It'll be practically like ruling Perilous itself. Wait a minute. How silly of me. It will be exactly like ruling Perilous. This *is* Castle Perilous, after all.''

"How fortunate for you,'' Sir Gene said. "I suppose I'll be a nonperson here as well?''

The anti-Linda shook her head. "Don't leave on my account, dear. I won't give you any trouble. Of course, if Incarnadine finds out you're here—''

"We already ran into each other.''

"How unfortunate for you. Don't worry, I won't sic my boys, here, on you. Put your sword away.''

Sir Gene harrumphed to himself and sheathed his weapon.

"It might be wise to keep you handy,'' the anti-Linda said. "I suspect you'll be ducking through an aspect to lie low, but keep in touch, will you? It's good to keep potential allies close at hand.''

Sir Gene gestured toward Linda. "What about her?''

"Well, that's a problem.'' The anti-Linda brought up her hand. Somehow a strange elongated pistol had materialized in it.

"A gun?'' Sir Gene said, perplexed.

The anti-Linda was looking at her twin. "Sorry, honey, but the best way to deal with you is just to get it over with. I hear you're very sweet, but you'd only be in the way. My apologies.''

Sir Gene began, "But a gun won't work—''

The pistol made a sharp hissing sound. Sir Gene turned toward Linda and looked wonderingly at the feathered dart that had blossomed in Linda's chest like a small deadly flower. Linda sank to her knees.

"Poison-tipped," the anti-Linda said. "Quick-acting, attacks the nervous system almost instantly."

Sir Gene made an instinctive motion to catch Linda as she teetered.

"Let her go, Gene. She's dead. No magic can block the effects."

Sir Gene straightened. The whites of Linda's eyes rolled up, and she fell over and lay still.

The anti-Linda smiled brightly. "Gene, how about lunch?"

# WEIRDWORLD

"THERE IT IS," Dalton said, pointing ahead.

"That look like a teeing green to you? Nothing but gravel."

"Well, there's the hole, way out yonder."

Thaxton shaded his eyes. "Where?"

"Out beyond that herd of animals."

"You mean we have to play through a herd of bison?"

"I don't think those are bison."

"Yes, there is something strange about them."

"They have six legs apiece."

"Well," Thaxton said, "they're an improvement over gryphons and basilisks. Do I have the honor, or do you?"

"You."

"Look at that bloody fairway. Full of rocks."

"It's a challenge."

"Right you are." Thaxton chose a driver and teed up.

They played the thirteenth. The herd moved off the fairway for the taller, more succulent grasses of the rough, and the men made their approach shots. They were on the green in three and two-putted for par.

"That was an easy hole," Dalton said as they followed a path away from the green and up a little hill.

"Yes. I hope they're not setting us up for something really dicey."

"We've pulled through so far."

"So far, so good, the man said as he fell thirty-nine of forty stories."

"I wonder who designed this course," Dalton mused.

"You think someone actually sat down and thought out this madness?"

"It has its inspirations, and there's a method to it all, however bizarre. Recurring themes, too."

"Oh, yes, and I'm just about fed up with the strange beastie motif."

They had come to the top of the hill. Below lay a shallow valley shrouded in impenetrable fog.

"Well, we're not going to be playing through that."

"Looks like there's no getting around it," Dalton said. "Next tee's bound to be somewhere in there."

"I'm worried about what else may be in there."

"What's a little fog to two seasoned hell-golfers?"

Thaxton hoisted his bag over his shoulder. "Right, what could be worse than . . . I won't say it. No telling what could be worse."

They descended into the mist. A blanket of whiteness enveloped them, bringing a moist, muffled silence. They walked down a gentle grade for a good stretch. When the ground leveled off they stopped.

"See anything?" Dalton said.

"Not a bloody thing. Are we still on the course?"

"I think we missed the tee."

"Then this must be the fairway. Let's retrace our steps."

"Wait a minute," Dalton said. "I've lost my bearings. Is that the way we came?"

"I dunno."

"Well, this is a fine kettle of fish. We'll have to wait for the fog to lift."

Thaxton eased down and arranged himself so that he was half reclining, elbows resting on his golf bag.

Dalton squatted on his. "How's the leg?"

"Coming along. I'm a fast healer."

A sound like the moan of a dying man came out of the mist.

"Good God, what was that?"

"He must have a bad lie."

Shrieks like the tortured screams of the damned. Then the flapping of great wings.

"That bloody roc again," Thaxton said.

"Or something else."

"Maybe a harpy. Actually I wouldn't mind. That barbecued harpy doesn't sound so bad now. I'm feeling a bit peckish."

"That salamanderburger didn't fill you up?"

"Like Chinese food," Thaxton said. "You know, an hour later . . ."

"I'm rather fond of Chinese. Moo shoo with plum sauce."

"Not my cup of tea, to coin a phrase."

"Of course, nothing can beat French cuisine."

"As a general rule I don't fancy wog food."

Dalton looked at him. "Wog?"

"Well, you know, the wogs begin at Calais."

Dalton glanced around. "Fog's lifting."

The mists took a few minutes to clear. Shapes in the distance came into view, craggy peaks against a black sky. Something was howling in the rocks to the right of the fairway where remnants of fog curled. To the left, a bloated yellow moon was rising, casting eerie light and purple shadows. In the sky were faint stars and glowing spectral clouds.

They had been sitting, as it turned out, right in front of the tee. The grass both on the tee and in the fairway looked like green crepe paper.

"Strange," Thaxton said.

"Yup. That moon's throwing enough light to play by, though. So . . ."

Dalton drove deep and straight. Thaxton teed up, swung, and sliced, sending the ball into the rocks. He cursed skillfully and at some length.

They hiked out onto the narrow fairway, Thaxton detouring toward the stony "rough."

"Take the stroke," Dalton called. "You'll never get it out of those boulders."

"I can try."

It was dark among the rocks, the weird moon throwing weirder shadows. Thaxton searched and searched, and was about to give the ball up for lost when he heard a bone-chilling howl, very close.

"Good God."

Suddenly feeling very alone, Thaxton threaded back through

the passage between the boulders, retracing his steps, whistling tunelessly.

He rounded a bend and stopped dead. A pair of eyes regarded him from the shadows ahead.

"I know where your ball is," a soft, epicene voice said.

Thaxton swallowed hard and cleared his throat. "See here. What do you mean by accosting people in dark places?"

"Sorry, didn't mean to scare you." A figure detached itself from the shadows. It was a hairy, generally man-shaped thing with yellow eyes, pointed ears, a snout, and canine fangs. Long claws tipped its pawlike fingers. "Thought you might want to know where your ball is."

"Well . . . actually, yes, I would like to know. If you don't mind awfully much telling me."

"Oh, I don't mind," the creature purred. "You might be able to do me a favor."

"Oh? What would that be?"

"Have any blood to spare? I won't take much, just enough to tide me over."

Thaxton said, "I beg your pardon?"

"I never get enough. Not many golfers get this far. You won't even feel it, just the tiniest pinprick on your skin. I wouldn't go for the neck. No, not that. Your wrist would be fine, just so I can get at a good artery."

Thaxton looked down his nose. "See here. Are you actually suggesting that I let you drink my blood?"

"As I said, I won't be greedy. You'll never miss it. Most folks go around with more than they need, and your body will replenish your supply in no time. So, you see, you'll be gaining a stroke and not losing very much at all."

"Good God, man . . . or whatever you are. Do you actually think I'd do such a disgusting, degenerate thing?"

"It takes all kinds, friend. Who are you to criticize people? We're born the way we are, and we have to do what we have to do. It's that simple. You shouldn't be so judgmental."

"On the contrary," Thaxton said indignantly. "I bloody well should be. Somebody's got to stand up for decent standards of behavior. Why, it's getting to the point where nothing's taboo anymore."

"You have to keep an open mind about these things, friend."

Thaxton harrumphed. "Bugger an open mind."

"Whatever makes your day."

"Well, my day's been sheerest hell, and it would please me greatly if you'd bloody well get out of my way. *If* you don't mind."

The creature bowed mockingly and stepped aside.

Thaxton strode past, then stopped. He turned and said, "Wait just a moment. You're a werewolf, aren't you? Werewolves don't go around drinking people's blood."

"Who told you?" the creature replied.

"But everyone knows that."

"Well, everyone's wrong, aren't they? I'm AC/DC. I just happen to like a little blood now and then."

Thaxton opened his mouth to say something, but thought better of it. He turned and left.

"Have a nice night," the voice behind him said.

Thaxton stalked across the fairway grumbling, "Have a nice bloody night," all the way. He came up to Dalton, who was sizing up a seven-iron approach shot, and threw his clubs down.

"I've bloody well had it."

"What's up?"

Thaxton delivered a mighty kick to the golf bag. "I didn't mind the weird stuff, didn't bat an eye at the volcanoes or the earthquakes or the acid hazards or even the bloody mythological beasts." Another kick sent the bag rolling and the clubs flying. "But when scrofulous *horrors* insinuate disgusting things at you out of dark corners, that's when I bloody well have to draw the line."

"Whoa, what's this all about?"

"Damn it all to hell. They've just got no right."

"Take it easy, old boy."

Thaxton smoothed his ruffled hair. He drew a couple of deep breaths and let out a long weary sigh. "Sorry. Didn't mean to go on like that."

"We have problems on the green, if you haven't noticed."

Thaxton pivoted.

"Don't look at it!"

"What?"

Dalton reached and whirled him around. "Don't look at the face. It's a basilisk."

"But how can you—?"

Dalton glanced over his shoulder. "It's turning the other way now. Take a quick gander."

Thaxton took a gander. The magenta-skinned hulk sprawled

alongside the green was a lizardlike creature about thirty feet long with a semicircular sail or crest running along its back. Its birdlike head was proportionally larger than a lizard's.

"A bloody pink iguana, that's what it is," Thaxton said.

"It's a basilisk. Look it in the eyes and you're a dead man."

"I wouldn't give it a second glance."

Thaxton retrieved his bag, took out a new ball, and threw it over his shoulder. He picked up the scattered clubs and rebagged them. Having scoped out his shot, he chose an iron and addressed the ball. He swung. Clinically eyeing the ball's trajectory, he picked up his bag and made his way toward the green.

The basilisk was lounging in the grass near the greenside bunker, into which Thaxton's ball had dropped. When Thaxton, wedge in hand, came trudging into the sand, the creature lifted its head to watch.

"Pretty good lie," the basilisk commented. "But that's packed sand. It can be tricky."

Thaxton ignored it.

"I'd say your best bet was to use the pitching wedge, not the sand wedge. You're not going to get very far just trying to blast it out."

Thaxton gritted his teeth and took his stance. He swung mightily. Exploding out of the sand, the ball ricocheted off the lip of the green and arched back into the bunker.

"Damn it all!"

"Told you," the basilisk said.

"Oh, go to blazes!"

The basilisk chuckled. "Temper, temper."

Thaxton took a few practice swings, then addressed the ball, now nearer the green. He changed his mind and fetched another club, the pitching wedge.

"Good idea," the creature said.

Thaxton mumbled something and swung. The ball bounded across the green and wound up a good distance from the cup.

"Best you could hope for," the basilisk said. "Not a bad shot, actually."

"Thank you," Thaxton said sardonically.

"You know, it's impolite not to look at someone when you talk to him."

"Sorry, busy day, you know. Can't stop to chat."

"Well, fine. No one ever does. Why should you be any different? It's still very rude."

"Look," Thaxton said heatedly over his shoulder, "I'm bloody sick and tired of being chatted up by *phantasms*. So if you don't think it too awfully rude of me, I'd like to play a bit of golf without being continually bothered by something out of a bleeding nightmare."

"I bet you can't look me in the eye and say that."

Thaxton spun around. "Look here, I can bloody well—"

The next thing he knew the bunker was in his face. He got up on his elbows, spat sand, and twisted around to see that Dalton had him by the legs. It had been a pretty solid tackle for an elderly man, and Thaxton was amazed.

"I knew the thing would goad you into it," Dalton said.

"Oh. Uh, thanks. Thanks, old boy. Lost my head, I'm afraid."

They got up and brushed off sand.

"One look at that fellow," Dalton said, "and you die."

"Next thing you'll say," the basilisk said peevishly, "is that my breath can kill, too. And then you'll repeat that old libel about my kind being hatched on a dunghill out of cock's eggs."

"Sorry," Dalton said. "Nothing personal."

"Yeah, I'll bet some of your best friends are basilisks."

With a haughty shake of its head, the creature wheeled its scaly bulk around and slithered away.

"The damnedest thing is," Thaxton said, "they're all so bloody *sensitive*."

"Well, minority touchiness. Are you ready to putt?"

Both putted, both for a bogey.

Walking away from the green, Thaxton yawned.

"Excuse me! God. Dalton, how long would you say we've been at this?"

"I've lost all track of time."

"Seems it's been days to me. Couldn't be, though. We haven't even played eighteen holes."

"Time runs differently in different universes."

"Yes, but I'm speaking of subjective time. I think we've been at this for over twenty-four hours."

"Could be," Dalton said. "It's been slow going. We lost a few hours resting your leg after lunch."

"Well, I don't know about you, but I'm bloody fagged out."

"Then let's book a room at yonder hotel."

"What?" Thaxton halted and looked. "Oh. Well, that's convenient, I must say."

"Told you this course was well designed."
"By an inspired psychotic. Look at that thing."

## TARTARUS INN
### Bed and Breakfast
### All Gentle Beings Welcome

The building was a Gothic monstrosity with turrets and cupolas, widow's walks and rosette windows. Rolling moors surrounded it, wreaths of mist draping the withered sedge and gnarled clumps of grass.

Lightning split the sky, and thunder rolled across the bogs.

"Oh, I can see I'm going to get a lot of sleep here," Thaxton said. "By the way, how do we pay for this?"

"Well, I still carry my American Express Card, out of habit," Dalton said. "I was going to flash it at the restaurant, until events obviated it."

"Why of course, sir," the gargoyle desk clerk said. "We take all major credit cards."

"Good," Dalton said. "A double with a private bath?"

"We have a wonderful room in the east wing with a view of the Blasted Heath."

"How nice," Thaxton said.

Dalton signed the guest register while Thaxton inspected the gift shop. Talismans, pentacles, and other occult paraphernalia were plentiful, along with the usual scented soaps, inscribed mugs, and saltwater taffy. He stared in fascination at the Cthulhu dolls. The bellhop came and he had to tear himself away.

The room was full of quaint furniture draped with lace doilies, and the beds had canopies.

"Charming," Dalton said. "You could have quite a nice weekend's dalliance here."

"No doubt," Thaxton said, lifting up the phone and scanning a menu he'd found on the dresser. "Hello, Room Service? Yes, room 203, here. Is supper still being served? Breakfast?" He looked at his watch. "Fine. I'll take tea, toast, orange juice, and all that, two cock's eggs, hard-boiled, and the biggest basilisk steak you have, rare. That's right. Room 203, and be quick about it."

# CITY

IT WAS STILL DARK when they boarded an omnibus heading for the suburbs. The sky was starless and the streets were almost deserted, a lone street cleaner, whirring its way along the curb, the only denizen stirring. The bus driver gave them a cheery smile when they got on.

"Getting an early start, eh?" she said. "Your shop storming for a quota overfulfillment?"

"Better and better!" Gene said.

"Every day!" she responded.

Gene's hand had instinctively reached into his pocket for fare, and he took comfort that the reflex was still there. The two days he'd been here had seemed the longest stretch of time he had ever experienced.

He held Alice's hand out of the driver's sight as they rode. The high rises continued for several miles, then thinned out, the gaps filled by older structures, some that were once single-family homes now carved up into tiny apartments. There were many vacant lots with old foundations still standing. The city had a raw look, as if it were being continually cleared for new development. The past must be obliterated and the present erected over top of it. Soon the landscape would hold nothing but faceless monoliths.

Dawn came, shading the sky purple.

"Do you know how far out the last stop is?"

Alice shook her head. "I've never ridden this line."

The city gave way to suburbs. There were a few factories and more high rises, but no houses. There were some boarded-up apartment buildings.

"Do you know the population of . . . whatever this is, the country, the state?"

Alice said, "The population? How many citizens? I don't know."

"Did it ever strike you that there aren't a lot of people, that there are less and less as time goes on?"

"Well, not really. What made you ask?"

"Housing doesn't seem to be a problem. Or is that because of heroic construction-worker efforts?"

Alice shrugged. "I've never thought of it."

They passed light-industrial parks, warehouses, yards full of building materials, lots with parked earth-moving equipment. Everything looked dreary and forlorn.

They rode for about fifteen more minutes, passing through the last of the suburbs. Finally the omnibus pulled over to the side of the road.

"End of the line," the driver announced.

They got off and walked along the road. There were overgrown fields to either side, trees bordering them.

"Let's cut across and get into the woods," Gene said.

Dew drenched their shoes as they made their way through the tall grass.

"Do you know where we're going?" she asked.

"Only generally. The place I want to get to is due east of the city. The roads are different here, but the lay of the land is the same. As far as I can tell, that road would be U.S. Route 30 in my world. We want to get as far along it as we can. Trouble is, we're miles from the place I want to get to. Maybe thirty miles. That's a lot to walk."

"We'll get there," she said gaily.

"Don't be so goddamned optimistic. I'm sick of the smiles, the phony cheeriness."

"Sorry."

He drew her to him and hugged her. "I'm sorry. I shouldn't have snapped at you."

"It's all right," she said.

"No, it's not. You're the only ray of light in all this darkness. You shouldn't exist. I—"

She drew back from him. "What's the matter?"

He turned away. "It's starting."

"InnerVoice?"

He nodded. "Nausea. There was a little on the bus but I was hoping it was just nervousness. Let's keep walking."

The woods were green and cool, alive with morning birdsong. They followed a deer path through thin maple trees and dense undergrowth: ferns, laurel, wild raspberry bushes, mayapple plants.

"What are you feeling?" she asked.

"Fear," he said.

"Bad?"

"Yes, getting worse."

She held his hand tightly. They came out of the woods and crossed a hayfield, entering the trees on the other side. A slope led down to the road, which had curved to the right and crossed in front of them.

"Let's chance the road for a while," he said.

They walked for about a quarter mile before encountering a garage with numerous official-looking vehicles parked in front of it. Most were trucks, but there were two cars, nondescript gray sedans. He led her across the parking lot to one of them. He tried the driver's door—it was unlocked.

"Get in," he said.

The interior was stripped down and functional, the dashboard made of unpainted metal with minimum instrumentation. The car had a standard transmission with a floor shift. As he suspected, the key was in the ignition.

He looked around a lot. No one was about. He depressed the clutch pedal and turned the key. The engine coughed, turned over, and started chugging and rattling.

He struggled with the gearshift.

"What's the matter?" she said.

"Feel weak. The nausea. Can you drive?"

"No. I never learned."

"Fine. I'll be . . . fine."

He got it into reverse and backed out of the parking slot. Jamming the lever into first gear, he started across the lot for the road.

A man in greasy overalls came out of the garage, stopping when he saw the car pulling out. He yelled something.

Gene floored the accelerator pedal, spinning tires on the gravel. He drove off the lot, swerving onto the road with only a cursory glance to see if traffic was coming. The engine howled but didn't put out much power. He kept his foot to the floor, though, and the speedometer soon read eighty—miles or kilometers or something else, he didn't know. He kept at that speed until it was apparent that they weren't being chased.

He slowed down.

"Well," Gene said, "the guy is sure to call the . . . the what? Would he call the army?"

"He might report the incident to the local Committee for the Investigation of Unsocial Behavior," she said. "They might call Constant Struggle."

"Does Constant Struggle always patrol the countryside?"

"I don't know."

"That's who picked me up. What were they doing out there? Do you have any idea?"

"No, Gene. I don't."

"There's gotta be more to this." He coughed. "Oh, God, I gotta throw up." He swallowed bile.

"Stop," she said.

"No, don't want to take the chance. If I have to puke I'll do it out the window. Hope you don't mind."

"I don't mind, Gene."

"The thing is the anxiety, the fear. It's not as powerful as it was that first day, but it's getting to me."

"I don't understand, Gene. You shouldn't have InnerVoice at all. You're a maladapt."

"Maybe this is psychological? Psychosomatic? I hope."

"If you're not a maladapt, maybe you have something that's fighting InnerVoice."

"I don't know what it could be."

"You must have something."

The road went into a series of turns and the motion sickened him even more. He slowed down, swallowing the lubricating mucus that had worked its way up his esophagus, preparing the way for the return of his breakfast of near-rotten potatoes. Then the road straightened again, his stomach rumbled, and the breakfast stayed down. He belched.

"Excuse me. Alice, have the maladapts ever gotten together to do something?"

"Like what?"

"Like a revolution? Guerrilla activity?"

"I don't know what you mean."

"Any attempt to bring down the system. To fight Inner-Voice."

"But how do you fight something that's inside people?"

She had a point. He belched again, feeling a little better. The road went serpentine once more, climbing a grade. Woods were dense to either side, an occasional connecting dirt road the only break.

At the top of the hill the woods cleared and they passed through an abandoned hamlet, its weathered houses and stores boarded up and deserted. To Gene it looked familiar and he thought it might be a variant of one of the highway whistle-stops along Route 30. If so, they were getting closer to the site where the portal would be if it hadn't vanished or shifted. There was still no calculating the chances of the portal still being in place. He put off thinking about what he would do if it wasn't.

The nausea was making a comeback, rising in yet another wave. His heart fluttered like a wounded bird. The anxiety was something alive in him, scrabbling to get out, wanting to scream, to run away.

The road was blocked off ahead, a red wooden barrier across it. The sign said simply: Road Closed. There was no detour.

He smashed through the barrier. Shards of wood fell off the hood and windshield. It was too far to get out and walk just yet. It would be risky traveling an interdicted road, but he wasn't ready to give up the car. Piece of junk though it was, it was something he could control. It obeyed his wishes, responded to the dictates of his body and will. It was power. He felt that if he let go of the steering wheel he would cave in and become some whimpering creature seeking only the alleviation of pain. He was afraid that he would give up and go back, do anything to make the hurt stop, even turn Alice in if it would help. The possibility of that scared him even more than the thought of being caught. He was feeling the lash right now. Would there be greater punishment if he was apprehended? Worse than this? He couldn't imagine it.

He realized he had speeded up. The speedometer read eighty-five. The fuel tank was half full, so no worry there. There was no water temperature gauge, no battery charge meter, but he wasn't particularly concerned with those readings. The car, clunky as it was, seemed to be in passable condition.

He screeched around a turn, braking in and accelerating out. They raced through another ghost village. Why were these sites abandoned? A matter of population decline, or was it part of a plan to redistribute population? Get people out of the countryside and into compounds of high rises so as to be more easily controlled? Perhaps. There were precedents in Earth history, though sometimes the flow went the other way, from the cities to the country. But dictatorships were notorious for shunting masses of people around, bulldozing villages, deporting ethnic groups, other high-handedness. The only people you'd need in the country would be personnel to work the fields of the huge state-run farms, like those he'd seen from the air, and those workers would live in residence complexes. There were no independent farmers, so no quaint farming villages were necessary.

He heard the whine of turbine engines above. He craned his neck to look. A VTOL craft was following, swooping low.

He floored the accelerator, taking the next bend fast enough so that the car went up on two wheels. The vehicle's weight was obviously ill distributed. Any good car would have taken the curve in stride. He cursed the industrial system that produced such shoddy design and manufacture. It felt good to get angry. Anger fought back the anxiety. Maybe that's what was keeping him going.

*"Stop your vehicle immediately! Pull over to the side of the road!"*

The voice boomed from the craft. He pressed his foot against the metal floor.

*"Pull over or you will be fired upon!"*

He glanced at Alice. She looked amazingly calm. What would be her fate? They would probably shoot her up with new nano-computers, better ones. No more evening walks, no more filching an extra dessert. Not even those peccadilloes would be allowed her then. Would it be better for her to surrender, or to die in a mad attempt to gain her freedom?

"What should I do, Alice?"

She looked at him with defiance in her eyes. As if she'd been reading his mind she said, "Don't let them take us. I'd rather die."

The VTOL fired, the sound like the buzzing of a chain saw. Dust rose from the shoulder. The miss had been deliberate. Gene began swerving all over the road. The craft's guns sounded again, and this time the miss may not have been intentional. Another bend came up, trees intervening between the car and the craft. The gunship veered away.

He looked ahead for cover, for a road to turn into, a building to hide behind, anything. There was nothing but dense forest to either side of the road, which was temporarily to the good, because the gunship had to keep well above the high trees and had a bad firing angle.

"Alice, get down."

She obeyed, tucking herself down between the dashboard and the seat.

The trees gave out and they were in wide-open country. He started weaving again. He couldn't see the gunship but could hear its vacuum-sweeper roar. The forest picked up again about a tenth of a mile down the road, and he decided to trade defensive maneuvering for time. He mashed the pedal and drove straight, hoping to make it to cover before the craft could maneuver for a killing shot.

There wasn't time. When he saw the craft again it was coming straight for him, its gun pods chattering. Asphalt exploded from the road, then the windshield shattered as the gunship whooshed overhead.

He spat out glass. It took him a few seconds to realize that he was miraculously unhurt. Wind from the rent in the glass tore at his face.

"Are you okay?" he yelled.

Alice nodded.

The car reached the trees and he thought that they had gotten through with no extensive damage, but telltale white smoke trailing from the hood told him otherwise. Slugs had probably hit the radiator.

He rolled another quarter mile before a red light appeared on the instrument panel. Engine overheating. A bullet must have taken out a water line. White smoke was billowing out of the hood now. Another red light came on—oil pressure dropping. He wouldn't be able to go another mile at this rate.

The right berm graded off to a steep drop, leading down to woods. He made a decision. He braked and pulled off the road, skidding to a stop.

"Get out!" he told her.

She did, and he put the transmission in neutral, got out, and let the car roll down the slight grade, steering to the right as he walked with the car. The car crossed the berm and headed for the edge. He closed the door and let it go. It rolled down the embankment and crashed through a wall of underbrush, and when it stopped at the bottom of the gully it was wheel-deep in a creek and was very hard to see from the road.

He took Alice's hand and led her down the embankment. She slipped on the loose shale and slid most of the way on the seat of her pants. At the bottom he hoisted her up and they splashed through the creek, ducking into woods on the other side.

They clambered up a hill. There was no trail and they had to hack through weeds and nettle. At the top they went straight until they came to the end of the woods and the edge of an overgrown hayfield.

They went to the left, keeping well inside the tree line. For the next few minutes they ran, trying to get as far from the road as possible.

When they heard the craft, they hid underneath a pine tree. The gunship whined irritably above them, searching the woods. The loudspeaker blared but the words were indistinguishable. The craft continued its pattern for a good ten minutes before going away. They listened to the engine sounds die in the distance.

Presently birds began singing again. A cricket chirped nearby.

They were lying on their bellies on a bed of brown pine needles. He rolled to his side and looked at her.

"You okay?"

She smiled. "Yes. How are you?"

"Adrenaline must do something. I feel better now."

"Good."

"But our situation isn't. We're still a long way from where we want to go, and now they're looking for us."

"We'll make it," she said.

"Yeah, even I'm beginning to believe it."

# SOMEPLACE

"Isis?"

A hand ran soothingly across his forehead. "Here, Jeremy."

"Jeez. Where are we?"

"I don't know, but we stopped."

"Was I out?"

"Just for a minute. We hit pretty hard."

Jeremy waited for his eyes to focus. When they did he saw a jumble of weeds and leaves pushed up against the view port. He looked around. The deck was canted sharply, but the interior of the traveler looked otherwise undamaged.

"Computer!"

"Someone get the number of that earthquake."

"You okay, still functioning?"

"I'll have to run a few tests, but from all appearances I am undamaged, Captain."

"Good. Report on the condition of the ship."

"Uh, that's not so good."

"How so?"

"Well, for starters," the Toshiba said, "the main drive is inoperable."

"What's wrong with it?"

"Cracked thermocouple on the primary coil, it looks like.

That's how I interpret the diagnostic readings, but you'd really have to eyeball it to be sure. Also, the graviton polarity generator is nonfunctional. No telling what's wrong with it."

"Damn," Jeremy said.

"Yeah. Also hell and botheration."

Isis said, "We'll simply have to fix it."

"Oh, sure," Jeremy scoffed. "Yeah, we'll just get out the old Sears toolbox and make a couple trips to the auto parts warehouse."

Isis sat down and gave Jeremy an admonitory look. "That's negative thinking again, Jeremy."

"Sorry. Okay, we'll fix it. Computer, d'you have any idea where we are?"

"Not the foggiest. Not the slightest glimmer of an idea. Not even the—"

"Okay! Make a guess, already."

"Very slim chance that we've hit one of the universes listed in the castle data base. The probability is that we're in one of an infinite number of quantum universes. We could be anywhere."

"Well, there're trees."

"Yes, this world looks Earth-like from first readings. Breathable atmosphere, tolerable temperature range, et cetera."

"Maybe we're on Earth."

"The odds are against it."

Jeremy sighed. "I guess we should go out and take a look."

"That'd be a good idea."

"You sure about the air and stuff?"

"I'm fairly sure you won't keel over dead the moment you open the hatch. But my sensors aren't equipped to scope out some of the real possibilities. Hostile natives, hungry fauna, infectious organisms, inconveniences like that."

"Right. But we gotta go out there."

"I guess you gotta," the Toshiba said.

Jeremy unstrapped and got up, bolstering himself with a hand on the bulkhead. "I'll go first," he told Isis. "No telling what's out there."

"Anything you say, Jeremy."

"It's Duke Wayne, as I live and breathe," the Toshiba said.

"Shut up, you piece of plastic junk, before I smash the crap out of you."

"Abuse! Abuse! Call my social worker."

Jeremy went aft and punched buttons on a small panel. The hatch popped open, letting in light and the smell of mountain laurel. He climbed out.

He slid down the flange of the hull and hit the ground. He turned and looked. The interdimensional traveler had landed in a copse of saplings and high bushes in the middle of a clearing. He walked around the bell-shaped craft. The front edge of the flange was hung up on rocks. The hull was intact. Whatever damage there was, it was underneath.

A dirt road ran by not far away. The surrounding woods looked very Earth-like. In fact, it looked for all the world like a deciduous forest of the familiar sort.

He went back to the hatch and yelled for Isis to come out. She appeared, and he helped her down.

"What's the situation?" she said.

"It doesn't look so bad, but that doesn't mean anything. See those trees over there? Looks like we clipped the top of them coming down. And then we whanged up against those rocks. See?"

Isis stooped and looked, nodding. "Bad luck."

"We could've been smeared. We could've hit anything, or wound up at the bottom of an ocean or something. We were damn lucky."

"I suppose that's right."

"You bet. But now we're stuck here."

Arms folded, Isis turned slowly around, inspecting the surroundings. Her high heels and daring black dress were incongruous in the setting. "It doesn't seem like such a bad place."

"Kinda . . . rural."

"Yes. I like it. It smells so nice."

Jeremy sniffed. "Like weeds and stuff."

"You city boys are all alike."

"Yeah, I'll take Manhattan. Or even Queens."

"What should we do, Jeremy?"

"Well." Jeremy shoved his hands in his jeans. "I guess we should take a walk down that road and see if we can get help."

"Good idea. I'd love to take a walk."

"Wait till I set up the security system, and then we'll go."

The road wound down a forested hill. The midafternoon sun was yellow, the sky blue, clouds a fleecy white—everything was as it should be. Tall maples and beech were in full leaf. A crow cawed in the distance.

"I love this place," Isis said. "I don't get out much."

"Me neither," Jeremy said. "I like to stay in and either work or watch TV. Though I haven't done much TV watching since I came to the castle. Kinda miss it."

"What kind of shows do you like?"

"Movies, mostly. That prime-time stuff is junk. Sports. I watch football. Mostly, though, I like to play around with computers."

"You're good at that. Don't you like to go out into the country once in a while, though?"

"Yeah. Sometimes. I used to go camping."

"With a girl?"

"Uh, no. I told you, I never had much to do with girls. Women. Girls. I never really had one. I mean . . . Look, that doesn't mean that I'm . . ."

She grinned at him. "What?"

"*You* know. I like girls. Women. They just don't like me."

"I like you."

"Yeah. Right."

"I *do*."

"Well . . . I do, too."

"You like you?"

"No! I like you, is what I'm saying. Not just because you're pretty, either. I mean, you are that. Very pretty."

"Thank you."

"What I'm saying is that you have smarts, and guts, as well as beauty."

"Thanks again."

"Girls don't usually . . . what am I saying? What I mean is, I used to think that a woman . . ."

"Hm?"

"Forget it. Anyway, the truth is, I've never had a girlfriend. Dates, yeah. A couple of those. But then I stopped doing it, because it never led anywhere."

She took his hand. "Well, you have a girlfriend now."

"Yeah."

"Come with me, Jeremy."

She led him off the road and into tall grass. She bade him lie down. Standing over him, she slipped off her dress. Underneath there was black lace, very little of it.

Jeremy's nostrils flared. He looked up at the computer-modeled perfection of her body, his eye following the rigorous geometry of her legs, her thighs, her hips, her breasts. He held out his trembling arms and she lay down with him and they were together.

A short time later Jeremy sat up and started unbuttoning his shirt. He froze when he saw the little girl.

Isis noticed his stare and turned. The little girl was watching them with big moon eyes, pale blue. She had on a shapeless, faded cotton dress, dirty and tattered, and her face was smudged. Her hair was pale yellow, almost white.

"Hello," Isis said.

"Hello," the girl said solemnly.

Jeremy sighed and buttoned his shirt. Isis got up and picked up her dress.

"Is your momma around?" Isis asked.

The little girl nodded and pointed down the road.

The house was a ramshackle bungalow with a gang of children playing in the junk-strewn front yard. The children fell silent when Jeremy and Isis approached.

"Can one of you kids go get your mom or dad for us?" Jeremy asked. "We want to speak to them."

A boy of about ten ran into the house. Presently a woman opened the front screen door and looked out. She was dressed in a threadbare housecoat. Her face was thin and her corn-silk hair was mussed and tangled. She eyed Isis up and down, then looked at Jeremy.

"Kin ah help you?"

"Yeah. We had a breakdown, up the road a little. Is—?"

"Say whut?"

Jeremy cleared his throat. "Our . . . vehicle broke down a little ways back up this road. Is there a town near here where we can get someone to help us fix it?"

"Y'say yore *vee*-hicle broke down?"

"Uh, yeah."

"An' you want someone for tuh *fix* it?"

"Yeah."

"Well, you jus' go right into Peach Holler, there, and see Luster Gooch and his brother Dolbert. They'll fix yore car."

"Peach Holler?"

"That's right, jus' right down this here road a piece, take you right into town. You go an' see Luster Gooch and see iffen he cain't help you any. Ah cain't stay and chew the fat with you, got somethin' on the stove. Good day."

She let the screen door close and disappeared into the odoriferous darkness of the house.

Peach Hollow (as the faded sign read) was a hamlet consisting of about a half a dozen houses, a few sheds, and the Gooch brothers' garage. The garage was a good walk from the road, and the front of the place was littered with wrecked automobiles and their rusting components. There were other sorts of junk, everything from old wringer washers to piles of bedsprings.

The big wooden barn doors were open. Jeremy and Isis walked in. The place reeked of oil and gasoline and decayed wood. A pair of dungareed legs was sticking out from under a battered car of indeterminate make.

Jeremy said, "Excuse me . . . hey, mister?"

"Yo!"

"You got a minute? We need some help."

"Start talkin', it's yore nickel."

"A woman up the road told us that you—"

"Say whut?"

"Uh, our vehicle broke down up the road a ways, and we need some tools and stuff, and, like, someone to help."

"Y'say yore *vee*-hicle broke down?"

"Yeah."

"And you want someone for tuh *fix* it?"

"Uh . . . yeah. We're in a big hurry and we're sort of in a spot. Can you help us?"

"Well, ah don't rightly know. What sorta *vee*-hicle d'you got?"

"Um. It's a foreign make."

The man under the car chuckled. "Hear that Dolbert?" he called.

A derisory cackling came from the back of the garage.

"Feller's got hisself one of them there *foreign* jobs."

The cackle rose in pitch. A shape came forth from the dim recesses of the garage. It was a short, chubby, homuncular man with a three-day growth of beard and most of his teeth missing. He was shirtless in grease-smeared bib overalls and wore big work shoes and a rat-chewed baseball cap.

The man under the car squirmed out and stood up. He was lanky and lean and wore patched dungarees over red longjohns. Thick blond hair came out from under a baseball cap that had

been gnawed by ferrets. He looked at Isis first and smiled,
touching the brim of his cap and nodding.

"Ma'am," he said, then looked at Jeremy. "Mister, ah don't
rightly know iffen ah kin fix one of them *foreign* jobs. Don't see
many of them around these parts."

"No?" Jeremy said. "Well, would you come take a look at
it?"

"Whut's wrong with it? Does she start? Kin you drive it in?"

"No, it won't start. The engine's . . . not working."

"Well, I guess you cain't drive it in, then. We're jus' gonna
have to git the truck and go up there and git it. This here's mah
brother Dolbert."

Dolbert's grin was gap-toothed and wide. His head bobbed
up and down as he cackled.

"And ah'm Luster P. Gooch."

"Nice to meet you," Jeremy said. "I'm Jeremy, and this is
Isis."

"Pleasure to make yore acquaintance. Y'say this vee-hicle of
yores is up the road a piece?"

"Yeah, not very far."

"Wull, let's go git it."

They piled into the cab of the ancient tow truck, Jeremy
squeezing next to Dolbert. Jeremy wrinkled his nose. Dolbert
quite obviously had very little experience in the soap-and-water
department.

Luster drove. "Where you folks from?"

"Uh, we're from the . . . the eastern part of the country."

"City folks?"

"Yeah."

"Uh-huh. Whutchyall doin' round these parts?"

"Oh, just driving around. You know."

"Uh-huh. We don't git many city folks out this way."

"No?"

"Nope. Pretty quiet hereabouts."

When they passed the dilapidated house, some of the children
waved. Luster waved back.

"It's right along here somewhere," Jeremy said.

"Cain't see nothin'."

"Just a little farther. There, right there."

Luster stopped the truck. "Whut the hay-ull is that?"

"That's our vehicle."

"Wull, what the hay-ull *is* that thing?"

"It's a . . . vehicle."

"Dolbert, you ever seen anything like that?"

Dolbert shook his head vigorously.

"Ah never seen anything like that in mah life. Whut the *hay-ull* is it?" Luster adjusted his cap. "Wull, whutever it is, let's take her in."

Luster backed the tow truck into the clearing, and everyone got out.

"There ain't even any proper wheels on this thing. Lookit these little tiny wheels, Dolbert."

Dolbert chittered his amazement.

"Don't that beat all? How the heck are we gonna hook this thing up?"

Isis said, "There are two retractable towing brackets along this edge."

Surprised, Jeremy said to her, "There are?"

Isis nodded. "They're controlled by one of the multifunction switches. I'll go deploy them."

When the brackets popped out Luster said, "Wull, ain't that slicker than owl spit. I guess we kin tow it."


"Whut the hay-ull is this?"

Squatting by one of the on-board jacks, Jeremy peered under the craft. Luster was on his back underneath, a stained piece of cheesecloth between him and the hard concrete of the garage floor. He had been a while unbolting the access plate; now he stared up in bewilderment at the arcane mechanical works of the *Sidewise Voyager*.

"Who the hay-ull built this thing? I never seen nothin' like this in all mah born days."

"Like I said, it's a foreign make."

"Don't that beat all. Dolbert? Crawl under here and take a look at this stuff."

Dolbert did. He shook his head and clucked.

"You ever see anything like this?"

Dolbert had to allow that he hadn't.

"You think you kin do anything with it?"

Dolbert shrugged.

Luster turned his head. "Dolbert usually does the foreign jobs when we get 'em. He kin fix anything."

"Can he fix this?" Jeremy asked.

"Dolbert, you think you kin do anything with this here contraption?"

Dolbert shrugged again, then nodded, chortling.

"Yeah, he figures he kin do it. You got an owner's manual for this here vee-hicle?"

"Uh, sort of. There's an on-board computer that has the complete technical specifications in its files. They're hard to understand, though."

"Yeah, I seen them types before. All them foreign words. Does it got pictures?"

"Yeah, it had schematics, but they're not easy to figure out, either."

"Wull, let's get a look at 'em and see iffen we cain't figure this gizmo out."

Jeremy led them into the craft. He sat them down at the control panel and knelt between the seats.

"Computer?"

"Yes?"

"Boot up the schematics out of the technical files and display the ones for the damaged components."

"Who are these two Paleolithic specimens?"

"They're mechanics. Show 'em the stuff. We gotta get this ship fixed."

"My tech files weren't even written for *Homo sapiens*, let alone *Homo neanderthalensis*. Or are we talking *Australopithecus africanus* here?"

"Never mind that crap! Do it!"

"Aye aye, Captain."

The Toshiba did it.

# Desert

THE SUN WAS declining when they had traversed the passes through the hills bordering the river. They came out into a wide valley. An intact temple, functional and unprepossessing, sat in the middle of it.

"That was simple enough," Incarnadine said. "Though I probably would have given this dump a glance and gone on."

"It is not what it appears," Jonath said.

"I'll take your word for it. Can we get much closer without tripping the spells?"

"A little farther. Then it becomes quite dangerous."

They walked on, Incarnadine leading his mount. The surrounding hills were eroded and bleak, etched with branching networks of gullies and ridges. Slides of talus cascaded down the slopes. The valley floor was level, cut with an occasional wadi and landscaped with heaps of rock.

Incarnadine stopped. "Strange. It looks different now."

"Yes," Jonath said. "It does."

"I could swear it got bigger."

They moved on. A few minutes later Incarnadine halted again. "Now, wait a minute. It looks bigger, but paradoxically enough it doesn't look any closer. How can that be?"

"All things are possible with Mordek."

"Of course."

They continued. The temple now seemed actually to recede from them. At the same time, it changed, growing more ornate and elaborate. The low sun caught the glint of gold.

"Some very fast remodelers at work over there. I wonder if they're getting time and a half."

The pair proceeded on, to no avail. The temple grew no closer, yet ever more resplendent. Golden friezes bridged columns of decorated stone. Atop was a roof of beaten gold bordered by gilt cornices.

"Nice place," Incarnadine said. "You've seen it like this before?"

"It is as it was in the days of my father's father."

The sky darkened, and the ground began to shake. Wind ripped at them and the dust that blew pricked like needles on the skin.

The area around them lit up in a flash. A golden beam of energy had hit above them and splayed out, as around an invisible hemisphere. Another came, then another, each hitting with an explosive concussion like thunder.

"Nothing like getting right to the point," Incarnadine said.

"Your forfending spells are potent," Jonath said. "Otherwise, we would be dead. You are indeed a powerful sorcerer."

"So far, so good. But that was just an opening gambit, I fear."

The ground trembled. Gouts of fire shot out of rents in the ground. The wind's force increased, and vague shapes began to fill the air, diaphanous things swooping and soaring. Eidolons appeared on the ground, and some of these coalesced into substantial figures. Some were winged, some not. Most had scales, some the heads of hawks and the bodies of two-legged lizards. All bore swords as they advanced on the approaching pair.

Incarnadine drew his sword. It was a magnificent thing, agleam with its own light, the blade of steel burnished to a mirror finish and the hilt wrought into silver involutes that defied the eye. He swung it and the air vibrated.

A hawk-head approached and slashed at him with a curving blade. He fended off the attack easily, then pointed the sword at the thing. A bolt of blue energy jumped from sword point to creature, and the latter exploded.

"Magnificent," Jonath said.

"It ought to be. I've been doing this silly bullshit for years."

A scaled one charged at him brandishing long and short swords. Incarnadine didn't wait to engage it; he pointed the sword and let fly. The thing resisted disintegrating, but didn't survive the second bolt.

Great birds stooped and dove, some attacking Jonath. Incarnadine had to be quick with the sword. Huge wings flapped in time with explosions of grue, and the stink of burnt flesh and feathers filled the air.

More airborne attacks came at them, these timed with ground advances. Blue bolts flashed left and right, into the air and at the ground as slithering things appeared: serpents with tails of fire. Other phenomena materialized—windmills of energy, blades chopping toward them; green ropes of luminescence that came at their legs and tried to ensnare; a poisonous orange mist that seared the lungs and scratched at the eyes. Hail the size of melons fell, shattering on the rocks. More golden fingers of energy shot out from the temple.

Manned by frog-faced drivers, chariots of fire rumbled out of the plains ahead, each drawn by five black horses snorting flames.

Jonath fell on his face and covered his head. When he dared look up again he saw not one but five Incarnadines, each wielding a fiery sword.

The next few moments were furious, profligate of energy and power. The flashes were incessant, the noise deafening. The ground heaved and rumbled, canting to one side, then the other. The heavens opened up and rain fell, lightning splintering the sky.

The concussions were so forceful that Jonath thought he would die. He hid his head again and prayed to be taken without too much pain.

The flashing stopped and the thunder gradually died, echoing from the far hills and ridges. The air cleared. The hellish creatures vanished, leaving behind the rapidly decomposing carcasses of dead horses and an idly spinning chariot wheel.

Jonath looked up and saw a lone magician, sword still at the ready.

Incarnadine scanned the horizon as things quieted down. He looked, sniffed the air, then made a few motions with his hands. He nodded with satisfaction.

He lowered his sword and turned to Jonath, smiling broadly. "Well, that was quite a workout!"

Jonath got to his feet and retrieved his cane. "You are more

than merely a powerful sorcerer,'' he said. "You must also be
a god.''

"Not quite. Never did aspire to it. Heady stuff, godhood. It
can get to you.''

"Nevertheless, you must be divine. No mere mortal could
stand up to such wrath and live.''

"You'd be surprised what a diet rich in oat bran can do.''

Something was building on the plain. It was an immense effort—waves of energy left the temple and froze into matter, ac-
creting layer upon layer. The thing grew, took on shape and
substance. The end result, when the last of the emanations had
solidified, was an enormous beast of mind-numbing lineaments,
an incongruous monster of disparate parts: leg of goat, head of
lizard, eye of cat, flank of lion, claw of bear, and on and on in
an incredible and ferocious mélange. The beast's tail was serpentine and spiked, and when it twitched boulders flew.

"What have we here?'' Incarandine mused.

"You might come to wish that you had aspired to godhead,''
Jonath said.

Incarnadine shook his head. "It's not good work. Too busy.
No organizing principle. But then again, such things can be
charming in their own catch-as-catch-can way.''

The beast roared in a thousand voices. It put one mighty foot
forward.

"Aesthetic criticisms aside,'' Incarnadine said, "there remains the problem of what the hell I'm going to do about it. It's
too damn big just to zap.''

The beast advanced, its footsteps thundering. Its shadow fell
across the pair below. It bent its head and lowered its body.

Jonath bolted, lost his cane, tripped, and fell. He got to his
knees and looked back. The gigantic mouth came down on Incarnadine and enveloped him. The mighty jaws closed. The beast
unbent, its head rising into the air, a satisfied smile on its saurian-
feline countenance.

It chewed and swallowed, then emitted a loud belch. Its eyes
scanned the ground below, its gimlet gaze finally falling on
Jonath.

Jonath began to pray again, on his knees now, as the beast
shambled toward him. A taloned foot came to rest beside him,
and the fetid stench of the thing was in his nostrils. Jonath collapsed and lay still on the ground.

When he came back to consciousness he lay unmoving for a

moment longer, then raised his head. The monstrous foot was gone. He looked around and saw the creature walking away. It had retreated about a hundred human paces when it turned around, a clawed paw on its abdomen. Its eyes narrowed, and what Jonath took to be a grimace of pain came over its countenance. The creature groaned, bringing the other paw up to clutch its middle. A bellowing roar escaped its mouth.

The creature exploded into a million glittering fragments, became a blizzard of confetti. The wind rose and blew the swirling cloud away to the hills.

On the spot where the creature had stood, Incarnadine got to his feet and brushed the sand off his doublet.

Jonath rose, fetched his cane, and went to him.

"I thought you had succumbed," Jonath said.

"It was the only way the deed could be done," Incarnadine said. "Blasting it from the outside wouldn't have even stunned it. But the insides of magical constructs are often shoddily put together."

"How did you manage to pass through the creature's maw unharmed?"

"A simple hard-shell protective bubble. Nothing to it. There wasn't much to breathe in there, though. I had to work fast."

"You have proven yourself worthy. Mordek is sure to vouchsafe you the sight of his beatific visage."

"I should be so lucky. No, I don't think he's through. You said it was a 'he,' didn't you?"

"Oh, most assuredly, Honorable."

"Goddesses are special problems. Well." Incarnadine turned to view the temple. "It's definitely closer. Let's see if we can't walk to it. We have to, anyway. My animal's run off."

They walked. This time the temple obeyed the laws of perspective and got closer. Its grandeur did not diminish. An imposing pylon gateway, decorated with painted reliefs, guarded the entrance. Gold leaf shone everywhere.

"Oh-oh. Wait a minute."

Incarnadine approached cautiously. He drew his sword and poked the air. The point hit something invisible and sparks jumped from it.

"Your basic invisible screen." Incarnadine began probing the air up and down, outlining the dimensions. "No doubt it goes all around in a big cube." Holding the haft with both hands he pushed the sword forward. A high-pitched note like that from a tuning fork was the result as more sparks flew.

"Hmmm." Incarnadine stepped back, put the sword between his knees, and spit on his hands. Then he used both to grip the sword again. He measured his swing, bringing the weapon slowly over his head and down in a sweeping arc.

"You gotta hit these things je-e-est right."

Jonath watched in fascination.

Incarnadine took a few more practice sweeps, then hauled back and swung in one powerful, graceful motion of calculated force.

The sword met the invisible wall with a flash. A spider's web of purple lines, like cracks in a pane of glass, expanded from the point of impact and propagated across an expansive plane paralleling the front of the temple. The cracking took right angles at the edges of the three upper sides and continued until it defined a gigantic cube around the structure. An ear-piercing high-frequency tone accompanied this process. Then, after a moment of shimmering and vibrating, the force screen shattered like so much plate glass, millions of fragments tumbling in a violet cascade. The debris disappeared in bursts of sparks as it hit the ground. When the roaring ceased, nothing remained.

"Pretty," Incarnadine said.

He motioned Jonath to come along and they approached the tapered walls of the facade. Two obelisks of red granite flanked the opening, but they did not stop to admire these, passing through the doorway and into the temple.

A vast hall, defined by a forest of columns with leafed capitals, greeted them as they came out of the dark vestibule. Light came from clerestory windows with screens of stone tracery. The scale was immense, bigger than anything in the Mizzerite valley. At the end of the hall was a wide doorway.

They went through and entered a chamber of somewhat smaller proportions but still breathtaking in its spaciousness, its high ceiling supported by columns sheathed in hammered gold that glinted in the light of a dozen ceremonial braziers. The scent of exotic incense hung heavy.

There were voices. An unseen chorus chanted a plaintive dirge.

The centerpiece of all this atmosphere was a gigantic golden statue of a creature with arms and torso of a man, the legs of a lion, and the head of a goat. The right hand held a sword, the left a knout.

As the pair came toward it, the statue began to move. The right arm brought the sword down until the tip was pointing at Incarnadine.

A voice boomed in the sanctuary.

*"You . . . have . . . incurred . . . my . . . wrath."*

Jonath fell to the floor and prostrated himself.

Incarnadine said, "Isn't it about time we cut the crap? I mean, you've put on a fine show for the faithful, you've done the wrath bit, but I do have pressing business and I *really* need to talk to you. So, if you don't mind . . ." Incarnadine sheathed his sword.

The statue ceased moving. The doleful chorus stopped with a ripping sound suspiciously like that of a phonograph needle skating across a record.

There was silence.

Presently a little man came out from behind the obsidian stone base of the statue. Bald, hook-nosed, and wearing black horn-rim glasses, he was dressed in an electric-blue leisure suit over a red paisley sport shirt with the shirt collar out over the collar of the jacket. His cordovan loafers shone with a mirror gloss. The top three buttons of the shirt were open, exposing a bumpy chest covered with gray hair. A gold medallion on a gold chain nested there.

Hands in his pockets, he sauntered over to the two visitors. On his face was a half-smile of mild annoyance. He came up to Incarnadine.

He shrugged. "So, talk to me, Mister Smart Guy."

# QUEEN'S DINING HALL

"I GOT HERE FIRST," Incarnadine said adamantly.

"The Hell you did," Incarnadine said just as adamantly.

The two men, identical in every respect save that one wore a crown and the other was bareheaded, stood facing each other. The crown wearer had made his point with a leg of honey-basted sage hen, which he then took a bite of.

A fight was going on in the other end of the room. The participants consisted of the following: one anti-Guardsman, hereafter referred to as a −Guardsman; one Guardsman, hereafter designated as a +Guardsman; one +Snowclaw; one −Snowclaw; another +Guardsman; and, for the sake of plot complication, one anti-anti-Guardsman, a category hereafter referred to as −2Guardsman.

"I'm telling you, I sent my men in here first. Everything was going swimmingly. Then you blundered in and buggered up the whole works."

"*I* buggered up the works? The castle was mine till you and your lot showed up."

"The mirror aspect showed up in my castle."

"In mine, too!"

"All right, in yours, too, but as soon as I found it I shot right through and hit with everything I had."

"As did I. I'm not one to pass up a target of opportunity."

The bareheaded one picked up a sparerib, took a bite, spat it out, and tossed the thing over his shoulder. "Cold. Lousy service in this dump."

"There's a war going on, you know."

"No excuse. Look, we're going to have to work something out."

"Doubtless," the crown wearer said. "But how?"

"It's a big castle."

"No, no, no. I'm not going to subdivide."

"Then we have to establish who has priority."

"Who's going to establish it? Are you suggesting we settle this in a court of law? Arbitration, maybe?"

"No, look. Two intelligent fellows ought to be able to work this out."

"Well, I'm not gainsaying it. But there has to be common ground from which to start."

"How much more in common could we have?"

"A point. A point."

"All right, then. Withdraw your boys and we'll talk."

"We are talking. It would be pretty silly of us to draw swords and start hacking away at each another, now, wouldn't it?"

"Of course."

The crown-wearer threw down the sage hen. "You're right, the food here stinks."

"Probably been sitting there for a couple of days. Okay, if you won't withdraw, then let's call a truce. This noise is distracting."

"Let's retire to my study."

"Where, here? It's not yours."

"My castle, then."

"You want me to walk into your lair?"

"All right, where?"

"Forget it, we'll stay here."

The crowned one rummaged through a salad bowl and came up with a radish, which he popped into his mouth. "Talk about generally futzing things up, *I* didn't come up with the brilliant idea of the yellow Snowclaws."

"Who says I did?"

"Well, it wasn't me."

"Wasn't me, either."

"Wait a minute. If it wasn't *you* . . ."

Both Incarnadines frowned and looked off.

"Holy hell. Another one."

"Nothing to prevent still another mirror aspect forming. Or more."

"I guess not. Which leads to some disquieting possibilities."

"And here comes one."

Another Incarnadine, this one in a fur coat and cossack hat, entered the dining hall surrounded by a phalanx of —3Guardsmen. He waved, shouldered past his men, and walked over.

"Greetings. Fancy meeting you guys here."

"Yes, we were just discussing that very fancy," the crown-wearer said.

"I suppose," the bareheaded Incarnadine said, "you're about to stake a claim to this shack?"

"No, I just came in to see what the hell's going on. What's all the ruckus?"

"The lord of this castle's not around. Disappeared."

"No, he didn't," the crowned one said reproachfully. "Tell him the truth."

"Oh, hell. When I found this mirror aspect I got a wild hair up my ass and stormed through. So did he, more or less at the same time."

"Whatever for?"

"Like I said, a wayward follicle. Just an impulse."

A chair came flying across the room, and the three ducked.

"Nothing like a good fight to work up an appetite."

"I hear this castle's owner doesn't go for blood sports."

"Yeah, I heard that, too."

"So you just blitzkrieged your way through for the hell of it."

"More or less."

"One hundred forty-four thousand worlds wasn't enough for you."

"You get bored, you know."

"Yeah, we live too damned long."

"Well, that's easily taken care of."

"You want to go Waltzing Matilda with me? We'll see who—"

"Gentlemen, gentlemen, please. Enough of that."

"Well, he threatened me."

"Stuff it."

"You stuff it."

"Can it! And you call yourselves Incarnadine."

"Who says we aren't?"

"Look, this mirror aspect stuff . . . it can't be real."

"*What* can't be real?"

"There's only one castle. Can't be more than one."

"Why not?"

"Well, it just stands to reason. Besides, the way you're acting . . ."

"Who?"

"You two. Neither of you can be the real Incarnadine."

"Get him. Let me guess. You're the genuine article?"

"Well, shit, I ought to know who I am."

"Now, it occurs to me that we could all say that. It's like the problem of solipsism. I know I'm real, but who are all you robots?"

"Look, I don't want to start splitting epistemological hairs with you. Let's table that issue for now and face up to the possibility that we have a problem on our hands. We have a castle with thousands of aspects, each one of which can turn into a mirror of the castle itself—"

"And each of those mirror castles has 144,000 mirror aspects in *it*—"

"And so on and so on, ad infinitum."

"Ad absurdum."

"Adirondacks. Yeah, it's a mess. What do we do about it?"

"Not sure we can do anything about it."

"That's what I mean. The real Incarnadine would be furiously busy doing something about it."

"Like you."

"Well, I'm here."

"So are we all."

"Let's not get into that again."

More combatants joined the fray. Tables overturned, and stale food went flying.

"Who was it that came up with the idea of cloning Snowclaw in the first place?"

"Who knows? What does it matter?"

"I suppose it doesn't."

"See here. It seems we should do something."

"Cast some sort of spell?"

"Yeah, but what kind of a spell would eliminate all the mirrors?"

"Whose mirrors would you be eliminating?"

"All of them."

"But don't you see, that would blink all of us out of existence except one, the real one."

"We're back to that again."

"Well, not necessarily. We could each have our separate reality, our own pocket universe, independent of the rest."

"Undoubtedly we do, but the notion of everything going poof is somehow unsettling to me."

"All right, let's not do a poof. Then what do we have? Pandemonium."

"Wait a minute. You're talking as if this poof spell were a foregone conclusion. Do you have such a spell?"

"Well . . ."

"Can you come up with one?"

"Frankly, not offhand."

"Okay, then the poof idea is moot until we do come up with one."

"That's how this castle's Incarnadine has us all beat."

"How so?"

"There's something going on up in the lab here. I think they have a mainframe computer working on writing a spell."

"Something I've always wanted to do—use a computer to do magic."

"Apparently the owner here has gone a long way along that path."

"Can we get in?"

"They have the place all tricked out with anti-intruder spells and I just haven't had the time to go up there and scotch them."

"Maybe we should all take a crack at it."

"I'm not sure our barging into something we know nothing about is such a good idea. They might be doing some good."

"They might also make us all go poof."

"That's a possibility. Anyway, I'm game. Want to go up and at least try to see what's going on?"

"Yeah, let's have a go."

"Okay. But we really should—oh, God."

"Hi, guys!"

The latest Incarnadine wore a black leather jacket, black T-shirt, jeans, and boots. He was smoking a funny-looking wrinkled cigarette. The room filled with −4Guardsmen.

"This is getting ridiculous."

"Hey, I'm kind of enjoying it."

"Is the kitchen open?"

"Oh, all the castle personnel are long gone. Hiding."

"I'm starved."

"Well, whip something up. You're a magician."

"I can't eat it when I do it myself. It's no fun."

"It'll do in a pinch."

"You do it for me."

"I'm no cook."

"You're a magician! What does it matter?"

"It still takes talent."

"True."

"But about the laboratory business?"

"Tell you what, let's get together for lunch in the King's Hall first—I'm starved, too—and then we'll all go up to the lab together and see what's what."

"That sounds like a fine idea. There's one problem."

"What?"

"Tried to do any magic yet?"

"No, why?"

"The magic's subtly different here."

"How can that be?"

"Well, there are a few differences among us. We're not identical."

"True. So, you think working any magic here is going to be a problem."

"Major magic at least. I think we're up to conjuring a good lunch."

"Well, if that's true, we all might as well go home."

"Let's have lunch first. Let the boys play, they're having a good time."

"We've got to get rid of those damned white-furred critters!"

"And the yellow ones."

"Them, too. Anybody got any ideas?"

"Without major magic, we're out of business."

"Not necessarily. We ought to be able to compensate for the subtle factors."

"This blasted computer stuff worries me. The owner here might be at a distinct advantage if and when he ever gets back."

"Where is he?"

"Haven't been able to find out."

"Then don't worry about him."

"Okay, guys, let's go to lunch."

"Forget about the King's Hall. We're not going to get any good food here in the castle. Let's head into the Nouvelle Provence aspect. There's a little café there that makes a great bouillabaisse. And the troubadours are superb."

"We might not be able to get through. If you haven't noticed, many aspects are screwed up."

"Not Provence. I had breakfast there."

"Fine. Well, let's go."

"Right."

They all trooped out of the Queen's Hall. In the corridor outside they ran into another Incarnadine.

"Where're you people going?"

"Lunch. Want to come?"

"Who's buying?"

"Separate checks. C'mon."

The new Incarnadine turned to his —5Guardsmen. "Go in there and kick some ass. I'll be back in a bit."

"Very good, sire!"

Incarnadine trotted after his colleagues.

"Hey, wait up!"

# MOOR

"THIS IS GETTING BACK to the roots of golf," Dalton said. "Nothing like a moor to play on."

"You're thinking of links land, along a seacoast. Nobody plays golf on a bloody bog."

"I stand corrected. But it still seems I should be using a brassie or a cleek for this hole."

The teeing ground was on a knoll above the moor. The land rolled from rise to bog as far as the eye could see. Purple-flowered heather grew all over, sedge and other grasses clumping in the marshy areas.

Dalton said, "Are we using the white markers?"

"Yes, unless you've turned into a scratch player overnight. Are you still keeping score in your head?"

"Yep. You're at—"

"Don't tell me, I don't want to know. Are we doing match play?"

"We're playing Nassau," Dalton said. "I won the first nine."

"Fine. Shoot."

"I'd be handicapping, but it's hard to do without a score-card."

"Forget the handicapping. This is a friendly game."

"Of course."

Dalton's drive went straight and true and landed in a bog.

"Still want that brassie?" Thaxton said mordantly.

"A two-wood's not going to do any good here, there being no true fairway."

"All rough and no fairway. Interesting concept."

"Get any sleep last night?" Dalton asked.

"Oh, some. Hard to get much with the bloody wind howling over the moor like a lost soul."

"It put me to sleep."

Thaxton drove deep and straight and wound up with a tall-grass lie.

"I'll need a sickle to get out of there."

"Hope we don't get literally bogged down," Dalton said.

They did. The sky was a thick leaden bowl and the land was dark and forbidding. Their spiked shoes sank into the wet peat. Dalton couldn't find his ball and lost a stroke. Thaxton hacked away at the grass with his seven-iron Ping Eye-2 until he could get at his.

"This is bloody preposterous."

A demonic howl went up from the bogs to the east and made the hair on the back of Thaxton's neck bristle.

"What in the world was that?"

"The hellhound!" Dalton said, chuckling.

"Don't bloody laugh about it."

Thaxton's approach went well and he was on the "green" (an irregular patch of unevenly trimmed bent grass) in two. He read the break brilliantly, successfully negotiated all the hills, bumps, and swales between the ball and the cup, and was in for par. Dalton chipped onto the green and putted for a double bogey.

"Where's the next hole?"

"I don't know," Dalton said. "But there's a path of sorts. See it?"

"Yes, but—"

Another blood-freezing howl, this one closer.

"Good God, bloody Basil Rathbone will show up next in his mackintosh and deerstalker."

"Look what *is* showing up," Dalton said, pointing to a rise where an enormous black dog had appeared at the crest. It was a monstrous animal, yipping and snarling and pounding full tilt straight for them.

The men dropped their bags and ran, Thaxton for some reason keeping his putter in hand. They didn't get far before the dog caught up and began to pace them almost teasingly, snapping and slavering at their heels, yellowed fangs bared, foam dripping from the corners of its mouth.

It chased them for a quarter mile before Thaxton stumbled and rolled in the heather. The dog leaped over him, chased Dalton for a few paces, then turned back. Thaxton reached for the putter and raised it in desperation against the inevitable attack.

The animal stopped and panted, its long pink tongue lolling in and out. Its tail began to wag.

"What the devil?"

The thing whimpered and its tail wagged faster.

"It's friendly?" Thaxton said incredulously.

Dalton returned. "Looks like."

"But it sounded as though it wanted us for supper."

"Dogs can be very territorial. Maybe this is his turf."

"Look at the thing. Paws as big as melons."

"Nice doggie." Dalton went up to it and scratched its enormous head.

The animal seemed to appreciate the gesture. Dalton patted its head and ran his hand up and down the neck.

"What sort of breed is that?" Thaxton asked.

"It's big even for a mastiff. Looks a little like one, though, around the droopy checks. It's a mutt, probably."

"Mongrel from Hell."

"Oh, this is a good dog—aren't you, fellow?"

*"Whuuff!"*

"Thank heaven it can't talk," Thaxton said. "I'm full up with bloody sentient beasts."

"It seems to understand."

"God, look at it drool. Looks like marshmallow sauce. It's making me ill."

"Looks like he wants to come along! Maybe he can find balls. Probably make a good hunting dog."

"I'll fetch the clubs, you entertain Baskerville, here."

"Wonder what his name is. Oh, wait, it says on the collar. You were right, Thax. He is a mongrel from Hell. 'Cerberus.' Good name for an occult canine. Hey, where're you going, boy?"

The animal shot past Thaxton and bounded across the moor. Thaxton stopped and both men watched. The dog went straight to one discarded golf bag, picked it up gingerly by the fake-leather strap, went to the other and somehow managed to get hold of both of them with its mouth, hoisted them up, then ran back and dumped them at Thaxton's feet.

"Never saw a dog do such a thing," Thaxton said.

The moor continued but became less boggy. They found the next hole, and from the tee it looked to present no special problems. Heather carpeted the rough, and this time there was an acceptable fairway of fescue grasses, though toughened with numerous rocks, deep swales, and pot bunkers. The green looked conventional.

"Let's call this par four," Dalton said.

"Looks a little long for a four. And a little difficult."

"Try a three-wood off the tee."

"Do you really think? It looks over five hundred yards, Dalton. Par five."

"That's about . . ." Dalton held his club out, using some undoubtedly arcane method of judging distance. "Four hundred fifty yards. A long par four."

"Oh, all right. Where did I put my bag? I—"

Cerberus was standing beside him, Thaxton's three-wood in his mouth.

"Hmm. Thank you. Good dog." Thaxton gave his partner a bemused look, shrugged, and took a square stance.

The sixteenth hole wouldn't have gone well even if the herd of wyverns hadn't shown up.

Dalton lost his ball in the rough. Cerberus found it for him easily enough, but it was a steep sidehill lie in the tall heather. Thaxton wound up in a deep swale and had to pitch his way out, but the lob shot merely put him into a fairway bunker.

Then the wyverns arrived, squawking and twittering, their stubby wings flapping noisily. Two-legged and green-scaled, they liked the tender leaves of tall bushes and could bend over easily to forage. As they did so, their long barbed tails writhed like angry snakes.

They got in the way. Thaxton's wood shot from the bunker hit one of them and sent the poor thing shrieking away. Cerberus chased them, woofing his delight, herding them this way and that and adding to the confusion. Wyvern claws chewed up the turf, wyvern teeth chewed up the rough, and wyvern innards landscaped the approaches to the green with wyvern dew. The place reeked.

Thaxton's ball landed smack in a huge pile. This didn't deter him. He hit a mean Texas wedge shot that splattered the stuff and sent the soiled ball bounding across the green and into a trap.

"Dung hazards!" Thaxton groaned.

"We shouldn't have to take this crap," Dalton said.

They putted as best as they could. Both wound up with triple bogeys.

"Rum show, that," Thaxton said.

"On to seventeen?"

"Of course. Why would we stop now? By the way, fairly soon we're going to have to face up to the problem of getting back to Perilous."

"That's certainly true," Dalton said.

"Have any ideas?"

"Why don't we start worrying about it after we've sunk the last putt? Or even after we've had a drink at the Nineteenth Hole."

"Right. What good to worry now?"

"That's the ticket."

They walked on, Cerberus tagging along. The moor petered out, giving way to rolling grass spotted with patches of sand. The sky changed, the overcast breaking up a little and revealing patches of blue sky.

"Looks like we're in for a bit of pleasant weather," Dalton said.

There was a new smell in the air: the sea. It sparkled to their right, its breakers washing a rocky shore.

"Here're your golfing roots," Thaxton said.

And indeed it was. What spread before them was an ancient course laid out on links land, the sandy grassland of the Scottish shores. Sheep grazed on the lee side of the hillocks.

"Lad, do ye ken the Highland fling?" Thaxton said.

"Aye. But I'd rather do the lindy. This is wonderful. I've always wanted to play on the real links. Wish we had some traditional clubs instead of these high-tech cheats."

"Well, to my way of thinking, anything that helps to . . . wait just a minute. Oh, no, not again."

A fog bank was quickly rolling in from sea. It was thick, impenetrable, and seemed to possess a reality all its own.

"Uh-oh," Dalton said. "Another change-fog."

"Oh, dear." Thaxton chose a flat rock and sat down. Cerberus lay down beside him and held his head up to be petted.

The mist rolled in, blotting out sea, sky, and land. It reached the golfers and their caddy-mascot and swaddled them in moist silence. Cerberus jumped to his feet and let out a few defiant barks, then lay back down and whimpered quietly.

"I have the feeling," Dalton said as he settled down to wait, "that the last two holes are going to test our mettle."

"I'm already suffering mettle fatigue." Thaxton gave his partner a wink. "Sorry."

"Well, you should be."

They waited.

# COUNTRY

THE COUNTRYSIDE WAS deserted, its fields silent, its eroded asphalt roads devoid of traffic.

They walked through overgrown hayfields and pastures, encountering the foundations of demolished farm houses and buildings, sections of rusted barbed-wire fence, and other remnants of what were once working farms. The fields had been allowed to go wild for so long that saplings had grown up in them, the surrounding patches of forest reclaiming lost territory.

They ate a lunch of wild raspberries. There was nothing to drink but creek water, which Gene didn't trust. They did find a well site but the pump was long gone. The raspberries' juice was enough to hold them, though, and they continued their cross-country journey, keeping away from roads and not staying too long in the open.

Occasionally they would hear the whine and roar of turbines and take cover. Rural areas were well patrolled. Gene wondered why.

He began to suspect the reason when they discovered a destroyed tank in an old cornfield. It had been hit in the turret with an armor-piercing shell. The top hatch had been blown off and the inside of the vehicle had burned out. Judging by the amount of rust and weathering, Gene put the event at four to five years ago.

They began to see evidence of recent battles—besides the hulk of the blasted truck, they found shell casings, ammo belts, and other military refuse. Nothing in great quantity: Gene got the feeling that this was debris missed in a general cleanup.

"Did you ever hear about what happened here?"

"No," Alice said. "Never. But . . ."

"What is it?"

"A while back there was a Citizens' Mobilization Training Festival."

"What was that?"

"We were ordered to report for training."

"Military training?"

"I guess you'd call it that. We marched around carrying wooden sticks."

"Not rifles?"

"No, just sticks to practice with. They didn't give us any guns."

"Then what happened?"

"Nothing," she said. "It lasted about a week, then there was a notice canceling the festival."

"Was there anything on the screen then about 'unsocial outside elements'? Anything at all?"

"Yes, a couple of mentions here and there, but no information."

Gene mulled it over. Thinking aloud, he said, "There was a battle or a series of battles fought here not too long ago. The area is still being patrolled. That might mean that the front lines are not very far away. Maybe fifty miles to the east. Which puts it close to the portal."

"Close to the what?"

"The thing that will take us to my world. A doorway. Never mind that for now. Let's reconstruct a possible history. This nation, whatever it was before, some variant of the United States, was taken over by this mysterious molecular entity called InnerVoice. The rest of the world wasn't taken over, or there were at least parts of it that remained free. These free nations or a group of them finally managed to invade the East Coast and work their way west as far as western Pennsylvania, meeting strong resistance all the way. Around here somewhere a decisive battle was fought, and the defenders threw back the invasion force. The front lines stabilized somewhere east of here, where they remain. Stalemate. The civilian population is kept in the dark, except for some hastily improvised mobilization effort. How does that sound to you?"

"I don't know. It could be true."

"It has to be true. No other interpretation fits the facts."

"How are you feeling, Gene?"

"Huh? Oh, fine. Fine."

It struck him then that he *was* feeling fine. No nausea, no anxiety. He wondered if the battle inside his body had been won. If so, how? What inner resources had he drawn on? Maybe it had been sheer fortitude and willpower, with a little adrenaline added to help.

Somehow he doubted it. He had been thoroughly cowed, beaten. InnerVoice and its mechanisms were almost insurmountable for the ordinary person.

But he was not an ordinary person—at least his experiences were not ordinary. After all, he lived in a magic castle in a world of magic. Was something supernatural working here? He couldn't see how, because he was not a magician himself; rather, he was a bad one. He could cast a few simple spells but seventy percent of the time he botched them completely. And those spells would not help him here in any event. So, what was happening to him? He felt the faint stirrings of something going on inside, but he couldn't put a finger on what it was.

They had come to the edge of a strip of woods. Ahead was a wide field and no cover until they reached the other side of a highway below, where trees started again.

Gene checked the highway, then the sky. He listened for half a minute. Nothing but birds, the wind through the trees, crickets in the field.

"We're going to have to make a run for those woods. There's no choice. We have to cross the highway at some point."

"We'll make it, Gene."

He smiled at her. "I like you."

"I like you, too."

"Let's go."

Holding hands, they jogged through the high hay. They were halfway down the hill when a helicopter came out of nowhere, followed by two VTOL gunships.

They dove into the hay at the first sound, and for a moment

Gene thought they hadn't been spotted. But the three craft began circling, and he knew his escape attempt was over.

He wished mightily for a gun, for any means of resistance, even for a handy cliff for them both to leap over. Anything was better than going back to InnerVoice. Anything.

But there was nothing he could do. He seethed with anger, wild desperate thoughts springing to mind. He imagined bolts of death leaving his fingers, striking down his tormentors. If only he had magic, like Linda and Sheila! Why? Why had he been left out?

He offered them no resistance. When they were handcuffing him he couldn't even look at Alice. He felt as though he'd betrayed her.

They put him in the helicopter, her in one of the VTOL craft. The noise of the rotor blades chopped at him, reverberating inside his head. It hurt. The helicopter took off and swung west. The faster VTOLs shot ahead and lost themselves in the sun. He stared out the window at the green earth below, mourning the silent meadows, the desolate farmlands.

The helicopter landed at what looked like a large rear-area field headquarters, an assortment of tents and temporary buildings not unlike Quonset huts but probably made of fiberglass. There were VTOLs in a field nearby and tanks hull-down in camouflage arranged around the perimeter.

They brought him to one of the fiberglass shacks, pushed him down a short corridor and into an office. He was made to sit.

An officer came in, a tall thin man with a bald head and wide shoulders. His uniform was crisp and new. The insignia he wore weren't recognizable but he had the odor about him of the rank of colonel or better. He came in and sat at the desk.

"I'm Group Leader Y-9," he said amiably. "You're Gene Ferraro, correct?"

"I can't deny it. How do you know my name?"

"Intelligence has been watching you since you were taken. You were obviously a setup. You were sent here to be captured, though what the strange papers and paraphernalia were about we haven't quite figured out yet. But we treated you like we treat most agents that you people drop. We usually interrogate them after we give them InnerVoice, but we wanted to see what you would do."

Group Leader Y-9 got up and began to pace. "We suspected

you were immune from the start. You put on quite an act, I'll have to admit. But you were immune to InnerVoice. This is something we've been waiting for." He turned and smiled. "And we're prepared for it."

"Prepared for what?"

"For the day when the Outforces developed a nanotechnology to deal with InnerVoice on a molecular level—when they found a magic bullet to kill it inside an individual who has been infected with it. You obviously have that magic bullet working inside you."

Gene shook his head. "I have no such technology. And I'm not from the Outforces, though I'm in complete sympathy with them."

Y-9 laughed. "Where did you come from, then? Or did you appear out of thin air?"

"Yes, as a matter of fact."

Y-9 regarded him curiously for a moment, then sat down.

"But we still don't know what you're up to. Care to tell us?"

"I'm trying to get back to Castle Perilous."

The Group Leader contemplated the ceiling. "We can't use InnerVoice on you. Drugs probably wouldn't work. We'll have to conduct the interrogation the old-fashioned way."

"It wouldn't matter what you did to me. I couldn't tell you anything."

"Well, we won't do a thing to you. We'll do it to her."

Gene's stomach twisted into a knot.

"We can't understand why you would compromise your mission for a temporary infatuation, but it seems as though you've done it."

"Leave her out of this."

Y-9 grinned. "You can arrange that by telling us what your mission is, how far advanced the defensive nanotechnology is, other things we want to know."

"I can't. Believe me, I can't tell you anything. I don't belong in this world. I come from something totally outside it."

Y-9 narrowed his eyes and looked down his nose at Gene. "Very interesting. You're asking me to believe that you're mentally unbalanced."

"I'm not asking you anything except for you to leave Alice out of it."

"Who?"

"The woman."

"I see. Well, we can't do that, I'm afraid. Only you can. The decision is up to you."

Gene could think of nothing to say or do.

"We'll let you think about it for a while. But you ought to keep this in mind. We know you people know about our research in biological transmission of InnerVoice. Well, you might as well be the first on your side to know that we've solved the main problems. Through gene-splicing we have come up with a bacterium large enough to carry the complete complement of InnerVoice nanomachines within its protoplasm. The ailment it causes is quite communicable and produces most of the symptoms of the common cold. All the world will soon have InnerVoice."

Gene shook his head. "But you think the other side has defensive measures."

Y-9 leaned back in his chair. "That's where we've got you. We've developed countermeasures, nanomachines that will defend the computers. We think they'll work."

Gene burned inside. He wanted to get up and choke the man.

Y-9 suddenly began coughing. He wheezed and choked, sounding as though he were having trouble breathing. His face turned gray as he gasped for breath.

Gene sat there, watching, nonplussed. By the time the Group Leader managed to catch his breath his face was purple. Recovered, he sat back, taking deep breaths. He coughed once more and straightened his collar.

His smile was sheepish and he seemed a little embarrassed. "Must be coming down with a cold myself." He stood. "Well, as I said we'll let you think about it. Let the guards know when you want to see me. Otherwise, the interrogation will begin tomorrow morning."

The man left, and the guards came in and took Gene away.

His cell was an unused windowless office with a cot. Two guards were posted outside the door.

He lay in contemplation, giving particular thought to what had happened in Y-9's office. Gene had wanted the man dead. And the man had begun to choke to death.

Curious. Was there some connection between Gene's wish and its fulfillment?

He tried to imagine a reason for there being such. If this thing stirring in him was supernatural, maybe it was the power of precognition. He had seen what was going to happen.

He had ESP? But why? How? It didn't make sense.

Maybe, just maybe, it was psychokinesis, the ability to influence matter, to manipulate things from a distance. Perhaps he had willed the Group Leader to start choking to death.

No. He knew it was something else.

*It was magic!*

He closed his eyes and tried to imagine what Linda had often tried to explain to him, the lines of force. They were supposed to crisscross, intersect, weave into nodes or focus points, and from those points one drew power. Could he sense them?

He tried. He thought of the weave of fabric, enmeshed strands of fiber. No. Farther apart, looser. Like intersecting pipelines carrying energy, they crosshatched the earth in an endless grid of power. You just had to know, first, that this network was there, and, second, how to tap its power.

How did you tap its power? He thought of a transformer on a high-tension line, stepping down the voltage into usable range, controlling the energy, transforming it into something that could serve useful purposes.

Like what, for instance?

He stood up to try a little experiment. He thought that it would be a fine idea if the shabby plastic cot would lift up in the air. Just rise up, of its own accord, and settle back down.

He had no spells, no incantations. He couldn't work that way. It was simply a matter of focusing power, of directing energy.

Nothing happened.

Okay, use an incantation. Something to concentrate his mind on the task. Maybe that's what incantations were for. Say something, say anything.

"Do it," he said.

The cot didn't do anything.

"Do it. Do it."

He pointed a finger at it.

"Do it. Do it. Do it now."

The cot moved, and it surprised him. Don't blow it, he told himself. It's real, use the power.

"Do it, do it, do it now," he intoned.

One end of the cot rose.

"Do it, cot."

The other end rose and the cot lifted into the air. It floated almost to the ceiling before stopping. He held out both hands and urged the thing back down. It came back down and settled to the floor.

Was that it? Was that his limit? Just being able to move inconsequential objects around? Or was he more powerful than that?

He was feeling very powerful, very powerful indeed. He knew now what had defeated InnerVoice. Not willpower, but magic power.

He sat back down. What would happen if, say, he wished the guards outside the door to lose consciousness? He asked himself how that would be accomplished. The best way would be to imagine the blood draining away from their heads. That would put them out cold. Or maybe it would be better to picture them just keeling over, don't worry about the mechanics of it. No need to—

Something thumped against the door.

He got up and went to it, listening. He heard nothing outside.

How to get out? Imagine the door unlocking, the metal tab pulling out of the slot in the jamb.

He tried the door, and it opened. One of the guards had been slumped against it and he spilled into the room. Gene looked at him. His eyelids were fluttering. The man would be coming around shortly. Gene didn't know how it would be accomplished, but he imagined the guard falling asleep and staying asleep for a long time.

He did the same to the other guard. Neither moved.

He reached for one of their guns, but had second thoughts. He'd never shoot his way out. Besides, he really didn't think he'd need the gun.

He went out a back window.

# GARAGE

"How you comin' under there, Dolbert?"

Dolbert gibbered happily as he turned a ratchet wrench.

"Okay, keep 'er up."

"How's he doing?" Jeremy asked.

"He says he almost has 'er licked."

"Good."

Jeremy went to the picnic basket and pulled out another leg of fried chicken—at least he thought it was chicken. It tasted a little strange, but good. Very good. The food had been supplied by Mrs. Gooch, the Gooch boys' mother, a tall, unsmiling, white-haired woman in a faded flower-print dress. She had brought the basket and left it without a word. Luster invited Jeremy and Isis to dig in, as he wasn't hungry and Dolbert was too busy. Isis had declined but Jeremy had been famished. Besides chicken there were biscuits and corn bread and several cold bottles of soda pop.

Something occurred to Jeremy as he munched. It made him put the chicken down and look at Isis.

She raised her eyebrows questioningly. Jeremy motioned her outside.

"What is it, Jeremy?" Isis asked when they had stepped through the door.

"How the heck are we going to pay for this? I completely forgot."

Isis frowned. "I hadn't thought about it. That is a problem, isn't it?"

"Yeah, they've been so nice."

"We could give them an IOU."

"Boy, I sure wouldn't trust *me* if I were them. And it's going to be hard to get back here to pay them even if they did."

Isis chewed her lip. Then she brightened. "The backup rectifier coil for the graviton polarity generator is wound with gold wire. We could do without it."

"Yeah! What do you figure it's worth? I mean, in Earth money."

"Well, there's approximately twenty troy ounces of pure gold."

"Wow," Jeremy said. "That works out to a bundle!"

"I suppose so."

"If they'll take it."

"Why wouldn't they?"

"I don't know. All I know is, this isn't Earth. A while back I made some crack about Luster's ancestors losing the Civil War. And he said, 'Whut civil war?' Maybe they don't deal in gold here."

"Gold is universally valued," Isis said.

"Let's hope it's interuniversally valued."

They went back in to find that Dolbert was bolting the access plate back on. When he was done he squirmed out from under the craft. He went to the picnic basket, pulled out a bottle of soda, bit the cap off, and spat it out. He upended the bottle into his mouth.

Luster poked his head out of the hatch, grinning triumphantly.

"Computer says everthing's workin' fine now. That grav-eye-ton polarity gizmo just had some metal shavin's cloggin' it up, and that thermocouple gadget weren't cracked at all. It was just busted off its mount. Dolbert put in a new bolt, and she's as good as new." Luster climbed down. "Ah don't know whut we would've done iffen we'd've had t'get parts for this here thing. Would've took months t'order 'em."

"Would have taken a little longer than that," Jeremy said. "Anyway, you guys did a great job."

"Weren't nothin'," Luster said.

"It was marvelous," Isis said. She took Luster's face in her hands, brought his head down, and kissed his forehead.

"Wull, thank you, ma'am," Luster said, beaming.

Isis approached Dolbert. Looking startled, he took off for the back of the garage.

"Dolbert's shy with the women folk," Luster said.

"Okay," Jeremy said. "What do we owe you?"

"Well, now, I'll have t'do some figurin'."

"Look. Uh . . . we don't have any money."

Luster smiled. "Ah kinda figured that."

"We can give you gold."

Luster guffawed. "Gold? Whut the hay-ull would we do with gold?"

"It's not worth anything around here?"

"Shore, iffen yore the gummint."

"The . . . you mean only the government can have gold?"

"That's plumb right. It's illegal t'own the stuff, 'cept fer a little jewelry. Now, there's some folks that deal in it, on the side, like. Know whut ah mean? But Dolbert and I, here—wull, we don't do nothin' whut's agin the law."

"No, no, I . . ." Jeremy scratched his head. "Then I don't know how we're going to pay you."

"Hmm." Luster took off his cap and scratched his head. "Now, that shore is a problem."

Isis took Jeremy's arm. "Will you excuse us for a moment?"

"Shore will, ma'am."

Outside, Isis led Jeremy behind a stand of rusting iceboxes.

"Jeremy, I'm going to offer myself to him."

"Huh? You can't do that."

"It's the only way."

"No. I'm the captain of the ship. I say you can't."

"Jeremy, we have to get back, and soon."

"No! There's gotta be another way."

"There's no other way, Jeremy."

Jeremy opened his mouth to retort, then closed it. He looked stricken.

"I still love you," she said, and kissed him.

She went back into the garage.

Jeremy sat down on an upturned wooden bucket and stared off into the bedsprings and the fenders and the piles of old tires.

A few moments later Isis returned with a strange look on her face. Jeremy stood up.

"He wants you."

Jeremy's mouth dropped open again.

He steeled himself and went into the garage, where Luster awaited him with an enigmatic smile.

"Take us for a ride," Luster said.

"Huh?"

"Take us for a ride in that there spaceship of yores."

"Oh. Well, I can't do that. First, I don't know if we can get back home. Second, I might not be able to bring you back here."

"That's fine by me."

"Really? But . . ."

"Shore would like to ride in that thing. Besides, you owe Dolbert and me forty-seven fifty."

"Uh, yeah. Well, heck, okay. There's room for two if you squeeze."

"Dolbert! C'mon. These here space people say they'll take us for a ride."

Dolbert came out of the oily shadows tittering his delight.

"Stand by to engage thrusters," Jeremy said.

"Standing by," the Toshiba said. "But we're not going to have any better luck this time than we did before."

"You have coordinates for the castle."

"Thing is, we're going to have to negotiate the interuniversal medium again, and it's all screwed up."

"We're not going to hang around in it this time. We have the readings. Don't we, Isis?"

"We have tons of good data," Isis said.

"So, what's the problem?" Jeremy said.

"The problem is that the supercontinuum is undergoing so much instability that it's going to make vector analysis an iffy proposition. That means there'll be no computing our relative velocity and therefore our momentum at the point of entry into the metrical frame of the destination subcontinuum."

"Spit that out again in English."

"We don't have any goddamn brakes on this thing."

"Oh. Well, do the best you can."

"R-r-roger!"

"Engage thrusters!"

"Engaged!"

The inside of the garage disappeared from view, replaced by a shifting, inchoate nothingness.

"Shore is pretty, space," Luster said.

"That's nonspace," Jeremy said.

"Shore is pretty, anyway."

"Hold on to your chitterlings, brothers and sisters," the To-shiba said gaily. "It's going to be a rough ride."

# TEMPLE

"UNCLE MORDECAI!"

The man in the electric-blue leisure suit squinted through thick-lensed glasses. "What are you telling me, I'm related to you?"

"Not by blood. You married my aunt Jacinda."

"Jackie! Good woman, rest her soul. You're—?"

"Incarnadine."

"I thought you looked familiar. You were young when I saw you last. You still look young. How old are you now?"

"Three hundred fifty-six."

"A baby. Still at the castle?"

"It's home."

"I enjoyed it when I lived there."

Incarnadine looked around at the opulence of the temple. "You have a nice place here."

"It used to be a good business back in the old days. Now nothing. Bad location."

"To say nothing of those protection spells."

"Hey, I got quite an investment here. You should see the insurance premiums I gotta pay for vandalism. It's murder today to run a business."

"Yeah, I'll bet. Uncle Mordy, you don't live here, do you?"

"Here, in this barn? No. I got a place in Palm Beach. I'm retired now."

Incarnadine was astonished. "You have a portal between here and Earth?"

"For years. Why?"

Incarnadine turned to Jonath, who was still prostrate on the stone floor of the sanctuary. "You think I'm a powerful magician? Here's one who can do something I can't." He turned back to Mordecai. "You're the only magician I know who can punch a portal between universes without castle power."

Mordecai shrugged. "It's a simple trick."

"I'll bet. Where is it?"

"Right in the back. Let's go back to the house where we can talk, I can offer you a drink, whatever. Come on. Oh, your helper, here. You're invited, too, pal."

Incarnadine helped Jonath up, then introduced him.

"A pleasure," Mordecai said. "Come on back."

Mordecai led them behind the base of the statue, through a doorway, and into a less voluminous chamber. Set into the base of the far wall was a small square opening.

"I just found out I got problems with this thing. When I heard the alarm go off in the temple I came running and found that it shrank on me. Look at that. Like a cat door. I had to crawl through the damn thing. You know what's going on?"

"Yeah," Incarnadine said. "The reason I'm here. The inter-universal medium is undergoing stress, and anomalies like this are happening all over."

"Well, let's get in here before it chops someone in half." Mordecai got down on his hands and knees and crawled through the opening.

The room on the other side was a large paneled game room with a bar, couches and chairs, and a pool table. Mordecai led his guests through it and up the stairs to the first floor of a very large house. A hallway came out into a spacious living room with a view of a manicured lawn and garden. The property ended at a canal and slip, where a large cabin cruiser was moored.

Decorator Swedish modern furniture graced the room, and modern paintings, among them what looked like an original Paul Klee, hung on the walls.

"Great place," Incarnadine said.

"My late wife, Leah. She had taste. And a lot of money, God rest her soul. Sit down, sit down. You want a drink?"

"No thanks." Incarnadine sat on the sofa. Jonath remained standing.

Mordecai seated himself in the matching white leather chair. "So, what's the story?"

"I was doing some military advising in Merydion—"

"*Those* clowns!"

"The same. Anyway, I detected some cosmic disturbance and checked the portal. It had constricted to a pinhole, and I was stranded."

"What were you going to do at the temple?"

"Cast a teleportation spell to get me home."

"Whoa, you were taking quite a chance. The magic there is a little tricky."

"So I found out. I had some trouble with your protection devices. Good thing they were on automatic. If I'd had to deal with you—"

"Forget about the teleportation thing. Those spells are monsters. You could arrive DOA back at the castle."

"There was the risk, but I had no choice. The portal was blocked."

"So, you're here now. What's the problem?"

"Reports are that the Earth portal went strange. It could mean that the connection between here and the castle is completely gone. It was anchored in Pennsylvania, and I guess I should go up there and check things out, but I'm pretty sure it's disappeared."

"I haven't been back to the castle in years," Mordecai said. "Wasn't the portal in New York for a while?"

"For a number of years, but Ferne moved it to Pennsylvania."

"Ferne. I remember Ferne. Beautiful girl. Gorgeous!"

"Yes. She died last year, I'm afraid."

"I'm sorry to hear that. I really am."

"Anyway," Incarnadine said, "now that I'm here I'll try to summon the portal, if you don't mind."

"Be my guest. You need any help?"

"Let me try alone first."

Incarnadine went to a blank section of wall and stood about five feet away. He stretched out his arms and began moving them in patterns, tracing a curvilinear figure.

He did this for about a minute before stopping. He sighed. "Thank the gods."

"What for?"

"The portal's still here. They reported at the castle that some strange world had popped up at the locus of the Earth aspect, and that made me worry that there was no wormhole at all between Earth and the castle. But from the indications I got just now, the wormhole still exists. Problem is, it's writhing around like crazy and there's no controlling it. It's wild, totally wild, as it used to be before I fiddled with it very recently."

"Then all you have to do is find it," Mordecai said.

"That's going to be tough." Incarnadine sat down. "Earth magic's always been my bugaboo. Had a devil of a job wrestling with it last time I was here. Ferne did the anchoring in Pennsylvania. My brother Trent's good at this sort of thing, too, but he's on vacation and can't be reached. And I have to get back soon. I must deal with the cosmic instability before it gets much worse."

"Well, you got a problem," Mordecai said.

"Yup."

"Good thing you came to me."

"Uncle Mordy, would you help me?"

"What, I'm going to refuse a relative? You're in trouble, you need a hand. Listen, I got nothing better to do."

"I would certainly appreciate it."

"It's nothing. You want to get going now, or you want some lunch first? The cook's off, but there's some corned beef in the fridge, a little coleslaw —"

"Time is a factor."

"Time, he says. There's always time. The universe has time out the kazoo. There's no end of it."

"Do you think we can summon the portal?"

Mordecai leaned forward. "You got a wild portal. Summon it you can't do. *Chase* it you gotta do."

"How?"

"Don't you worry how. We'll find out how. When was the last time you ate?"

"Days."

"Days!" Mordecai appealed to Jonath, who stood solemnly by. "Days, he says. Magic he can't do without, food . . . *phfft*! Who needs it. Uh, listen, fellah, why don't you sit down and take a load off your feet?"

Jonath dutifully sat on the couch.

"He don't say much, does he?" Mordecai commented.

"Mordy, Jonath has never seen Earth, or anything like it."

"I forgot. Pardon me, Jonath."

Jonath silently nodded.

"Anyway. Listen, son, you gotta eat. The body can take a lot of punishment, but you gotta take care of it."

"How old are you, Uncle Mordy?"

Mordecai held a hand up. "Don't ask!"

"I won't. Getting back to business. Has anything untoward been happening here? I was wondering if the cosmic disturbance has had an effect."

"Yep. Big earthquake in California."

"Ye gods, the big one in L.A.?"

"No, in Frisco. Terrible!"

"Then there's less time than I thought. We really have to get going."

Mordecai shrugged. "So, let's get going. We'll pick up something to eat on the way."

He led them downstairs again, turning left at the foot of the stairs. They went through a steel fire door and into a huge garage. Three automobiles were parked there: a silver Rolls-Royce, a white Mercedes, and something of an antique—a gargantuan mint-green 1959 Cadillac Coupe de Ville, bulbous chrome agleam, wicked rear fins razor-sharp and eager to impale pedestrians. In its exuberant and flamboyant crassness, the car was nonpareil.

They got in, Incarnadine in front, Jonath in the rear. Mordecai took a black plastic box out of his pocket and pressed the stud on it. The wide garage door opened. Mordecai started the car and drove out.

"Nice house," Incarnadine said as the Cadillac rolled down the driveway.

"It's comfortable," Mordecai said, clicking the door control again. "What do you think of this old buggy, eh?"

"It's one *rara avis*."

"You can't buy quality like this anymore. They built them solid then."

"That Rolls didn't look shabby."

Mordecai waved disdainfully. "Overpriced. This I have outfitted with a couple spells. Trouble is you can't find leaded gas anymore, so it sits."

They cruised through palm-lined residential streets, sumptuous homes to either side.

"This neighborhood's certainly not for the hoi polloi," Incarnadine said.

"Some nice people around here. Some not so nice. But you live and let live."

After six or seven blocks, Mordecai turned onto a main boulevard lined with boutiques and trendy shops.

"What you got here is Rodeo Drive East," Mordecai said. "The prices would scare you."

"No doubt," Incarnadine said.

"Start with the portal-summoning. First push that third radio button. That trips a facilitation spell."

Incarnadine pushed the button and began concentrating. He tested the ether with his right hand, angling it this way and that. "I get the feeling it's east of here. Out to sea?"

"In the Bermuda Triangle," Mordecai said. "Where else? Maybe we should take the boat out." He shook his head. "Nah, we'd never catch it in the boat."

"I'll try to reel it in."

"You do that. Open your window. The air-conditioning's busted."

They swung through town and veered onto a business-clogged four-lane highway.

"Listen, there's a nice deli in West Palm Beach. Friend of mine used to own it. A nice Cuban fellow bought it and he's doing a wonderful job."

"No time, Uncle Mordy. There."

Mordecai looked. "McDonald's?"

Mordecai wheeled into the lot and stopped in front of the take-out ordering station.

A woman's voice came through a tinny speaker. "Good afternoon, can I help you?"

Incarnadine spoke up. "Give me a fish sandwich, a large order of fries, and a small Coke. Jonath, are you hungry?"

Jonath nodded.

"We also want a large Chicken McNuggets."

"Any fries with that?"

"Right, large fries and another Coke. You're gonna love this, Jonath."

"Me," Mordecai said, "I like to sit inside when I eat, have a nice piece of fish. Give me a strawberry milkshake, honey!"

They pulled around the building to the pickup window. After

208 *John DeChancie*

a short wait, the food came through. Mordecai paid, and they left.

"It's moving in, Uncle Mordy," Incarnadine said, mouth full of fries. "The f'cilitation spell's working."

"It's a doozy. Makes everything happen."

The huge Caddy swerved between lanes, drawing honks from annoyed drivers.

"Blow it out your keister!" Mordecai drove with one hand on the mint steering wheel, the other casually holding the milkshake. "Listen, Inky. You say you don't know where in the castle the portal's other end is?"

"No, if it's whipping around here, it's doing it castleside, too."

"Hmm. I can get the car through, a portal's got fuzzy edges. But if we come out into a hallway . . . Remember to push that second button if we get into trouble. That's a protection spell."

"I'll remember," Incarnadine said. "All I can do is try to influence the other end. I'll try to make it come out in the laboratory. It's mostly empty floor space and there should be some stopping room. With the protect spell we ought to be all right."

"We'll be fine," Mordecai said with a serene smile.

"How do you like the food of the gods, Jonath?" Incarnadine asked, looking back.

Jonath swallowed. "I have never tasted such fare."

"Try it with the sweet-and-sour sauce."

Mordecai turned off onto a ramp and squealed around the long turn down to the Interstate.

"What are you getting now?" Mordecai asked.

"It's close. I think it knows we're chasing it."

"Damn frisky things, portals."

Mordecai bulled into the traffic stream, attracting more retaliatory honking. Still smiling, he took a sip of milkshake, left elbow angled out the window. The wisps of blue-white hair on the back of his head stood out straight, fluttering in the window wash.

"Up ahead somewhere," Incarnadine said. "It's weaving in and out."

"It wants to be caught," Mordecai said.

Incarnadine wolfed down the rest of his fish sandwich and wiped his mouth. "Can you get up more speed?"

"We got three hundred and ninety cubic inches in the engine and a four-barrel carburetor."

Mordecai eased the accelerator pedal to the floor and the car's engine throbbed with gas-guzzling power. Expertly and with equanimity, Mordecai piloted the huge vehicle through foaming channels of traffic, blithely weaving from lane to lane. More horns blared, dopplering in anger.

"I see the little devil now," he said. "There she is."

"You have sharp eyes, Uncle Mordy."

"These glasses are fake, you know. Nothing wrong with my eyes at all. Twenty-twenty. Well, maybe not that good, but I really only need them for reading. How d'you like Florida, by the way?"

"Nice and hot."

"Ever spend much time here?"

"No, not much. I can see it now."

Ahead was a fuzzy area of grayness, a shimmering sheet like heated air rising from the hot asphalt. It seemed to move with the traffic, shifting from side to side.

"There we go," Mordecai said. "We'll have you back in the castle in no time."

Behind them, a siren began to whoop.

Incarnadine looked back. "This could be trouble."

"Don't worry. I got handicapped plates."

Mordecai shifted lanes, passed a bus, then swerved back to overtake a car via the inside lane. The speedometer was edging past eighty-five, muggy Florida air blasting through the open windows.

The siren was getting closer. Mordecai swung into the outside lane again.

"Whoops, there it goes!"

"There's an exit," Incarnadine said calmly.

The portal had veered to the right, heading off the road. Mordecai careened toward the exit and nearly took the front end off a camper. A chorus of horns screeched their execration.

The caddy shot onto an exit ramp and thundered down it in pursuit of the portal, the siren following. The ramp merged with a two-lane road, which Mordecai roared onto, ignoring the stop sign.

Trees flanked the blacktop, edging a wide shoulder. The police car was gaining now, its whirling red lights dancing in Mordecai's rearview mirror.

"We may not make it," Incarnadine said.

In the back seat, Jonath, quite unruffled, popped the last McNugget into his mouth. A smile crossed his lips.

"You married?" Mordecai asked.

"Yes," Incarnadine said, eyes caged front.

"Children?"

"Two, boy and a girl."

"Wonderful," Mordecai said. "A man should be married."

"I think we lost it," Incarnadine said, leaning forward to peer through the wraparound windshield.

The road bent sharply to the left up ahead. The portal was nowhere in sight.

"We better think about slowing down," Incarnadine said. "I'll pay your ticket—or bail you out."

"Don't worry about it. I got friends in this county, and a wonderful lawyer."

"Wait till the cops get a load of our getups—*Mordecai*!"

The portal had stopped just around the bend and was waiting for them, a vague patch of wavering nothingness. Mordecai's foot didn't have time to hit the brake pedal.

# Inferno, Then Paradiso

THE LAVA FLOWED, the ash rained down. Smoke and fire rose from gashes in the earth. The tee was a bed of cinders that set the soles of their shoes to smoking. Thaxton had the honor, and drove into a magma flow. One lost stroke. He hit another and the ball bounced among the rocks and disappeared into a crevice.

Two. Gritting his teeth, Thaxton got out a new ball and shot again. The ball fell on the narrow fairway, where a herd of hippogriffs pecked and scratched. One got to the ball and gobbled it.

Thaxton threw his club into the bubbling tar pit. "Right! That's it, that's the bloody end! I'm damned if I'll put up with any more of this!"

Dalton said, "I don't blame you this time."

Above, harpies shrieked their dismay, and great dragons soared on thermal updrafts. Smoke poured from the great volcanic cone that rose against the sun to the right. The air was filled with flying debris.

"Oh, damn. Damn!" Thaxton stamped his foot. With an air of resignation, he took out his three-wood, teed another ball, and drove. The ball bonked a hippogriff and hid in tall grass.

"To hell with it," Thaxton said, rebagging his club.

After Dalton drove they struck out for the wastes, Cerberus following. They passed basilisks sunning themselves on the rocks. None spoke, none seemed to care; needless to say, the men paid them no mind.

Tremors shook the ground, steam-venting chasms opening up here and there. Dalton nearly fell into one, Cerberus clamping down on his shirttail to save him. His ball was lost, so he calmly played another.

Thaxton finally found his ball and chopped at it to get it out of the rough, then hit a good four-iron toward the green. The earth split where the ball landed.

Without saying a word, Thaxton dropped his last ball.

The erupting volcano exploded, raining ash and fire down on the course. By the time the men got to putting, the surface of the green was a smoking ruin and they were dodging boulders the size of cars. Thaxton virtually herded his ball into the cup.

"Make your putt!" he shouted over the din.

Dalton putted for a sextuple bogey, and they got out of there.

The land seemed to change as they ran. The thunder faded, and the smoke cleared. It was like passing from one diorama to the next in a museum. The sky became blue and trees sprang up. The grass thickened and greened, as did the shrubbery. Wildflowers bloomed in the rough. A soft breeze began to blow, carrying the scent of jasmine and lilac. The sun was bright and beautiful, sparkling off the lake and drenching the course in a yellow glow.

The fairway ahead was long and broad, few bunkers to mar its manicured prettiness.

On an oak near the tee was a sign:

## HOLE 17½

Underneath, on a picnic table, was a bucket of ice with a magnum of champagne in it. Two inverted glasses rested on a sheet of white linen.

"How nice," Dalton said. "Compliments of the management, I assume."

"Or the Devil," Thaxton said, taking the bottle out and ripping off the foil top. He deftly worked the cork up until it popped and flew. He poured.

Dalton sipped. "The real thing, from the Champagne region."

"I'll take your word for it." Thaxton gulped it down and poured himself another glass.

Their clothes were in tatters, great holes burned in them. They were snowy with ash and their shoes were scarred and burned. Thaxton poured out a stream of champagne for Cerberus, and the dog lapped it up with relish.

All three were slightly tipsy by the time they were ready to play golf, but this didn't seem to affect the play. Both players drove deep and true.

The fairway smelled of fresh-mown grass; ducks, simple un-mythological ducks, paddled and dipped in the lake, and birds—robins, sparrows, and blue jays—twitted in the bordering woods. The sun shone down. Apple trees were heavy with late-summer fruit, and bees buzzed among the clover in the rough. They were through the fairway and onto the green in three.

The green was quiet save for the *plock* of balls dropping into the cup. Both men putted for par.

Thaxton replaced the pin and smiled. "Well, that's that."

Dalton sighed. "Yes. Best game I ever played. I'll always remember it." He slid the putter into the bag.

"Who could forget it?" Thaxton shouldered his bag. "And now we pay the piper."

"Yes." Dalton solemnly nodded. "Yes, we do."

They walked through trees, following a path that bore gently uphill.

"I'd like to think I lived my life as well as I played that game," Dalton said.

"Did you?"

"No, not as well. Sometimes I gave up, withdrew, didn't care."

"We all do that," Thaxton said.

"But you get older, and you learn. There's always time for redemption, for changing, for doing better. It's never too late."

"Well, I learned a few things, I must say," Thaxton said. "Never say die, keep your pecker up, and all that."

"Good outlook."

When they came out of the woods the Devil was waiting for them.

He was sitting on a bench by the first tee reading a newspaper and smoking a thick green cigar. His scaly legs were crossed, the talons on his feet long and sharp. When the men approached, he lowered the newspaper, and a fangy smile spread across his gargoyle face. He took the cigar from his mouth.

"Enjoy your game, gentlemen?"

"Very much," Dalton said. "I don't think we ever want to do it again, but it was an experience."

"Oh, but you must do it again. In fact, that's the whole point of this place."

"Uh, what's the point?"

"Wait a minute. You're lost souls, aren't you?"

"No."

The gargoyle frowned. "You're not?"

"Not quite," Thaxton said. "I'm afraid we blundered into your domain quite by accident."

The gargoyle took a puff. "Well, I don't see as how that makes a difference. You're here, and you have to play."

"Why?" Dalton asked.

The gargoyle snorted derisively. "*Why.* Now, see, that's the kind of question that really bugs me. This is my universe, I run it, I set the rules. It's my show. When you run the show, certain rights and immunities accrue to you, one of which is not to be constantly annoyed by piteous wails about how absurd it all is, about how senseless and futile it seems, and so on. Screw that noise! It's the only game in town, so play already. Quit belly-aching."

"I think we've learned that," Dalton said. "But you only have to go around once. Once is enough."

"Not if I say it isn't," the gargoyle said. "There's the first hole. Go tee up."

"There comes a time," Dalton said, "when you have to stand up to the big guy and say, hey, that's enough."

Frantically Thaxton shook Dalton's shoulder and pointed. "There it is!"

The portal, or what could have been it, was flitting about in the meadow behind the gargoyle. The phenomenon was a region of vagueness that now and then took the shape of a doorway. It floated, dipped, scudded, then rose into the air and settled once again.

"Run for it!" Dalton shouted, dropping his bag.

"Wait just a damned minute," the gargoyle said, throwing down the cigar and rising.

Cerberus leaped on the monster and knocked him back against

the bench. The bench flipped and dog and gargoyle went rolling in the grass. The two duffers took off across the meadow.

The gargoyle got up and retrieved his cigar. Puffing thoughtfully, he watched them chase down the strange doorway and disappear into it. Then the phenomenon vanished, leaving the meadow to its bees and flowers and other peaceful inhabitants.

The gargoyle turned to Cerberus, who had also watched.

''Hell, I was going to take them to dinner.''

# LABORATORY

OSMIRIK WAS SITTING at the workstation reading when something hit with a crash. He fell off his chair, then lurched to his feet. Frightened out of his wits, he looked toward the rear of the lab.

The *Voyager* was back. It had materialized at a good clip and smashed through some old lab equipment, finally hitting the far stone wall. The hull was intact, though the front end was crinkled a bit.

By the time Osmirik reached it the hatch had opened and a strange towheaded man in a battered baseball cap had his head poked out. He was grinning.

"Is this here another planet?" he asked.

"You are in Castle Perilous," a surprised Osmirik responded.

The man looked around. "Shore is somethin'." He climbed out, and was followed by an even stranger man.

"This here's Dolbert, and ah'm Luster."

"Osmirik," the librarian said, bowing.

"We got it, Ozzie!" Jeremy poked his head out. "We got the data!"

"I am pleased," Osmirik said.

Jeremy waved a mini-disk. "It's all here."

"Are you harmed?"

"Oh, we got shaken up a bit, but we all had seat belts on."

Jeremy got out, followed by Isis, who threw her arms around him. They embraced.

"No time now," Jeremy said, breaking away. "Got to get this into the program!" He started running across the floor.

"Jeremy, look out!"

Something huge and green flashed by Jeremy, barely missing him. There was a roar and a tremendous crash.

Everybody looked toward the adjacent wall. Out of nowhere had come this huge gaudy automobile. Now it was crumpled against the wall with its hood sprung and most of its windows shattered. Fenders fell away and white smoke issued from the engine.

They all rushed to it.

"Lord Incarnadine!" Jeremy tried to open the deformed door; it wouldn't budge.

"I'm okay," Incarnadine said, crawling through the window. Luster and Jeremy helped. "Get the old man out. Careful, he may be injured."

"Injured, schminjured," Mordecai said, his head popping above the roof. "You hit the button in time, we're okay. Okay?"

Isis and Dolbert helped Mordecai out of the wreck, then were surprised to discover Jonath. Jonath wasn't surprised in the least. More gods. Fine.

"Where did you come from?" Jeremy asked in astonishment.

"Florida," Incarnadine said. "Never mind, explain later. Now, about that data from the interuniversal medium—"

"We got it."

"You got it?" Incarnadine caught sight of the *Voyager*. "I see. Well, good work. Let's go take a look at that cosmos-fixing program."

As they walked to the workstation the lab door opened and at least a dozen Incarnadines filed in. The first one said, "There you are! Nice operation you have here. Can we take a look at it?"

"We're busy," Incarnadine said. "Look around but don't get in the way."

"Well, excuse us for existing."

"I'll deal with that later," Incarnadine said.

# WORLD

HE CROUCHED IN THE TALL GRASS between two fiberglass buildings. Two soldiers walked by on the company street between the tents and the buildings. He waited till they passed, then stood up and began running his fingers over the outline of a window on the side of the building.

He knew Alice was inside. Clairvoyance? Call it "knowing the location of things and people that matter." This was his magic; he had discovered it, so far as he knew. He could invent the nomenclature.

The window fell out, its screws and washers loose and falling free. He caught it and put it carefully and quietly down.

"Alice?" he called softly.

She came to the window. Inside was a storage space converted to a cell. She came through the window headfirst and he eased her to the ground.

They crouched in the weeds. More soldiers passed on either side of them. Voices. There didn't seem to be any way to get out of the compound without being seen.

He suddenly had a wild idea. Why not?

"Alice, listen. We're going to get up and walk out of this camp. No one will see us. They won't be able to see us. Understand?"

She nodded.

He took her hand and they stood. He led her out of the weeds and onto the street. Two soldiers were coming toward them. He steered a path past them, not hurrying, trying to be nonchalant, confident, cool.

The soldier on the right looked at them, slowed, and frowned. He stopped and narrowed his eyes. He shook his head. Then he looked away and caught up with his companion.

They kept walking. Three more soldiers passed them; there was no reaction at all.

They walked right out of the camp, heading toward the VTOL field. He had another wild idea.

The cockpit of the VTOL was carpeted with dials and gauges, all incomprehensible to him. It didn't matter. He sat in the pilot seat and grabbed the controls. Alice sat beside him. He reached for the hatch and locked the compartment.

He closed his eyes and thought about gremlins. Little gremlins who knew every rivet and bolt in the craft, who knew its every function and capacity. He was in command of those gremlins, those little imps. He would tell them what to do and when to do it. They nattered and mumbled, crawling all over the craft, climbing on the wings, getting into the engines, squirming through the wiring. They were everywhere, and he commanded them.

He set them to work.

Start the engine.

The starter motor cranked, turbine blades began to whir, then picked up speed. Fuel pumps pumped, and kerosene ignited with a roar.

Take her up.

Slowly the craft began to lift, its directional engine nozzles funneling the exhaust toward the ground. The vectored blast provided stability and safety, creating a magic carpet of force that defied gravity, working its own kind of magic.

He put his hand on the thrust lever and the other on the stick. He slid his feet onto the pedals. He didn't know how they worked, but it didn't matter, either.

Guide me.

He turned the craft east and vectored forward. The craft gained altitude and speed. He pushed forward on the throttle, and the nozzles automatically rotated toward the horizontal as the air-speed increased, their attitude computer-controlled.

The craft rose over the trees and headed for the darkening sky. He looked at Alice. She was smiling, confident as ever. He smiled back, then glued his eyes to the instruments he didn't understand.

He found the altimeter. It already showed five hundred something—feet, meters? The airspeed indicator was marked out in tens, and the needle pointed to one hundred. He pushed the throttle forward, keeping the foot pedals even. The craft jumped forward into full aerodynamic flight. Now the craft was a jet airplane. He didn't know how to fly a glider, let alone a jet airplane.

But for a master magician everything is easy. Let your familiars do the work. Anything goes. Pumpkin, become a carriage. In you go, Cinderella, honey. You're late for the ball.

They streaked east, deserted farmland rolling beneath them. It wasn't long before pursuit craft came up behind, faster than he had thought of going. He pushed both the throttle and the stick forward, and the craft dove and picked up speed.

His pursuit mimicked him. The lead craft fired a preliminary burst, nothing serious, just letting him know that they were around. They probably didn't want to lose an expensive VTOL. After all, where could he go? They'd just follow until he either gave up or was forced to land.

But he wasn't worried. The more he did and the longer he did it, the more powerful he felt, and the more things he felt himself capable of doing. He thought he'd try some more experiments. This aircraft had a certain operational speed capacity—or "capability," as engineers insisted on saying. Nothing could push it over that limit. But what would happen, say, if from out of nowhere, extra fuel materialized in the combustion chamber and added to the mixture? Just that. A little extra fuel. Like an afterburner. Whoosh.

The craft shot forward, and the flashing lights of the pursuing gunships dwindled.

That had been most satisfying. Keep it up, gremlins. The bleak countryside rolled by, darkening in the twilight. He banked to the right, using the pedals and the stick, correcting course. The portal was . . . where? Ahead. Another few miles yet.

The pursuit was catching up. Apparently these craft had real afterburners. Yes, now he understood. How about a little more fuel in the combustion chamber. No, let's not do something that might tempt physical reality. Don't want to overheat the chamber or cause it to explode. Do something else.

Invisibility? It had worked before. But maybe he couldn't do it for something as big as the aircraft. Anyway, the pursuit probably had infrared scopes and heat-seeking missiles.

He imagined what they would see through those scopes when they looked, and what the missiles would see with their heat-hungry eyes.

Multiple images! A hundred targets in their sights. A thousand! Diverging now, all heading in different directions, scattering to the winds.

That is apparently what they saw. The pursuing ships fell back in confusion, then split off in different directions.

He continued on. The portal was below. He powered down and the computers took over, rotating the nozzles and laying down the magic carpet.

The craft floated to the ground, blasting the tall hay in the twilight. The landing gear deployed and the craft settled. The whine of the engines died.

"We're here, Alice."

Alice looked out at a lonely hillside. She didn't see the standing rectangle of darkness near the craft.

"There," he said. "See that? It's the entrance to my world."

They got out and walked toward it. A night wind was up. It was almost dark.

A VTOL came screaming out of the dusk, guns chattering.

He became angry. He had had enough. He raised his hand, finger pointing. He knew now that he could do anything, that he could, if he wanted, be a god in this world, a world that was beyond strangeness, beyond hope.

A bolt of yellow fire left his finger and lanced toward the attacking craft, enveloping it in blinding luminescence.

The VTOL blossomed into a fireball. The burning wreckage fell out of the crepuscular sky.

They watched the dry brush burn.

"I didn't want to do that," he said. "But I did. I'm only human."

"You did what you had to do," she said.

They stood before the portal. He could see the stone of the castle's walls.

He grasped her shoulders. "Alice, do you want to come with me? This is not my world. I have to leave it, and I won't be

back. This is your world. Do you want to leave it forever, leave
it in the hands of InnerVoice? Or do you want to stay and change
it, fight InnerVoice?''

The wind blew the hay around and stirred the trees, the sound
almost drowning out the soft chirp of crickets.

"I want to stay," she said.

"I thought you would. Listen to me. I'm a great magician,
and I'm going to cast a spell on you. It will be a very special
kind of spell. I will give you the gift of immunity. They can
never saddle you with InnerVoice again. Your body will fight it
off. You will be immune to it. But there's more. You will be
able to pass on this ability to anyone you meet, anyone you come
in contact with. It will be like passing on a disease, but it will
be a benevolent disease. And the people you give it to will be
able to pass it on to other people. It will be a gift that will be
shared among people all over this world. In time, InnerVoice
will be eradicated, and there will be freedom. Do you understand me?''

"Yes, Gene."

"Good. I'm going to leave you in a moment."

A few stars were out. The Big Dipper was up in the northern
sky. He followed the pointers to the polar star, then turned east.

He pointed. "The Outforces are that way. I want you to get
into the aircraft and fly about thirty miles east."

"But I can't—"

"Yes, you can." He laid a hand on her forehead. He imagined
all the power and all the knowledge that he had flowing from
him and into her through the channel of his arm. A tingling went
through him, and she gave a little shiver.

"I've just given you the power. This kind of thing could happen in this world only once. The power comes from some kind
of flux, some kind of flow between two very different universes
when there's a tiny opening between them, as there is now. I
don't know how long it will last. I don't think it will last very
long, Alice, so you must leave now."

She drew close to him. "Thank you. Thank you for all you've
done. I'll always remember you. You gave me my name."

They embraced. Then she turned and went to the craft.

He watched her get in and close the hatch. She looked as
though she did it every day.

The engines started and the exhaust beat the hay around. The
craft levitated straight up, rotated its nose toward the east, and

moved off. It flew over the trees and out of sight. He listened to the sound of her engines fading in the night.

He looked at the stars again. They looked the same as they did on the world in which he was born.

He turned and walked back into the castle, his powers fading with every step.

Back to reality.

# KEEP—NEAR
## THE GUEST RESIDENCE

"I'VE NEVER BEEN more hungry in my life," Thaxton said.

"Me neither," Dalton said.

Something strange was coming down the hall. It looked a bit like Snowclaw, but it was yellow.

The strange creature ran past them, and for some reason, despite the fact that it was the most fearsome kind of beast one could imagine, it looked frightened.

It had reason. Something was chasing it. They heard a strangely familiar chuttering sound and turned. The thing that made the noise looked for all the world . . . actually there was no question about it. It was a giant floating chain saw, buzzing loudly and angrily, and it was hot on the beast's tail.

The erstwhile golfers watched the anomalous machine go past. It paid them no mind at all.

"What do you make of that?" Thaxton wanted to know.

"No comment. Obviously a lot has been going on."

They continued down the hall until they ran into Linda Barclay and the beautiful, red-haired Sheila Jankowski.

Linda ran up to Dalton and threw her arms around him.

"Whoa, girl," he said. "We're all right!"

"We were so worried about you!" Linda looked with dismay at their smudged faces and the singed and tattered remains of their spiffy golf outfits. "My God, what happened to you? What were you two doing?"

"Golfing," Thaxton said.

She kissed them both, then said, "You wouldn't believe what's been going on here. First, all the aspects went on the fritz, then some goofy twin of Gene shows up and stirs up all kinds of trouble, and then some goofy double of Incarnadine barges in with six hundred nasty Guardsmen, and then I almost freak out when *my* double tries to *kill* me, and—" She started coughing and couldn't stop.

"Take it easy," Dalton said, thumping her back. "Calm down, Linda, honey."

Wearing a beautiful vacation suntan, Sheila said, "She's been through a lot. She told me all about it. The thing about her double is weird."

"What I want to know," Dalton said, "is what the animated chain saws are all about."

"It's a spell we cooked up together," Sheila said. "The castle was full of people who didn't belong here. The situation was a complete mess. We wanted something really frightening that would chase them all back to where they belonged, and that's what we came up with. The saws pick out strangers, anyone who isn't from this world, and, like, harass them. A lot."

Linda coughed and said, "Yeah, they really did the trick. All the strange Guardsmen are gone, and most of the yellow Snowclaws."

"That's the other thing I wanted to ask about," Dalton said. "The yellow Snowclaws. But maybe I better wait."

"We'll talk about it over dinner," Linda said. "Are you hungry? Some of the castle cooks came back already, so there might be some food up in the Queen's Hall."

"Well, let's go. But what's this about your nearly getting killed?"

"It was my double. I must have some sort of deep nasty streak in me, because—"

Linda stopped when she saw Gene come out of a side passage.

"You're still here?" she said coldly.

"Hello," Gene said.

"Where did you get that baggy outfit? It looks ridiculous. By the way, aren't you surprised to find me still alive?"

Gene looked at Sheila, then at Thaxton and Dalton, then back at Linda.

Linda said, "When I saw her pull the gun, I materialized a bulletproof vest under my blouse. I didn't expect darts, of course, and the dart did penetrate the vest, but it didn't break the skin. I faked passing out, and then . . ." Linda stopped, disturbed by Gene's curious stare. Only then did she realize who it was.

"Gene!"

She jumped on him and nearly knocked him over.

# LABORATORY

THE MAINFRAME HUMMED and bubbled, whirred and clicked. Tiny sparks ran through a glass tube in one component, wheels spun in another. It was the strangest of machines. But it was working superbly.

"The program's running fine," Jeremy said, his eyes fixed on the screen. "It's nearly done."

He took a bite of Hostess Twinkie.

Isis, Luster, Dolbert, and Mordecai stood behind him. Osmirik and Jonath were talking in another part of the lab. Osmirik was showing him some very interesting books.

"Shore is an interestin' place," Luster said.

"Oh, you'll love the castle," Mordecai said. "It's like a resort in the Catskills. All that's missing is the social director."

"I wish we could get some results," Isis said. "I hope Lord Incarnadine will let us know what readings he's getting on his instruments."

Jeremy turned around in the swivel chair. "He said the effects wouldn't be spectacular. Things will just right themselves, calm down, and that will be that. But just think. What we're doing in this room is affecting the whole universe. All the universes!"

"It's a big responsibility," Isis said. "It was a big job. But you did it, Jeremy. You got us through."

"With a little help from you, Isis. With just a little help from you."

"But that's simply my job. I'm a program, remember. I serve the user."

"You serve me just fine." He smiled up at her.

"Ah'd like to see the rest of this here castle," Luster said. "Iffen it wouldn't be too much trouble."

"I'll be glad to show you around," Mordecai said. "I still remember how the place is laid out. You have to watch yourself, though. It can be tricky."

"Yeah," Jeremy said. "Be careful the first few weeks. After that you'll get used to the place and it'll be like home."

"Wish there was a way t'get word to Momma," Luster said.

"We have the coordinates for your universe. If you guys can fix the *Sidewise Voyager*, we can take you right home. Think you can do it again?"

"Well, ah don't rightly know," Luster said. "Dolbert, you think fixin' that there contraption will be a problem?"

Dolbert thought about it, then guffawed.

"Dolbert says it'll be a challenge," Luster interpreted, "but he thinks we're up to it."

Jeremy and Isis exchanged looks.

Jeremy said, "Luster, how can you understand Dolbert? He doesn't talk."

"Beg pardon? Why, he'll talk yore arm off, iffen you let him. Oh, I know he's hard to understand sometimes, but—"

"Dolbert must have his own language," Isis said.

Luster scratched his head. "I guess he does, so t'speak."

"He fixed the *Voyager*. He must be brilliant."

"Wull, Dolbert's about the smartest man I know. He stays up nights readin'."

Dolbert chittered some comment.

"Dolbert says he's 'specially partial to the poetry of Sheats and Kelley."

Jeremy nodded, then did a take. "Shouldn't that be 'Keats and Shelley'?"

Dolbert chortled.

"Not where we come from," Luster said.

Dolbert thought that was very funny indeed.

# QUEEN'S DINING HALL

". . . so SHEILA AND I went back to the weird aspect where the cloud was," Linda was saying. "We reversed the thing's rotation, and it started *absorbing* the clone Snowclaws. We told all of them to report back to the aspect for . . . well, for getting sucked back up into the thing, and they went. Snowclaw's clones are good troupers."

"That's because Snowclaw's a good trouper," Dalton said. "But the question that arises is, what did they feel about vanishing into the oblivion from which they came?"

Linda waved the issue away. "We didn't ask. And I don't want to think about it."

"If you start thinking about things like that when you do magic," Sheila said, "you'll never sleep at night. I still have a submarine crew I created sitting around doing nothing—but that's another story."

Dalton took a sip of coffee. "By the way, where's the real Snowclaw?"

Linda froze, then put down her toast and looked at Sheila. "Did you—?"

"Well, I thought *you* knew where he was," Sheila said.

"Oh, my God," Linda said, hands up to her face. "You don't think he got . . . ?"

"Oh, I expect he's around somewhere," Dalton said. "He can certainly take care of himself."

"Well, anyway," Linda said, "it's been a crazy couple of days. I hope the cosmic disturbance is over. I wouldn't want to go through that again."

"You're sure all the strangers have been shooed out?" Dalton asked.

"Whoever's left, the Guardsmen ought to take care of," Sheila said.

"What about the bogus Incarnadines?" Thaxton said.

"We don't know about those," Linda said. "They all seemed pretty much immune to whatever we were doing. In fact, they all seemed to be having a pretty good time."

"I hope Lord Incarnadine managed to get back," Dalton said.

"I sent a page up to the laboratory to check. He ought to be reporting soon. I kind of suspect Incarnadine returned okay. Things are quieting down."

"There he is," Sheila said.

Gene and Snowclaw had entered the dining hall.

"Hi, guys!" Snowclaw said, throwing down his broadax.

"I found him sleeping in my room," Gene said.

"I was tired. Besides, I was sick of looking at myself all over, so I thought I'd get some sleep. Great White Stuff, am I hungry!"

"Dig in," Linda said. "I had the cooks bring your beeswax candles and Thousand Island dressing."

"Thanks! Sometimes I like beeswax, sometimes paraffin. It depends on my mood."

Snowclaw dipped a candle into a bowl of dressing and popped it into his toothy maw.

Thaxton looked disgusted and put down his Reuben sandwich.

Other Guests entered the hall, laughing and chattering away. Deena Williams waved and said hello.

"Hi, there!" Sheila called.

"I'll bet they all have stories to tell," Linda said. "And I'll bet you have one, too, Gene. Whatever happened to you?"

"Got into a strange universe. But that's nothing new."

"What about school?"

"Forget it," Gene said. "I've had enough reality to last me awhile. Give me swords and sorcery. Can't get enough of that stuff."

"Well, you came to the right place," Dalton said.

# KING'S STUDY

THE ROOM WAS FILLED with books and curios. The ceiling was high, supported by rib vaulting. Bookshelves reached almost to the ceiling. Star charts and astronomical gear—orreries and such—were concentrated in one corner of the study. A rank of instruments resembling grandfather clocks ran along one wall.

"What readings you getting?" one Incarnadine asked of another.

"Things are just about back to normal."

"Well, that doesn't solve our problem."

The other Incarnadines grumbled agreement.

"What exactly is our problem?"

"There is the ultimate ontological question."

"Meaning?"

"Who's real and who isn't."

"Why don't we let reality take care of itself?"

"Ultimately it will, but I for one can't regard myself as the product of some glitch in the supercontinuum."

"Me neither. I don't hold with the notion of there being an infinite number of castles."

"Why not?" asked still another Incarnadine. "Any rigorous quantum interpretation of things would accommodate them."

"Well, quantum physics is so much whistling in the dark as

far as I'm concerned. There's an irreconcilable conflict between quantum theory and relativity, and everybody pretty much agrees that relativity is right. You can't have both.''

"It depends what particular subuniverse you're talking about,'' said a third Incarnadine. "The paradigms are polar opposites, but most continua are compromises between the two. Earth, for example, is pretty much fifty-fifty. The ratio has something to do with the amount of magical leeway per given continuum, but just what the mapping function between the two is, is unclear.''

"Let's drop all this chalkboard chicken scratching. I just want to know who the real McCoy is.''

"Damn it, Jim, I'm a doctor, not a philosopher!''

"Very droll. I tell you, it's relative.''

"It's not relative. There can only be one of us.''

"Why? Are we supposed to be a god, or what?''

"Well, that's never been very clear.''

"A demiurge, at the very least.''

"Anybody want to buck for Glaroon?''

"That's a special pocket continuum, and it's copyrighted.''

"Look, we're not getting anywhere. Why don't we all return to our respective . . . whatever you call them. Continua, quantum glitches, Erewhons, reflections of reflections—''

"I kind of like this place a little better. Some nice equipment here that I don't have.''

"See? What you're saying is that we aren't merely reflections.''

"I never said we were.''

"I'm getting confused.''

"It is a confusing situation.''

" 'Mirror, mirror . . .' ''

"Who's got the mirror? Endlessly regressing fleas, and all that. I say the question's purely academic, and I say to hell with it.''

"Well, we tried to settle it by force, and that didn't get us anywhere. Nobody ever gained anything by playing chess with himself.''

"Why don't we flip for it? Anybody have a coin?''

"Why don't we all meet in an aspect somewhere, bring guns, and start banging away at one another?''

"Primitive, but it ought to settle something.''

"That's what I was talking about at lunch. Some of you guys are just a little too bloodthirsty for my taste.''

"Well, all you liberal pantywaists can hold a raffle for the door prize."

"Who's a pantywaist?"

"Who's a liberal?"

"Wait a minute. Something's happening."

They all looked at one another.

"You're all fading," said one of them.

"So are you," said another. "I can see right through you."

"Anybody know what's going on?"

"The disturbance has been quelled. The problem is taking care of itself."

Gradually the figures in the room grew transparent, save one.

One of the disappearing ghosts raised a hand. "Anyway, fellows, thanks for lunch."

"See you around," another said, his voice an echo.

Presently there was only one man in the room. He exhaled and got up from the chair he was sitting in. He checked the instruments again, nodding in satisfaction.

"So much for that," he said.

On his way out he passed a mirror, and stepped back to consider his reflection.

"Anyway, I *feel* real enough."

His image winked at him.

"You and me both, pal."